High Meadow

FREYA BARKER

High Meadow

ISBN: 9781988733722

Cover Design: Freya Barker
Editing: Karen Hrdlicka
Proofing: Joanne Thompson
Cover Image: Jean Woodfin—JW Photography
Cover Model: Rory Mills

An emergency call to pick up an injured stallion on the side of the road sends Alexandra Hart, the new owner of Hart's Horse Rescue, into action. A recent addition to the area, she is not impressed when the animal's taciturn owner shows up. With his less-than-stellar disposition, he's the kind of man she normally avoids at all costs, unfortunately, he owns the ranch just down the road.

However, when the manhunt for a pair of escaped prisoners gets a little too close for comfort, Jonas turns out to be a better neighbor than she expected

The *Alex* who shows up at his ranch to help with his prize stud's recovery is not exactly who Jonas Harvey expected. This is the same bleeding heart he met on the side of the road. Worried she's not up for the job, he'd prefer to keep a close eye on her but his High Mountain Trackers team gets called in to track down a group of domestic terrorists.

But the slip of a woman proves him wrong. On all fronts. Alex not only charms his horses but him as well, and when trouble comes calling she proves to be a worthy ally to boot.

One

JONAS

"J!"

I turn in the saddle to see Ama waving from the porch.

"It's the movers!"

Shit, what now? It's been one thing after another with these guys and I already regret hiring them to drive Dad's stuff here. It should've been here last week.

It had taken me two years to convince my father to sell his place near Amarillo, Texas and move up here with me. He's getting up there and managing his small ranch—even with the help of the couple of hands I'd hired him—was quickly becoming too much to handle. Hard for me to get down there regularly to pick up the slack with my own workload up here. Giving up his life's work had not been easy. Dad doesn't like sitting idle, which I assured him he wouldn't be.

I own High Meadow, a busy horse ranch near Libby,

Montana, and can always use an extra pair of hands and eyes. Especially with my other business picking up again after the winter season. Most of my guys do double duty and having someone I can trust to manage the ranch while we are out on a search will make life a lot easier.

"Sully, grab Blitz, will you?"

I swing my leg out of the saddle and slide off the young, spirited Arabian I was able to pick up at auction last month. He's got a lot of fire I'm slowly working out of him. He could be a nice addition to my stable as a stud, but the way he is now he could do serious damage to the mares.

Sully takes the reins and starts walking him to the stable, the horse's tail high as he prances along.

Ama hands me the phone when I reach the porch.

"Harvey."

"Mr. Harvey, it's Jessica at Titan Moving and Transport. I'm afraid there's been a slight delay."

"Again," I grumble.

"Our truck broke down just south of Denver. I've already dispatched another truck to pick up your belongings and continue on to Montana, but it means we have at least a day's delay. Maybe two," she adds quickly.

As much as I'd like to voice my displeasure, it's no use yelling at the girl. In the grand scheme of things I guess a few more days is not such a big deal.

"Before the weekend," I demand.

Dad insisted on driving himself up here. In part because he wanted to stop off in Wyoming to visit an old army buddy of his. I don't expect him until next week, but I want to make sure we've got his rooms ready for him.

"For sure," she says sounding confident.

"Let me guess, they won't be here tomorrow," Ama observes when I hand her back the house phone.

"Got it in one."

"Well, that sucks." She pats my arm. "But don't worry, we'll get it done before he gets here," she adds.

"Yeah."

"By the way, I'm heading into town to run some errands. Anything you need?"

"Yes, can you stop at Homesteader's and pick me up some iodine?"

A quick and easy disinfectant for nicks and cuts, we go through the stuff like water.

"Again? Maybe I should start ordering extra."

We usually get our feed and sundries delivered by truck once a month, and Ama manages the order. Hell, Ama manages just about everything. Married to one of my trusted men, James Watike, Ama has become my major domo. She runs the house, the kitchen, the office, the orders, the men, and me.

I lucked out when I was able to pull in James, along with some of my other former teammates. Not only was he a great asset, but his wife turned out to be the glue holding this place together.

When I bought this place a little over a decade ago, after I aged out of my unit, I didn't expect to miss the work. Horses are in my blood, but apparently tracking was as well and I started missing the thrill of the hunt. I was occasionally asked to help search for a lost hiker—something we see quite a bit of here in the Montana mountains—and the idea for High Mountain Trackers was born.

James, Bo, Sully, Fletch, and I had all been part of the same Special Ops tracker team. We'd get called in on a wide variety of operations in a lot of different geographical locations. Sometimes our only task was tracking down a target. Other times it also involved the extraction of said target.

The job required a specialized set of skills my team had in spades.

As it turned out, I wasn't the only one who missed flexing those particular muscles. It took me a year, but eventually I was able to convince four of my former teammates to join me and HMT was in business. We haven't been lacking for work, requests to help families locate missing loved ones, but also calls for help from different levels of law enforcement. On our downtime we work the ranch, but especially this last year we've had to hire more hands to keep this place running. That's where I hope Dad will come in handy.

I catch up with Sully, who already set Blitz loose in the paddock out front and is carrying the tack into the stable.

"Any word from Bo?" he wants to know.

Yesterday, Bo, Fletch, and James took the trailer up to Eureka, just south of the border with Canada, aiding in the search for a hiker. The guy got separated from the small group of friends and has been missing for four days now. The nights still get cold up here and with limited gear and no shelter, it can be a challenge to survive the elements. Time is of the essence.

"Nope. Nothing yet."

My guys wouldn't have stopped for nightfall. A lot of gain can be made in the dark, since most people—even those who are lost—have the common sense to hunker down and stay stationary until sunup. My men are outfitted with infrared night vision so the lack of daylight wouldn't hamper them. They also carry a satellite phone, since cell reception is spotty at best in the mountains.

Sully dumps the saddle and bridle in the tack room before turning to me.

"Want me to take the bird and head up there?"

The bird is a Matrice 210 RTK, a high-end drone outfitted with cameras, a datalink allowing for real-time monitoring, and a positioning beacon. The bird is Sully's baby and the best twenty-grand investment I've made. Only problem is, even from the air, the mountains hide a lot. There's a lot of luck involved unless we know what direction to search in.

I shake my head. "Give it another day and see if the guys can get a bead on the target."

"Sully!"

One of the hands pulls his horse to a halt in the barnyard when I poke my head out of the doors. Sully steps up beside me.

"What's wrong?"

The kid dismounts and startles when he catches sight of me. He looks instantly panicked.

"Fuck, Dan," Sully prompts. "What's the hollering about?"

"It's Phantom."

My back straightens and my attention is piqued. Phantom is my prize stud and is out in the back meadow enjoying the last days of freedom before breeding season confines him closer to the barn.

His eyes flit to me before returning to Sully.

"He got out."

～

Alex

. . .

There's something about the mountain air that centers me.

I'm on my porch sipping my second coffee of the day as I take in the view. The hints of spring add a softer green against the permanent shades of pine and spruce more prevalent in these mountains. The peaks in the distance still white with the snow that overwhelmed me all winter.

It's a harder life than I was used to—not that I've ever been afraid of hard work—but it's also more gratifying. Since moving here my life feels more balanced.

A soft clucking sound has me look in the direction of the corral where Lucy is exercising our latest addition. She's a skittish mare we picked up from a ramshackle house along the Kootenay River, just outside Jennings. Poor thing had been chained to a tree, the skin on her neck rubbed raw by the weight of the metal. There were two dogs on the property in a similar condition and we took them as well.

Lincoln Sheriff's Department had been called in by a neighbor and they in turn contacted us. A deputy met us out there in case the owner showed up. The horse had been a challenge to get into the trailer, but the dogs had come willingly. They were a tad shy but seemed happy someone was there to look after them.

Doc Evans came by to check all three of them out the other day. Not much he could do about their emaciated state—it would take time to fatten them up—but he cleaned up their injuries and left me with some antibiotic ointment.

As soon as I turn to head inside both dogs, who had been lying down at my feet, got up to follow. One looks to be a blue heeler or some derivative thereof, and the other is a mix with the coloring of an English shepherd but smaller and with a shorter coat. Oddly enough he seems to be the leader.

"You can stay out here, boys."

They've been following Lucy and me around like skinny shadows, as if they're afraid we won't return. It's gonna take some time to build their trust, just like it will with the mare out there. Maybe we should start by naming them.

I let the storm door slam shut behind me as I make my way to the kitchen and dump my empty mug in the sink.

The kitchen is old, like the rest of the house, but the bones are good and everything seems to work as it should. Other than the wallpaper stripping and painting we've done over the winter, we haven't really done more to upgrade the place. Most of my money is going toward the care of the animals and the rest will have to wait until I can start generating some income, hiring out my services treating animals with behavioral issues.

Not an easy feat as it turns out. Most folks up here don't subscribe to what a lot of them consider to be whoo-whoo psychobabble. They'd rather write an animal off than pay someone to modify the unwanted behavior. If only someone would give me an opportunity to show what I can do.

The phone on the kitchen counter rings and I eagerly rush to answer.

"Hart's Horse Rescue."

"Yes, hi, this is Esther Grimshaw. I'm about two miles south of you on US-2, and I just drove past a horse in the ditch on the west side. It was trying to get up, but I think it may have broken a foreleg. I was hoping you could help."

This land is vast but however spread out, the community seems small. So it doesn't really surprise me a neighbor I haven't met yet seems to know plenty about the newcomer.

"Have you contacted Doc Evans?" I mention the vet I've

7

come to know over the past four months since I bought this property.

"Can't get through, but I left a message. Thought I'd try you."

"Okay, thanks. I'll grab a trailer and head down. If Doc Evans calls you back, will you tell him I'm on my way there?"

"I will."

I hang up, grab a halter and a rope off the hook by the door, and head out. I almost trip over the dogs, who've taken up guard right in front of the door.

"Lucy!"

"Yeah!"

"Gonna need you. Got a call about an injured horse along the highway."

"Let me set her loose. I'll be right there."

Lucy has worked with me for close to six years and moved up here with me from Billings. My place there barely had room for a handful of horses and when I heard through the grapevine of this property in the mountains, with substantially more acreage, it was like a dream come true for me. Lucy, who is about ten years my junior and without any attachments in Billings, was up for the adventure.

The dogs follow me to the truck. I don't really want to lock them in the house and I don't trust them alone on the property yet, so I open the cab door. Without hesitation they hop in the back seat. I back the truck up to the trailer.

Lucy joins me after releasing the mare in the field with the others—seven horses and one donkey—and it takes us a couple of tries to hook the trailer up to the truck, but we finally get it done.

"Where are we going?" she asks, climbing into the cab beside me.

"About two miles south, along the highway." Highway is a big word for the two-lane road, but it's the main drag in these regions.

I turn left out of the driveway, heading south. I don't have to go far to see another trailer parked on the side of the road, a Sheriff's Department cruiser already there. I pull in behind it and get out; Lucy jumps down as well.

I can hear the restless snorting of a horse come from the larger trailer up ahead. A man wearing a dirty old Stetson is chatting with law enforcement when we walk up.

"Can I help you?" the deputy asks.

"We're from Hart's Horse Rescue up the road. We got a call about an injured horse?"

"Yeah, he's mine," the cowboy says with a Southern drawl, and I take my first good look at him. I can't see his eyes with the brim pulled low, but his mouth is pressed in a firm line beneath the gray scruff.

"What are you gonna do with him?" I ask, knowing most ranchers won't bother with a broken leg; they'll euthanize the horse first. Not only for the cost of possible repairs —which can be substantial—but because the chances of recovery aren't always great for a horse. Still, I currently have two animals that we've been able to rehabilitate successfully, and I won't give up on a horse without trying everything I can.

"Not your horse, not your concern," the cowboy says dismissively.

"That may be, but I'd like to offer an alternative to killing—"

Ignoring me and without another word, the big lug turns on his heel and disappears around the trailer.

"It *is* his horse. He can do what he likes," the deputy offers. Typical.

My stomach churns as I watch the truck and trailer drive off with the injured horse in the back.

"Who is that anyway?" Lucy asks the cop.

"That's J. Harvey. He's well known around these parts."

I bet he is. He may be an exceptionally handsome man, but he's an arrogant prick.

Two

JONAS

"Easy, boy."

Doc Evans finishes wrapping the foreleg of the sedated stallion. It was the only way Doc could get close to his leg.

The high-strung quarter horse is my most prized stud, and as soon as I know he'll be okay, I'm going to have a talk with the idiot who let him escape and fire his ass.

The good news is that Phantom's leg is badly sprained but not broken, yet he also sustained a deep gash that needed to be cleaned and stitched.

"It'll need to be cleaned daily. I suggest you give him plenty of stall rest and light walking exercise a few times a day." Doc comes out of the stall and closes the door before he turns to me.

"He's got a busy stud schedule coming up," I note, thinking about the appointments lined up for next month.

"He's gonna need some time to heal. Let's see how he

recovers in the next couple of weeks. We can reassess then," he adds regretfully.

Shit. Hope it doesn't come to that.

Phantom stands at a decent fee. Last year the seven-year-old bred sixty-two mares. That goes a long way to keep the ranch going. Of course we breed our own mares as well, and the offspring makes a decent penny at auction, which helps. I'm hoping next year Blitz will be settled enough to go on the stud roster, but until then we're dependent on Phantom for the bulk of our income.

"I'm gonna leave you a five-day course of antibiotics he'll need to finish," Doc says, packing up his bag. "Clean those dressings daily, and I'll be back in a few days to see how he's doing."

We walk out of the barn and he points at Missy, my paint mare, who is due in a month or two, lazing in the smaller paddock.

"She's looking good. You have her on enriched food, right?"

"Started two weeks ago."

"Good. When I come back to look at Phantom, I'll quickly check her as well."

"Sounds good, Doc. Thanks for coming out."

"Not a problem. Esther Grimshaw from up the road saw him and left me a message so I was already on my way over when you called."

"Still, I appreciate it."

The older man tips his hat and climbs into his rusty 1970 Ford F-100. He calls it a classic, but if you ask me, it's a miracle the thing still runs. He won't consider an upgrade though, stubborn old coot.

I watch him drive off, slap my leg for Max—my Bernese mountain dog—to follow, and make my way over to the hay barn. Sully, my foreman, was supposed to sit on Dan, the moron who was working on the fence at the north pasture. Phantom's pasture. The kid's only saving grace is he beelined it straight back to the ranch when Phantom slipped past him. I know my horse; he's skittish around people and would never have come close had Dan been right there. I'm guessing he was either taking a piss with the fence not secured, or he was playing with his damn phone, which he does every chance he has. Luckily, the trailer had still been on the back of my truck and I hauled right out of here to look for the horse.

The kid is mucking stables when I walk in and peers up with a guilty look on his face.

"Do you like working here?" I ask him.

A sound draws my attention and I catch Sully leaning a shoulder against the doorway to the tack room.

"Yeah," Dan mumbles, ducking his head.

"Hmm," I grunt. "You're gonna have to do better to convince me. See, that horse you let escape pays for your wages. He coulda been killed. What do you think woulda happened?"

"I'da lost my job?" He glances up.

I bark out a bitter laugh. "Fucking right you would have. Who's to say you won't anyway? You better hope and pray Phantom heals up good in the next three weeks or I may not have a choice but to send you packing."

"I'll do anything to keep my job."

I hold his eyes for a moment when I recognize desperation in his voice.

"Yeah, you will. You'll be the one walking Phantom around the ring at least twice a day. Once in the morning before your regular shift, and once more when your shift is over."

"He hates me."

"Fuck, son, then you better make sure you win him over, because your future at High Meadow depends on it."

"Yes, sir," he concedes meekly.

Christ, he's young. Nineteen, maybe twenty, his body may be strong like a man's but his face looks like a teenager's.

"And every day you are to hand your phone in to Sully here. He'll hold onto it until you're ready to go home."

Shock steals over his features.

"But..."

"You want this job? Then that's a condition. Can't have you around my horses when you're distracted playing games or chatting up girls," I state firmly, but a moment later my conviction wavers when he mumbles something. "What was that?"

"It's my mom. Not games or girls."

"You're on the phone half the day with your mom?"

Some disbelief may have filtered through in my tone, because the next minute his earlier drooping shoulders snap straight and anger fills his eyes as he juts out his chin.

"Yes, I am. She's sick. She ain't got no one else."

Well, shit. The kid is fighting tears, making me feel like I've kicked a puppy.

Part of me wants to ask what is wrong with her, but Dan isn't volunteering more and I don't want to pry. Still, I'm gonna have to come up with a solution.

"Like I said, Sully's gonna hold your phone so you don't get distracted, but you'll have it back during lunch break. Also, you're gonna give your momma the house number so she can get hold of Ama in case of an emergency."

And I'm going to have a talk with Ama to find out a bit

more about Dan's situation as soon as I'm done here, but I keep that to myself.

"Yes, sir," he mumbles.

I nod at him and share a meaningful look with Sully before I turn on my heel and head for the house, Max following at my feet. I glance over at the corral where the stallion is still tied up.

"And get Phantom into a stall!" I yell over my shoulder.

"Yes, sir!" comes back firmly.

I'm tempted to stay and make sure the kid can handle it, but I trust Sully to keep an eye on things.

Getting Phantom into the trailer had been a challenge, even for me. His full body had been shaking, and he couldn't put weight on that leg. God, I was worried he'd be done for.

Needless to say, by the time that woman from the new rescue place showed up, I wasn't exactly in a good mood; I may have been a bit curt.

Pity, from what I could tell, under the baggy flannel shirt and that ball cap, she was mighty pretty.

Alex

"How about Buttercup?"

"How about no?" I fire back at Lucy, who is trying to keep the heeler from escaping the big galvanized-steel trough we're trying to bathe him in.

Both dogs were filthy when we found them, but we wanted to wait until they were a bit settled in before subjecting them to the trauma of a bath.

We've been trying to come up with names, but Lucy keeps going for the cheesy ones.

"Buttercup sounds like the name of a cow," I add.

"Well, then you come up with something," Lucy snips as she wrestles the dog, while I try to pluck another tick out of his fur.

The shepherd is cowering on the porch, keeping a close watch on what is being done to his buddy. We're going to have a hell of a time getting that one in the tub.

"How about Hope for the mare? We can name the shepherd Chief—he seems to be in charge—and we can call this one Scout?" I suggest, glancing at Lucy.

"I guess I can live with that," she grumbles and I grin at her.

Lucy is like a pineapple: a prickly, hard exterior to protect the soft and sweet on the inside. It put me off at first, until I saw how she was with the animals. She doesn't hold back with them, not even a little. Over time she's become a good friend. My best friend, probably. We get each other, share a passion, work shoulder to shoulder, share the same ideals, and it wasn't really a surprise she was already packing to come to Montana before I had a chance to bring up the possibility.

Sharing the large rambling farmhouse these past four months—she had her own place in Billings—has been an unexpected pleasure. I had no idea Lucy could cook like a freaking gourmet chef, and we even have the same taste in Netflix shows. In the mornings neither of us is particularly approachable—especially pre-caffeine—so we tend not to get in each other's way.

All in all, it's a pretty sweet setup. At least for now.

I fully expect some handsome cowboy to notice the treasure behind the barbed wire Lucy is wrapped in and snatch her up. All that blonde hair, those feminine curves, and that pretty face draw enough attention. I, on the other hand, look more like an aging tomboy. The once dark red hair now is streaked with silver, more freckles dot my skin, and even age hasn't added any curves. Still no hips, no chest to speak of, or that hourglass figure I used to dream of. Not that I care anymore, though, I've already known the love of a good man who thought I was perfect just the way I am.

I hope Lucy finds someone who feels that way about her, but in the meantime I'm happy for her company. It's been nice having someone around the house again, especially since Jackson left to join the army two years ago.

Thinking of my boy is like a punch to the chest. I'm in equal measure proud as hell and terrified beyond belief. I remember when he told me, after his second year of college, he'd changed his mind and decided to follow in his father's footsteps. Bruce was killed by a roadside bomb in Afghanistan when Jackson was only eleven, but now that little boy is grown and serving his country in Iraq.

I shake to clear my head. If I think on this too long the fear becomes crippling.

"I think his pads are starting to prune," I comment. "Why don't you get Scout out and I'll go grab Chief."

When we're done both dogs are clean, but Lucy and I both need a shower and a change of clothes.

This time when I walk inside, I hold the screen door open so the dogs can follow me in. They hesitate briefly before stepping over the threshold, but once inside move more quickly, their respective noses inhaling every scent they can catch.

By the time I get downstairs, Lucy is already outside heading for the barn, both dogs by her side. We have the stalls to muck today and there's a fence on the south field that needs a few new boards. I grab my bottle and fill it with cold, filtered water from the fridge, when the phone on the counter rings.

"Hart's Rescue."

"Alex? It's Doc Evans."

"Hey, Doc, how are you?"

"Good, good. How are your new guests doing? Any problems?"

This is part of what I love about living out here. Find me a vet in the big city who'll call to see how his patients are doing? I certainly never encountered one.

"They're coming along. No longer looking quite so gaunt. Lucy is working with the mare daily and the dogs seem to be adjusting well. We actually just brought them in the house for a bit."

We kept the dogs in the old chicken coop at night the past week, mostly because they were clearly used to being outside. Now they've attached to us, I'd like to see how they do being indoor dogs. Overnight anyway.

"Great. Listen, I have another reason for calling. One of my ranchers has an injured horse. He was spirited already, but since getting hurt he's almost impossible to approach. Dressings need changing daily, which is becoming a bit of a problem. Any chance you could go have a look? See what you can do with the animal?"

A little bubble of excitement forms in my stomach. This is the kind of stuff I live for but I haven't been given much of an opportunity to do since moving here. Behavioral adjustments were our bread and butter in Billings, and I'm hoping to build up that same reputation here.

"Absolutely," I respond, trying not to sound too eager. "Where do I go?"

The easiest would be to bring the horse here, where it's

easier to look after and work with him but without first earning their trust, there isn't a rancher who'd let me take their animal.

"High Meadow. It's only about ten minutes south of you."

That's not bad at all. I could head out there this afternoon, after we tackle the barn and that stretch of fence. Should only take us a couple of hours.

"I can be there..." I glance at the kitchen clock. "Between three and four?"

"I'll get them to give you a call to sort that out."

I'm grinning wide when I head outside. I can't wait to tell Lucy we may have landed our first paying gig.

Three

ALEX

Oh, hell no.

I almost do an about-face when I see who is leaning casually against fence around the horse corral, a smug grin on that annoyingly handsome face.

That arrogant bastard on the side of the road last week.

"Well, I'll be damned. To what do I owe the pleasure?"

His voice, rich with a lazy Southern drawl, is as attractive as the man himself and thus grates on my nerves.

Guess now I know who owns High Meadow Ranch. When the woman called twenty minutes after I hung up with Doc Evans, she mentioned someone named Jonas. I had no idea she was referring to J. Harvey, the name given to me by the officer. She also indicated this morning would be better for me to drop in, which worked out well for me since the fence took us longer than anticipated.

What a shitty bit of luck it's the same guy. Still, I can't let that incident get in the way of this opportunity, so I straighten my shoulders and lift my chin. I can do this. Hell, I've always had an affinity with animals, especially with horses—something Doc Evans has been able to see firsthand —and combined with my training as a veterinary assistant, it comes in handy. All I need to do is show this guy what I can do.

The woman who called didn't give me many details, but assured me that the horse's owner would fill me in.

"You're Jonas Harvey? Doc Evans called the rescue center, said you needed help with a horse."

"I am, and I do." I bristle when he scrutinizes me from the tips of my boots to the ball cap covering my hair as I walk up to him. "You're Alex?"

"The one and only."

"Well, shit, I thought—"

"Short for Alexandra," I interrupt him.

I don't tell him a lot of folks think they're dealing with a man when my name is mentioned. I like it that way. Archaic as it may seem, some of these ranchers would sooner deal with a guy than a woman, so I use the confusion to my advantage. All I need is an opportunity to show them what I can do and by then they hopefully won't care what gender I am.

"Ahh." He grins and lifts his hat, running a hand over the bald head hiding underneath. A very nice bald head that suits the lined face and silver scruff. If I had to venture a guess, I'd say he's late forties, not that much older than I am. "I have to apologize then, I automatically assumed—"

"A man," I finish for him. "Yes, I get that a lot, but there is no man. I'm sorry to disappoint."

"I'm far from disappointed," he assures me with a smile.

Oh, he's a charmer, this one, and I can't say I'm unaffected. From the way his eyes crinkle, it's clear smiling is something he does a lot. Hmmm. Seems a far cry from the asshole who blew me off. Maybe I caught him on a really bad day last week, but he almost doesn't look like the same man.

I catch myself staring and quickly avert my eyes over his shoulder, where a pregnant paint leans her head over the fence of a small paddock.

"Is she your problem horse?" I tilt my head in her direction.

"Missy? God no, she's a sweetheart. A little slow now, with only a month or so to go, but her disposition never changes."

The gentleness in his voice as he talks about the mare does more to break down my defenses than his charming smile does. Actually, that's probably a lie; both seem to be effective, but I can't forget the growling bear from before. I don't know this man and would do well not to get distracted. I've got a job to do.

I walk up to the fence and reach out my hand. The mare lifts her head, sniffs my hand, and moves her lips restlessly over my skin, probably looking for some treat.

"I don't have anything for you, honey," I mumble before turning to Jonas. "She's beautiful."

"She is, isn't she?" he says with fatherly pride. "But she isn't the problem. It's her foal's sire, Phantom. He's in his stall." He points at a large stable. "I'll show you."

I'm very much aware of the man beside me as we walk through the large doors of the gorgeous green barn. This whole place is amazing, with well-tended grounds and nicely kept buildings. Aside from this barn there is a second, smaller one on the other side of the exercise ring, and I noticed a nice house sitting on a hill overlooking the property when I drove in.

"This is Phantom," he says, indicating the stall farthest back in the barn.

I peek over the half-door to find a beautiful quarter horse huddled in a far corner. His nostrils are flared, and his eyes are wild and restless. A tremble seems to ripple over his dark buckskin hide. A stunning animal.

Then he stomps his hoof in the straw and I notice the wrap around his foreleg.

I glance at Jonas, who looks amused at my shocked expression. I'd been so sure the horse was going to be euthanized.

"Is that the horse injured out on the road?"

"One and the same." He slightly tilts his head. "You thought I'd put him down."

I'm slightly embarrassed having jumped to conclusions, but more so that he could read me so easily.

"I did," I admit, but then add a bit defensively. "But you have to admit that's what most ranchers would do."

"Not me," he counters. "And not when the horse in question is a working stud."

I glance back at the horse and can see the quality. Quarter horses are very popular for a wide variety of uses and this boy is a beauty. I'm sure he brings in a decent buck in stud fees.

"I stand corrected," I concede, before reaching for the stall door.

"What are you doing?"

My hand stills.

"I thought you wanted me to have a look at him."

"I do, but I don't want you to get hurt. As you can see, he's skittish. That's a lot of horse for a little thing like you."

There's nothing I can do to stop the automatic eye-roll

his remark invites, but I manage to keep the sharp words inside. Not like it's the first time I get a reaction like that, but it only makes me more determined to get close to the horse.

"Do you have a halter for him?" I ask, trying for a casual tone. "I'd like to get him outside in the ring."

"I can get him out for you," he offers.

Sucking in air through my nose I conjure up patience.

"Mr. Harvey, I—"

"Jonas. Please," he adds as an afterthought.

"I promise you, I know what I'm doing. I have worked with animals who have been abused and beaten, who have every reason to distrust the human race, for quite some years now with great success. If you want me to help Phantom here, you're going to have to trust me."

His jaw is working while he appears to consider my words. Then he turns on his heel and marches into the tack room, only to return moments later with a halter which he hands to me.

"Be careful," he mumbles. "He doesn't play well with others, except for Missy out there. They have a special bond."

Not exactly a vote of confidence but I'll take it.

∼

Jonas

I watch Alex ease her way into Phantom's stall, his halter casually in one hand and the other held out in front of her. The horse's nostrils twitch, trying to catch her scent, but he seems less panicked than he was a few days ago. I don't move, not wanting to interrupt the trust I see her slowly building.

I had my reservations at first, sending the slip of a woman into his stall—afraid Phantom could crush her with one powerful kick—but she'd assured me she knew what she was doing. Despite her confidence, I continue to stick close; ready to pull her out at the first sign of danger.

It's been a few days since Doc was last by to tend to Phantom—once again under sedation—and his dressings are starting to smell. Alex had balked when I suggested yesterday to call the vet back in, claiming it would set her back building trust with the animal. She promised she'd get him out of his stall and into the exercise ring this morning, after which she thinks she can change the bandages.

She's not what I expected. When she showed up yesterday, I was pleasantly surprised. I admit, when she'd mentioned Hart's Horse Rescue at the side of the road last week, I never thought she owned the place. Call me a sexist bastard, you'd probably be right. But in my defense, the horse business is still very much a male dominated industry, especially up here in the boonies. I'm sure some have strong reservations around a woman handling these strong, powerful animals, but I'd like to think I am more open-minded.

She definitely gained my respect with the way she handled Phantom yesterday. She wasn't able to coax him out of his stall, but spent some time softly mumbling to him as she carefully soothed him with slow strokes of her hand. He visibly relaxed in her presence. Enough for her to promise today she'd get him into the corral.

We'll see. I made sure my guys are all working far enough away from the stable to minimize the risk of Phantom startling, but I'm staying right here.

"Hey, buddy. Are you ready for some fresh air today? Can't be fun cooped up in here all the time." I grin at her running monologue as she inches closer to the stallion. "How about a quick hi for Missy? She's about to pop. You should see her, she's positively glowing."

When I mentioned the two horses have a special bond that dates back to their early years, it had been her suggestion the pregnant mare might actually have a calming effect on him. I put up a makeshift pen right next to the corral to keep her separate so Phantom couldn't inadvertently injure her, but he'll be able to smell, see, and touch her. We'll have to wait and see how it goes, but I'm up to try anything at this point. Phantom is my most popular stud, making up almost half of my business, and I'm eager to see him better.

In the stall, Alex gently rubs the horse's head—something she wasn't able to do yesterday—before deftly slipping the halter over his ears. Instead of immediately grabbing hold of it, she continues stroking him.

"Want to open the door, Jonas?" she asks, in the same tone of voice she uses for the animal. Phantom looks my way when I do as she asks, but he doesn't startle.

With one hand on his halter, the other rubbing his nose, and her nonstop verbal soothing, she starts moving and slowly guides him out of his stall. He hesitates when he passes, his body curving away from me, but seems to take his lead from Alex.

I'm impressed. I'm good with the horses, but aside from having the patience of a saint, this woman has something special. Not only that: she's smart, passionate, and seriously pretty. It isn't exactly a hardship to watch her work. Or...just watch her.

When they step out of the barn doors Phantom sticks

his nose up, sniffing the air. He seems to catch Missy's scent and turns his head her way, whinnying softly.

"Wanna go see your girl?" Alex coos, walking him into the ring and over to the fence where Missy's already waiting. She lets them rub noses for a bit, before she calls me over. "Can you bring the bucket? We'll try and do it here."

I grab the water and the clean dressings and slip in the ring, amazed when other than a quick look; Phantom doesn't seem too disturbed by my presence.

I smile appreciatively at Alex, and this time I get a wide grin back. One that goes straight to my gut.

With infinite patience—a quality I'm unfortunately short on—she rubs the wet sponge over his neck, getting him used to the water before she eases it down his injured leg. She never once stops talking in that same calming tone as she makes sure the dressing gets soaking wet.

Every so often Phantom stomps or jerks his head up, but Alex eventually is able to peel away the bandages.

"Doesn't look too bad," she mumbles for my sake as she gently probes the wound. "Can you hand me the ointment?"

I watch her carefully apply the antibiotic when I hear the crunch of footsteps behind me. Phantom does too and jerks his head around, his nostrils flaring and ears twitching restlessly.

"Thought I'd told you guys to stay away," I call out as calmly as I can.

Sully's voice comes back.

"Sorry, Boss. Urgent call."

Alex turns her head to look behind me.

"It's okay. I've got this," she says. "Go take the call."

I back away from the fence before turning and walking toward Sully, who holds out the phone.

"It's the sheriff, something about an incident north of Libby. Insists on talking to you."

"Keep an eye on them," I tell him, nodding in the direction of the paddock.

Then I aim my attention on the call.

"Harvey."

"Jonas, it's Wayne Ewing."

Ewing ran uncontested in the last election for the sheriff's office. I don't see eye to eye with him on a lot of things, but he's a decent man. A fair one.

"What can I do for you, Sheriff?"

"There was an incident about a mile south of Kootenay Falls on US-2 early this morning. US Marshal's Office lost touch with a prisoner transport from Castlegar, BC, north of the border to Kalispell. We've got two prisoners missing."

"What kind of incident?"

"One that has federal agents from Kalispell all over the damn scene," he grumbles, clearly not happy with the FBI's involvement.

That means either this 'incident' was not an accident, or the missing prisoners are high profile. Or both.

"Can't tell ya much more," Wayne continues. "Been told to warn some of the bigger ranches to be aware we've got some escaped prisoners—probably armed—running loose in these mountains."

Wait a minute...

Last weekend the team came back after finding the hiker at the bottom of a gully, barely clinging to life with significant injuries from the tumble he took. While talking to law enforcement, Fletch picked up a rumor the Royal Canadian Mounted Police had made a significant arrest near Castlegar.

"Tell me these aren't the guys who set off those bombs in Helena last year."

The silence on the other end tells me enough.

"I don't even wanna know how you figured to ask me that," he says eventually. "None of that's public knowledge and I suggest you keep it that way."

"Of course," I quickly ease his mind.

"Lock your doors."

"I will. Want our help?" I offer.

"If it were up to me, I'd probably take you up on it, but it ain't. Feds are in charge."

Wouldn't be the first time we're called in to help the FBI track down a criminal, but that was only after they'd exhausted all their own resources.

"We're here if they need us."

"I'll pass it on."

The line abruptly goes dead after that. I'm sure the idea these homegrown terrorists are possibly hiding in his county doesn't sit well with the sheriff.

We've had trouble with groups of disgruntled militants up here before—mostly the sovereign citizen types, who are anti-government and think the law doesn't apply to them—but the bombs outside state buildings last November went well above and beyond that. The attack was claimed by a thus-far unknown group calling themselves the Montana Sovereign Posse and had law enforcement scrambling.

The blatant daylight attack came at the cost of life. Car bombs went off in two different locations. One at the Montana State Capitol in Helena, where an FBI agent was killed and several civilians injured. The second one was set off at the Department of Justice building where two were killed—a security guard and a civilian—and half a dozen injured. Although the attacks appeared well-coordinated, the bombs were rudimentary. Within days local, state, and federal law enforcement launched a massive manhunt for the two men identified from the CCTV feeds. When after a few weeks no news was forthcoming, most of the press moved on to more current events. The first I'd heard anything since last December was the bit of information Fletch picked up last week.

I make my way back to where Sully has taken a seat on the fence and is watching Alex walk Phantom around the paddock.

"We're asked to keep our heads up," I mention, leaning my arms on the railing beside him.

"Oh yeah?"

I share the conversation with Wayne and my own conclusions.

"I'll tell the guys to carry at all times, just in case."

"That'd be good."

Sully's gaze wanders to Alex.

"What about her? The rescue is right down the road. I think I should make sure—"

"Like hell you should," I growl, cutting him off. "I'll talk to her."

I ignore the shit-eating grin he throws my way.

"She *is* real pretty," he taunts.

Four

ALEX

I rush into the kitchen, jonesing for one more hit of caffeine before I have to rush out the door.

I got up late after a night riddled with restless nightmares. Even though I'm not easily scared—or prone to dreaming—I suspect the warning Jonas passed on yesterday had my imagination running in overdrive. Two escaped prisoners, possibly armed, did not make for a peaceful sleep.

Neither did the occasional appearance Jonas made...for different reasons altogether. It's left me with a permanent blush and clumsy hands all morning while trying to do my chores here.

"Lunch?" Lucy asks, making sandwiches at the kitchen island.

"Thanks, but I should get going."

A smile creeps on her face as her eyebrows inch up to her hairline.

"In a rush? That horse must be something special."

I know she's fishing, but that doesn't stop my cheeks from flushing deeper.

"He is," I confirm, pouring brew into my travel mug.

"Are we still talking about the horse?" she asks teasingly. "You forget, I met the man. Intimidating and sinfully handsome, but also a bit of an ass."

"He was stressed and concerned about his prize horse being injured. He's really quite nice," I defend him.

I recognize my mistake when the smile turns into a shit-eating grin. I snap my mouth shut and fit the lid on my mug, making for the door.

"That's what I thought," she calls out after me, and I flip her the bird over my shoulder.

I'm just getting my feet wet here, I have better things to do than to get any fancy ideas around the first handsome cowboy I bump into. That won't do much for my professional reputation.

What the hell is in the water at High Meadow Ranch anyway? There's not a damn frog in the bunch. I wonder if good-looking is a prerequisite to work there.

Anyway, Jonas *is* nice. That's simply a fact.

It starts raining when I pull into the long driveway up to the main house. Damn. There was no mention of rain in the forecast. I hope it's just a shower because I don't want to bring Phantom out in the paddock if the ground is too saturated. If he slips or freaks out, he could make that injury a lot worse.

By the time I park the truck, the few drops have turned into a monsoon. Lovely. Looks like I'm going to get wet. I grab my ball cap from the passenger seat and fit it on, looping my ponytail through the hole in the back. I'm wet to the skin by the time I'm halfway to the barn.

"Alex!"

I swing around to see a woman standing on the porch of the house, waving me over.

"Get your butt in here, you're getting soaked!"

I throw one last look at the barn before jogging up to the house.

"Come in," the dark-haired woman says, ushering me past her into the front hall. "Stay put. I'm gonna grab you something dry to wear."

I start by kicking off my boots to put them beside a couple of pairs of giant ones on the mud tray under the coatrack. Then I shrug out of my coat, which is dripping puddles on the tiles, and hang it up along with my ball cap. Max, the gorgeous dog I've seen following Jonas around, comes lumbering up, giving me a good sniff.

"Who's a good boy?"

His tail starts swishing slowly from side to side as he allows me to stroke his head. Only for a moment before he disappears down the hall again.

"I'm Ama, by the way. We spoke on the phone."

The woman steps into view from the same doorway the dog just disappeared through. She has a stack of towels and what looks like some sweats in her arms.

Ama is a beautiful woman, tall and shapely, with striking features and gorgeous long, sleek black hair with just a few shimmers of silver. If I'd venture a guess, I'd say she has Native American heritage. The bright colored and intricately patterned woven jacket she's wearing over a pair of jeans only adds to that impression.

"I was just letting Max in," she chatters on, just raising her voice as she ducks into what I presume is a bathroom under the stairs going to the second level. "He's been moping on the porch since Jonas left this morning."

When I spoke to her on the phone, I got the impression she was an employee, but now I'm not so sure. I don't know why I assumed Jonas to be single, but I'm feeling all kinds of stupid now. Especially after last night's dreams. Heat flushes my face. She and Jonas make a handsome pair.

"You can change in here." She steps out and waves me over. "Just toss out your wet stuff and I'll put it in the dryer. I was doing laundry anyway."

"I really appreciate the towels, but you don't have to go to the trouble. I don't want to get your stuff dirty when I head to the barn."

"Nonsense. Besides, the weather will have blown over and your clothes will be dry by the time we've had our coffee," she replies in a decisive tone. "These spring downpours never last long."

I guess we're having coffee.

The sweatpants and shirt she gave me are obviously a man's and I'm drowning in them, but they're dry and warm. I step out of the bathroom carrying my wet stuff rolled in the towels.

"Through here," Ama calls from the rear of the house.

Not much escapes her, I'm sure.

I follow her voice to a bright kitchen that surprisingly opens up to a large living and dining space. I would've thought the living room would have been at the front of the house but it looks like the front of the house is closed off.

"I see you're swimming in those," Ama points at the gray sweatpants.

"A little."

"I'll take those. Have a seat."

Ama grabs the wad of towels from my arms and indicates the large harvest table in front of the floor-to-ceiling glass doors. I pull out one of the rustic chairs and sit as she disappears through a door beside the fridge. I assume the laundry room.

I use the opportunity to scan the living room. A beautiful stone fireplace bisects two large picture windows on the back wall, a wide-screen TV sitting on its mantle and a large, U-shaped, tanned-leather couch facing it. The coffee table looks as rustic as the dining set does, and the only thing on it is a stack of magazines and the burned-out stump of a fat candle.

In fact, there is little decor anywhere. No picture frames to sneak a peek at, just one throw pillow in a corner of the couch and a substantial landscape painting on the wall over it. Against the side wall is a large shelving unit filled with books. That's it. No curtains on the windows, no knick-knacks on any of the surfaces, just the bare bones.

Even the kitchen, although clearly high-end, is sparse, almost industrial-looking. It's hard to imagine a woman looking like Ama—heck, any woman really—not to have a couple of pictures, or maybe a plant or two to liven up the space.

The view is incredible back here, however, and I can see why the living area is at the back of the house. A handful of horses graze in a sloping meadow behind the house and beyond that the Rockies rise up in their full glory.

A sound has me whip my head around as Ama walks back in and grabs a big thermos and two mugs from the kitchen before joining me at the table.

"This is beautiful," I comment when Ama slides a mug in front of me. "I don't think I'd get anything done with a view like this. Don't get me wrong," I hurry to add. "The view from my front porch is nothing to sneeze at, but nothing like this."

Ama pushes milk and sugar containers my way. "I

know," she muses, staring out the doors as well. "Trust me, it never gets old."

"How long have you—"

My question is cut off when Max—who was hiding under the table—suddenly starts barking and beelines it toward the front door.

"I guess they're home," Ama announces.

∾

Jonas

Fucking rain.

Already a steady stream of water runs down the channels on the sides of the driveway. That's not what the forecast indicated for today, but then again, you never know what the weather's gonna do in the mountains.

One moment the sun is out and the next you get a downpour like this. The only thing you can be sure of is that it's gonna snow in the winter and is relatively dry and warm in July and August, but everything in between can run the gamut from frigid to comfortable. This morning we had frost on the ground and a stark blue sky, and look at it now.

The early morning callout was for an industrious five-year-old who somehow managed to unlock the deadbolt on his parents' farmhouse about twelve miles south of here. The frantic father had knocked on a neighbor's door, hoping the kid had wandered over there. The neighbor happened to be a friend of James, which is why we trailered a couple of horses at the break of dawn to help with the search.

Luckily, we found the boy quickly. Only clad in his pajamas, he was hypothermic by the time we got to him, but he should recover just fine.

I notice Alex's truck when I pass by the house. She's probably in the barn with Phantom. Hope she missed the downpour.

"Let's get these horses inside," I tell James as I get out of the truck.

Fortunately the rain seems to have slowed down a bit when I round the back of the trailer and unlock it to reveal the two horses. James grabs Cisco and I back out Sugar—my preferred ride. High Meadow houses mostly quarter horses, but we also have a few quarter-draft crosses. We prefer the rugged breed for search and rescue. They're surefooted and durable in the sometimes-rough terrain, and they have impressive stamina. Perfect for our kind of work.

I lead Sugar into the barn and am surprised to find Phantom in his stall, but no Alex in sight. I rub down Sugar's wet coat with some straw.

"Can you feed them?" I ask James as I start toward the house. Only place I can think of she may have gone.

"Say hi for me," James calls out behind me and I flip him the bird over my shoulder.

Sully and his big mouth.

A dark-red Dodge Ram is coming up the driveway. *Dad*. I grin and shake my head when I recognize the massive white Stetson barely visible behind the wheel.

I get my height from my mother's side of the family. Dad likes to claim he's five foot eleven, but I bet he's no more than five eight. His whole life he's compensated for it with big hats and big trucks. This one is new, a massive 1500 dually. Dad is a bigger-than-life character, loud, boisterous, flashy, but underneath all that is a kind, hardworking man with a good heart. A good soul.

The smile lingers on my face as I approach the truck.

"*Goddangit.*"

The strangled curse comes from the other side of the cab where I find my father standing in a puddle, his snakeskin boots—probably worth a mortgage payment—covered in mud.

"Damn rain," is the first thing he says when he catches sight of me.

His seventy-nine-year-old, scraggly face is barely visible under the wide brim of his hat, but blue eyes matching mine peek out, still young and sparkling with mischief.

God, I missed him. Haven't seen him since last Christmas.

"Couldn't you've ordered me some damn sunshine, Son?"

I grab his offered hand. My father doesn't hug. A pat on the shoulder or back, maybe, but any other public displays of affection were reserved solely for my mother when she was still alive.

"Good to see you too, Dad. Got your stuff in the truck?"

He waves me off.

"We'll get it later. Take me inside, already. I've gotta shake hands with the major, I'm about to wet my damn pants. Drove straight here from Bozeman."

Jesus, that's over six hours. I can't even hold it for that long.

"Should'a stopped, Dad," I admonish him, but again he waves me off.

"Don't start. I'll be fine once you show me to the bathroom," he grumbles pointedly.

I can hear the barking inside when I step up to the front door.

"Max, settle down," I intercept the big dog when I enter the house.

Last thing I need is him knocking Dad to the ground and, God forbid, breaking his hip.

"Hold on to me."

I grab Dad's hand and steady him while he kicks off his expensive boots. Then he pushes past me, shuffling on stockinged feet to the bathroom.

"That your father?" I hear Ama calling from the kitchen.

"Yup. He just drove all the damn way from Bozeman without stopping," I respond as I make my way to the back of the house.

But when I step through the doorway my eyes are instantly drawn to Alex, who is wearing my clothes.

Fuck me.

Not like my favorite workout shirt is revealing—in fact, it hangs on her like a potato sack—but I swear she looks sexy as hell.

Ama clears her throat and my eyes snap her way. She's flashing a big grin.

"Got her in out of the rain," she explains unnecessarily. I could've figured that out for myself. "Looked like a drenched cat so her clothes are in the dryer."

"I should probably get to work," Alex says immediately, shooting to her feet.

"Sit. It's still raining outside."

She glances out the back before turning to me. "Hardly."

"Sky's starting to break up. Give it ten minutes and it'll be dry," I insist.

She seems undecided until Ama adds, "Your clothes will be dry in another ten or fifteen. Time for a refill."

"Goddangit, almost sprang a leak there," Dad says as he shuffles into the kitchen.

"I'd better not find splatter on the floor," Ama grumbles as my father makes his way over to her, grinning wide as he wraps her up in a hug.

"My aim is still good. Always so warm and welcoming, Ama, does my rickety heart good."

"Nothing wrong with your heart, old man. It'll still be ticking long after that skinny body of yours gives up. Have you eaten at all since Christmas?"

This is nothing new. Since Dad's very first visit to the ranch—when he tried to order Ama around—these two have been bickering like an old married couple. Underneath all that bluster they adore the heck out of each other.

I keep an eye on Alex, who appears to be taking in the friendly spat with a healthy dose of humor. But when James walks in, and instantly hooks Ama behind the neck laying a wet one on her, Alex is clearly shocked.

"I eat," Dad says with a stubborn look when suddenly he notices Alex sitting at the dining table. His face transforms on the spot and the charmer appears. "Well, well, well, who have we here?"

Alex drags her eyes from the couple and focuses on Dad.

"Alex, this is my father, Thomas Harvey. Dad, Alexandra owns Hart's Horse Rescue down the road. She's working with Phantom."

My father shakes his head. "Too much horse for a pretty filly like that."

Shit. I should've known that would be his reaction. My dad is a bit of a traditionalist.

I quickly jump in before Alex has a chance to climb down Dad's throat.

"Actually, she's very good with Phantom. None of us—not even Doc Evans—managed to change his bandages without sedating him first."

"She did?"

Dad directs a surprised look at Alex, who is clearly not used to compliments. A bit of a blush crawls up her cheeks. I fucking love that freckled pale skin, it shows everything.

"It's what I do," she states simply, before she walks over to my dad and holds out her hand.

Dad takes and holds on to it as he glances outside.

"Rain stopped. If you want me to believe that, you're gonna have to show me."

Alex juts her chin in the air proudly.

"Let me get my clothes on and I will."

She pulls her hand back and marches toward the laundry room, turning back at the last minute with a sparkle in her eyes.

"But...you may wanna use the facilities first," she says, a grin pulling at her lips. "This is gonna take a while."

Ama's loud hearty laugh bursts loose and gets the rest of us going. Even Dad, who shakes his head as he turns to me.

"She's a fiery one."

Five

"She's got your father wrapped around her finger as well."

Sully walks up and rests his arms on the fence beside mine.

In the corral, Alex throws her head back and laughs at my dad. Phantom doesn't even flinch at the sudden sound. She looks beautiful. In her element. Free.

I'd like to find out more about her, her life, how she ended up here. She has me curious and that's new for me. I may feel the occasional attraction, but I can't recall ever being this fascinated with a woman.

"You're being outplayed by your father," Sully teases, interrupting my thoughts.

Dad's ended up in the corral with Alex and Phantom the last couple of days and I've taken a back seat. I trust my father. He's been a horseman his whole life, and his father before him. He may be turning eighty this year, and working full days running a ranch may be too much, but working with Alex may be just the thing to make him feel useful.

"I'm not playing."

Sully's silent for a moment but I can feel his scrutiny.

"I stand corrected," he concedes before abruptly changing the subject. "Have you heard anything from Ewing?"

"Nope."

"Don't understand why we're not out there looking."

"Not up to the sheriff's department, Sul. The feds are on it."

"Right, and they're pinching pennies while those guys are getting farther and farther away."

I clap him on the shoulder and head to the stable. It's time I give Blitz a good workout.

When I return to the ranch an hour or so later, Alex's truck is gone but Dad is coming down the porch.

"He's a beauty," he says as he walks up, rubbing a hand along Blitz's muscular neck.

The horse flicks his head a few times.

"He's got an attitude." I swing my leg over the horn and slide down. "Too much fire and he battles me every step of the way."

"Gonna breed him?"

"That was the plan, but not as long as he's like this."

I take his reins and start walking toward the barn. Dad falls into step beside me.

"You could ask that filly to see what she can do. Betcha she could sweeten him up some."

"She's got her hands full with Phantom. She also has a rescue to run."

Dad shrugs. "Wouldn't hurt to ask."

"Maybe."

"Who's that?"

He looks back at the house where a black SUV is just pulling up.

"Not sure. Can you take Blitz? One of the hands in the stable can help you with his tack."

Dad huffs loudly when I suggest asking for help, but he takes the reins.

Two people get out of the SUV and start walking to the house. I instantly recognize the white lettering on the back of their jackets, *feds*, but I'm not familiar with the agents.

"Can I help you?" I call out, closing the distance.

The older of the two men turns his head and changes direction, walking toward me.

"Jonas Harvey?"

"That's me."

"Special Agents Schroeder and Wolff. We'd like to speak with you."

"Come on in."

I gesture toward the house, where Ama is already poking her head out of the front door. The woman doesn't miss a beat.

"What can I do for you, gentlemen?" I ask when we settle in my office at the front of the house.

The younger agent, Wolff, stands by the door like some sentry while Schroeder takes a seat on the other side of my desk. The hierarchy is easily established.

"I understand Sheriff Ewing already spoke to you about the incident near Kootenay Falls?"

"If you're talking about the two escaped prisoners, then yes," I state bluntly.

I don't have the patience to beat around the bush.

"Right. I hope you understand this information is confidential. Last thing we need is the press getting hold of this."

I sit back in my chair and fold my arms over my chest.

"I assume you've done your due diligence before you came here, which means you are aware of my background and know damn well I run a team of professionals. Not like it's the first time we've been called in by the FBI to assist. Now..." I lean forward and plant my elbows on my desk. "My guess is you're here because you need help tracking down Adams and Wright."

I purposely use their last names so Schroeder knows he can stop holding his cards close to the vest. If we're going out there to hunt these guys down, you better believe I want every scrap of information I can get my hands on. The safety of my team is at stake.

"Looks like I'm going to have to have a talk with Ewing."

"No need. The sheriff didn't share that information."

"Then how—"

"Lucky guess. Now, can we get to the point of your visit?" I prompt.

I don't like Schroeder. Either he's a little too full of his own importance, or he's feeling the pressure and is trying to defer responsibility. Either way, he needs to get his priorities straight.

Not happy with my less than subservient attitude, he clenches his jaw.

"We're not entirely sure what happened but we found the van in a ditch, and the two US Marshals transporting the prisoners killed, their sidearms missing. No sign of Adams or Wright. Our dogs were able to track them along the Kootenay River to where Fisher River branches off to the south. That's where they lost them."

"I bet you they went into the river. The Kootenay is too

deep, but it wouldn't be hard for them to trek through Fisher River."

I should know, the river borders the east side of my property and intersects with US-2 a mile and a half south of here.

"We figured. Unfortunately the dogs weren't able to pick up the trail from there. We've explored all the mountain roads, had a helicopter flying over, but no luck."

That doesn't surprise me. There's still a lot of land that isn't easily accessible. It's like searching for a needle in a haystack.

"I'm told your unit is good at finding people."

"We are," I confirm without hesitation.

"These are not five-year-old runaways, though," he feels necessary to point out.

Prick. Guess he heard about the kid the other day.

"Neither were the insurgents we flushed from the mountains in Afghanistan," I snap. "You're the one looking for help. If you're worried we're not qualified, then why did you come?"

Now it's Schroeder who leans forward.

"I need to find these guys."

His voice is almost pleading. So it's pressure making him an asshole, or maybe just a worse one.

"I can have my team and my horses at the mouth of Fisher River tomorrow morning at eight."

"They could be gone by then."

I snort. "That might've been a valid point if you hadn't spun your wheels for days before calling us in. If you're right, they were likely gone days ago. If not, they're holed up somewhere and we'll find them. Tomorrow morning at eight. We'd appreciate a briefing from your search team leaders so we don't waste more time doing double duty."

He nods. I look past him at Agent Wolff, who is now leaning casually against the wall, a smirk on his face. Looks like the younger agent isn't a fan of Schroeder either.

It takes twenty more minutes to get Ama to fill out a standard contract, which I have Schroeder sign on the spot. I don't trust him not to try and stiff us in the end.

I watch from the porch as the SUV takes off down the driveway when Sully walks up from the barn.

"Feds?" he guesses correctly.

"Get the gear ready. We're heading out at daylight."

Alex

"Hey, good boy. You ready for your exercise?"

Phantom rubs his nose against my coat pocket. Smart animal, knows I keep a few treats in there.

"You can have one later," I mumble, sliding my hand under his mane to stroke his graceful neck.

He doesn't flinch at my touch anymore, which is why I'm going to try a saddle on him today. Test the trust I built with him.

I've been working with him daily for a week and a half now. Normally, I'd opt to give it a bit more time before testing him, but his leg is healing nicely and from what Ama told me, his stud schedule starts the first week of May. That's a week away. It wouldn't hurt my reputation if Phantom would be able to go ahead as planned.

The only thing that has me second-guess myself is, for the last couple of days I haven't seen hide nor hair of Jonas. In fact, the only guys I've seen around have been Dan and

Toby, the young ranch hands, and Thomas, Jonas's father. I wonder if he'd be upset if I don't wait for him.

Thomas mentioned they're assisting on a search but didn't elaborate. I've been wondering if it has something to do with those missing prisoners Jonas warned me about. If you ask me, it's a little odd—not to mention potentially dangerous—to have a group of civilians join in a manhunt by law enforcement. I have a feeling there may be more to it but for all his chattering, Thomas was pretty tight-lipped.

"You sure about this, Filly?" Thomas says coming out of the tack room with Phantom's saddle.

"Yup," I state firmly as I lead Phantom out of his stall.

The horse doesn't even look twice at Thomas or the saddle, which bodes well.

Showing me this isn't his first rodeo, Thomas hands me the saddle blanket first. I take my time letting Phantom sniff it and then rubbing it along his flank. This is a trained horse, so it's entirely possible he would have accepted the saddle without incident, but I prefer approaching things as if it were his first time. It's not just the saddle he needs to trust, it's me too.

But just as I'm about to lift the saddle on his back my phone rings, startling the horse. He rears up, his blanket sliding off his back to the ground.

"Just let him go," Thomas says.

I do as he suggests while pulling my phone from my pocket.

"Not a good time, Lucy."

"Sorry, but I'm in a bit of a pickle."

"What's up?"

I take a step closer to the fence, leaning against it as I watch Phantom on the other side of the corral trying to nip at a few clumps of grass growing around the base of the post.

"I'm stranded a few miles up the road from home. We missed the deadline to put in a delivery order so I just went by Homesteader's to pick up the feed and I've got the truck bed full of bags. I can call a tow truck, but we need the feed at the rescue."

Shit.

The truck Lucy drives has been acting up the last few weeks. We've talked about investing in a new vehicle, but that would take a good chunk out of our budget we hadn't counted on. We're in better condition now than two weeks ago—the paycheck for working with the stallion helps a lot —but we still need to be careful.

I glance over at Thomas, who is eyeing me closely.

"My assistant's truck full of animal feed has broken down," I explain.

"Then go. I'll take care of Phantom."

I'm sure doubt is etched on my face. "I don't know…"

"Not gonna put the saddle on, gonna leave that to you, but I haven't forgotten how to work a horse on the lunge line. Go," he insists.

"Is that the luscious Jonas?" Lucy asks in my other ear.

I decide to ignore her and instead tell her I'm on my way before hanging up.

"Positive?" I make sure one last time.

"Good Lord, woman. Will you get outta here already?"

I climb over the fence, leaving Phantom in the corral.

"I'll be back as soon as possible," I promise Thomas.

"Just get your business sorted. I'll see ya tomorrow."

I swear the old man blushes when I lean in and kiss his leathery cheek. Then I jog up the hill to my truck.

Lucy's old Chevy is off on the shoulder on the opposite

side of the road, about three miles up from the rescue. When I pass it, I see a large tow truck pulling up right behind it. I wait for a gap in traffic, make a U-turn, and pass the old truck before I steer my vehicle onto the shoulder.

A tall man is getting out of the big truck as Lucy gets out of the stalled pickup. The guy has a ball cap pulled low over his eyes but he looks familiar.

"I'm sorry I caught you at a bad time," Lucy starts.

I wave her off.

"Don't worry," I reassure her. "What happened?"

"I have no idea. It did that weird shudder again, except this time it died. Can't get it going."

My eyes turn to the guy, who has come to a stop behind Lucy.

"Hey, you called for a tow?"

Now I know where I've seen him. I had my Ford in a few months ago for an oil change at a place that was recommended to me. Something Automotive. It suddenly comes to me.

"Standish Automotive, right?"

His smile lights up his whole face.

"Yes, ma'am, that's me. Name's Hugh."

I cringe at the *ma'am* but let it go.

"Well, Hugh," Lucy jumps in as she swings around. "I'm the one who called for a tow." She indicates the back of the old Chevy, which is loaded down with a pile of fifty-pound bags. "But we need to move these bags to that truck first."

She nods at my Ford as she drops down the gate and climbs in the bed.

It doesn't escape my notice that Hugh follows her movements carefully. The guy is probably mid-thirties, maybe

55

older, and definitely not blind. It takes him a moment to jump in.

"Let me," he says, grabbing two bags at once and tossing one over each shoulder.

Then he saunters off to my F-150 and leans over the side as he drops them in the back, making for a nice view. Before he turns back, I avert my eyes, only to catch Lucy with her eyebrows up in her hairline. Guess she doesn't miss much either.

I feel a little useless as Hugh hauls all eight bags to my truck.

"I'll try to have a look at it today, otherwise first thing tomorrow," he says to Lucy.

"Don't do any work on it yet, though," I jump in. "I want to make sure it's worth repairing."

"Sure. I'll tell you fair and square."

"Appreciate it."

I start walking toward the Ford while I hear Lucy rattling off our home phone number behind me.

I'm behind the wheel with the engine running by the time she opens my passenger door, a smile playing on her lips.

"Look who's all flustered now," I tease her as I pull away from the shoulder.

From the corner of my eye, I see her making a face at me before straightening in her seat.

"Shut up and drive."

Six

JONAS

"Anything?"

I dismount Sugar and glare at Schroeder who clearly has been through our stuff, judging by the open zipper to the tent we set up.

Last thing I need is to have our base camp invaded by the feds.

It's been a frustrating couple of days, after we looked to be off to a good start. It had taken us just a couple of hours of searching, along both sides of the Fisher River, to find evidence of someone climbing up the bank about four miles south of where the river branched off from the Kootenay. The partial footprint would've been missed by the FBI search groups from shore, but Sully and Cisco were scanning the bank from the shallow water.

On the other side of the road, running alongside the river, was a logging road—no more than a dirt track—running up into the mountains to the west. They were smart enough to steer clear of the dirt road, but left a trail maybe twenty or so yards into the tree line running parallel to it. We were able to follow the tracks a couple of miles in before we lost the trail.

By that time it was getting late and rather than heading blindly into the woods, we opted to go get the trucks, set up camp right here on the side of the logging road, and plan a search for the next day.

That was three days ago.

We only covered about a third of the search grid we'd set out and with every day passing, without picking up the trail again, my frustration grew.

"No. Nothing yet," I grind out trying to keep my temper.

"Every day you spend dicking around they could be farther away," Schroeder grumbles.

Sure, and whose fucking fault is that? I just manage to keep that thought to myself and resort to staring him down. Fletch takes Sugar's reins from my hands to tend to her while I face off with the agent.

I try for a reconciliatory tone. "Look, no one is dicking around." Except maybe Schroeder himself. "We know they're up there somewhere and are methodically searching a grid we laid out."

I explain there's a big difference between looking for someone who is missing versus someone who doesn't want to be found. The first is relatively easy, since everyone leaves some evidence behind, but it gets significantly more difficult when someone's main objective is to stay invisible.

"I get the sense these two guys are no strangers to the wilderness. Maybe hunters or even survivalists. Is there any background you can give us on that? Wasn't the attack in Helena claimed by a militant group?"

Best way to take the wind out of his sails is to get him involved.

"The Montana Sovereign Posse, yes," Schroeder confirms. "We haven't been able to find a lot about these guys. Neither Wright or Adams talked, no mentions on social media, and the only reason we knew who to look for in the first place was the overnight CCTV footage from the hours before the bombs went off."

"So who were these guys?" Sully pipes up.

"Adams is a twenty-seven-year-old garbage collector from Helena and Wright a forty-one-year-old, local truck driver from Park City, just outside Billings."

"That's not next door to each other," Sully observes. "A three-and-a-half-hour drive."

"True, but they do have one thing in common," Schroeder shares, his eyes coming back to me. "And that goes back to your earlier question about them being outdoorsmen. We discovered through interviews with family and neighbors, both men were hugely into big game. Bear, bighorn, bison, you name it, they were on it."

"That covers about the entire year," I quickly calculate.

If you'd mark those individual hunting seasons on a calendar, you'd have about two-thirds covered. Except perhaps part of February through middle of April, and the months of July and August would be the only ones left open.

"Yup," the agent confirms. "Both men were loners—although Adams has an ex-wife—and they both were gone most weekends, and last year each of them took a three-week vacation in October."

"Same dates?" I want to know.

"Yup. To the day."

"Do you know where they went?"

When Schroeder appears to hesitate with an answer, I prompt him sharply, "If you want us to find those guys, it won't help if you keep holding back information."

"We found a single charge to Adam's credit card for the Cenex gas station along US-2 in Happy's Inn. That was on October seventeenth," he reluctantly shares.

"That's twenty-five miles from here," Fletch observes. "You figure they spent that time in the area?"

"October is in black bear season. We've got plenty of those," Sully points out.

"Can we assume they were together?" I ask Schroeder.

"They only keep their security feed for a few months, but we showed around their pictures and one of the clerks there remembers them coming in together. They stood out. Both were dressed head to toe in camo."

Damn.

"They're familiar with this area," I muse out loud. "Which could mean they're not just on the run, they have a destination in mind."

"That changes things," Sully adds.

Schroeder immediately reacts to that.

"How so?"

"Running, they'd be on the move and we'd eventually find some evidence of that. They'd need food and water at some point. But I'm guessing there's hundreds of hunting shacks, cabins, and hideouts scattered through these mountains, and they may be holed up in one they stocked with supplies that could sustain them for months last October," Sully explains. "It changes the way we need to search."

He's right. We're wasting time searching on a grid, when we could be pinpointing locations to focus on.

"We need a new plan."

I'm still pissed with the FBI agent when we're heading

back to the ranch. If we'd had this information from the start, we might've already found them. Instead we packed up camp and are heading home.

As I tried to explain to Schroeder, who wasn't too receptive, we need a decent bed for a night—sleeping on the rocky ground is wreaking havoc on my damn back—give the horses a little break, and plot a new course. We'd look at satellite to pinpoint structures, working our way outward from where we'd set up camp. Sully can bring his drone, which will allow us closer views to see if we can spot evidence of recent activity, and once we've identified possible locations, we'll head out on horseback.

The only light point in these new developments is that I'll see Alex tomorrow morning when she shows up. For the past four days my eyes have been focused on my surroundings, but my thoughts have been on the pretty redhead.

∽

Alex

"Let's wait and see what the mechanic has to say."

I hold back a chuckle. In previous discussions on whether or not to invest in some younger wheels than the old Chevy, it was always Lucy who was *for* buying something else. I'm the one who was holding off. Looks like those tables have turned.

The other thing that strikes me as amusing is the fact she tries her best to sound uninterested in 'the mechanic,' but I saw her response to him yesterday. She's definitely interested.

"Sure thing. Next driveway," I tell her.

She's dropping me off at High Meadow before she takes Chief over to Doc Evans. He got tangled up in a coil of rusty barbed wire some idiot left lying around the woods behind the back paddock. He'd followed me out last night when I walked back there to check on Daisy.

She's the senior donkey we took in back in Billings. She'd spent most of her life in a petting zoo but a few years ago started biting the kids. We'd taken her in and had her looked over. As it turned out, the poor thing was suffering with severe arthritis and in constant pain. That's why we keep her out in the field as much as we can now, so she stays limber. She's on medication and that combined with movement is keeping it in check. She's not alone, a couple of the horses are out there as well including Flint, the young gelding who seems to have taken on the role of companion to Daisy.

Chief went off sniffing in the woods, and a few minutes later I heard him yelp. I had to use the flashlight on my phone to get him untangled. Luckily the cuts were superficial and we were able to clean them last night, but this morning I noticed he'd been licking one wound on his front leg in particular, and he was limping. Maybe something got embedded we didn't see so Lucy's going to get Doc Evans to check it out.

Next on my list is to get rid of that damn barbed wire and anything else that may have gotten dumped back there. I'm ashamed to say we've been here now almost five months —granted most of those were winter months—and we've never bothered to go beyond the fence lines. Beyond it is mostly wilderness. The property was listed as forty-six acres, but I have maybe three or four of those acres in use. The rest of it goes back a ways.

I wasn't exactly looking for something this big but the

property was in foreclosure, was in a good location, the house and stable in decent condition, and the price on it ended up less than most places a quarter the size. It had been a no-brainer.

"Jesus, look at you," Lucy says beside me as the house comes into view. "You've got a damn welcoming committee waiting for ya."

My heart starts beating just a little faster when I spot Jonas on the porch along with his father, Sully, and a black guy I saw only once before but was never introduced to. Every single pair of eyes is aimed at my truck.

I tell Lucy where to park and take my time giving Chief some attention while trying to compose myself before I get out.

"Hey!" Lucy calls after me and I turn to see her top half hanging out the window. "Call me when you're ready for me to pick you up."

I hear the crunch of footsteps behind me but before I can turn around a hand lands on my shoulder and Jonas steps up beside me.

"No need. I'll drop her home. Hi, I'm Jonas Harvey," he says, letting go of my shoulder and walking up to the window, his hand outstretched. "I don't think we've met before."

"I'm Lucy Lenoir. And actually, we have met. I was with Alex when your horse got injured, but I see I didn't leave much of an impression."

"That's because he's losing sight at his advanced age," a deep voice sounds behind me, and the man who was standing on the porch beside Sully walks into view.

Even with a big smile on his face he makes an imposing picture. Not quite as tall as Jonas, but built like a linebacker.

He doesn't spare me a glance, his focus entirely on Lucy who eyes him suspiciously.

"And my only comfort is that you're not that far behind me, Bo," Jonas responds with an amused shake of his head.

Whoever this Bo is, it's clear he's on good terms with the boss to exchange the lighthearted barbs. It opens my eyes a little more to the different faces of Jonas. It only seems to add to his appeal.

"Good to meet you, gentlemen." Lucy gives each man a nod. "I've gotta run." Then she flashes me with a wide-eyed look that has me chuckle. "Good luck with this lot. Call if you need me."

As I watch her drive off in my truck, Jonas walks over.

"Hope Bo didn't scare her off," he says.

"Oh, no. She has to get one of our rescue dogs to Doc Evans. He got himself caught in some barbed wire last night."

"Dogs too?" Bo saunters up. "I thought you rescued horses."

"We do, but we won't turn a blind eye to any animal in distress."

"Bo, this is Alex Hart. Alex, meet Beauregard Rivera. He's one of my guys," Jonas explains as the man reaches out his shovel-sized hand and flashes that big grin at me.

"What he means is I'm his favorite guy."

The big hand swallows mine but his shake is gentle.

"Why don't you go ahead, I need a minute with Alex."

I'm almost annoyed those words launch butterflies in my stomach. I remind myself this is a job and I'm a professional. I better start behaving like one.

The moment Bo returns to the house I turn to Jonas and ramble off my report.

"Phantom is progressing nicely. His leg is looking good,

the skin has closed over and his limp is getting better. He's also less jumpy. He's even getting used to your father. He had him out on the lunge rope yesterday. Oh, that reminds me, I had to leave early yesterday. Lucy's truck stalled an—"

"Alex," Jonas interrupts with a smile. "I checked on Phantom last night and see the improvement. I've also talked to my dad and he filled me in on everything. That's not what I wanted to talk about."

"It isn't?"

He steps close, closer than perhaps is wise. I have to tilt my head back and catch him shaking his head.

"Nope. I'm busy this morning but Dad'll be around to give you a hand. I was hoping we could have lunch today. I have a few things I'd like to discuss with you. Blitz is one of them," he adds.

"Oh."

Blitz is the high-strung Arabian. For a minute there I thought... I shake my head. Good, he wants to talk business. That's a good thing.

"Sure, that's fine." I toss him a friendly smile and step to the side so I can maneuver around him. "I best get to Phantom."

"Think you can be done around noon?"

"I'll make sure I am," I respond over my shoulder.

He doesn't say anything else, but I can feel his eyes on my back as I force my legs to keep walking toward the barn.

It's not until I step inside, I hear the storm door at the front of the house slam shut.

Seven

JONAS

This plan was hatched after four this morning when I heard Dad get up to use the bathroom, and I couldn't get back to sleep.

His space is an in-law suite on the opposite side of the upstairs hallway from the master. Unfortunately, living alone for decades, Dad makes no effort to be quiet. He turns on all the lights and slams doors, which startles Max every night...thus waking me up.

It's not a big deal—my alarm goes off at five every morning anyway—so I haven't bothered mentioning it. At least he's as regular as clockwork.

This morning I use the extra hour trying to find a way to spend some time with Alex. Sully is checking a few locations we were able to pinpoint on satellite images last night with the drone to see if he can get a closer look. If any of them look promising, James, Fletch, Bo, and I will head out there with the horses for on-the-ground recon. That way we can find the closest access road with as little time as possible traipsing through miles and miles of wilderness if it's not necessary.

"It's all here," Ama says, walking in with a bulging saddle bag and setting it on my desk.

"Perfect. Thanks, Ama. I owe you."

She snorts as she turns to walk back out.

"I'll add it to the pile," I can hear her mumble to herself.

I get up, clip a radio on my belt so the guys can get hold of me, and sling the saddlebag over my shoulder.

When I get to the barn, I notice Dan already has Blitz and Moonbeam saddled like I asked him. I give him a thumbs-up. He's done everything I asked since he let Phantom get away. Handing his phone in to Sully or Ama in the morning, walking Phantom twice a day, and everything else I've thrown at him.

"How's your mom?" I ask, catching him coming out of the tack room.

"Same old, same old," he responds, still not telling me much. Then he adds, "She's stable."

"That's good." At least I hope it is. "Thanks for getting the horses ready."

"No problem," he mumbles as he moves past me, the weight of the world on his shoulders.

"Hey, Dan?"

He stops and turns.

"The slate's clean, all right?"

His mouth goes slack. "Sorry?"

"We're square."

This time he gets it and I can read the relief on his face. He gives me a nod and heads for the doors, but his shoulders are squared and his step a lot lighter.

I can hear Alex before I see her. She's talking in that

soothing melodic voice in Phantom's stall. My father's in there with her.

"How'd it go?"

"She got the saddle on him," Dad shares and Alex lifts her head with a smile.

"He was good. I'll get on tomorrow. See how he does with my weight," she says.

Phantom is not an easy mount, which is why Sully or I are usually the ones exercising him. I'm about to caution her when I catch the slight tilt to her head and amused expression on her face. It's exactly what she's expecting me to do, so I keep my concerns to myself. Dad reads the situation well and chuckles.

"Dad, Ama is looking for you," I lie before he has a chance to make some smart-ass remark.

"What for?"

"How should I know?"

"I told Alex I'd put away the tack."

He points to the saddle slung over the stall door. I should never have told him what I'd planned, but at five this morning—over coffee—I clearly wasn't thinking straight. I know he's just needling me. The sparkle in his eyes tells me he's enjoying himself.

"Don't worry about that, I've got it," Alex jumps in.

Like hell.

"I've got it," I bite off.

Shit. I'm annoyed with Dad but end up snapping at her.

I see Dad's big Stetson shaking as he walks out of the stall, Alex exits right behind him and closes the latch. Good thing I love Dad and he's old because sometimes I'd like to take a swing at the pain in my ass.

"I'll be right back and we'll go."

I try for a friendlier tone and grab the saddle from the door.

"If you're busy, we can do this another time..."

"I'm not. I'll be right out."

Alex is leaning against the side of the barn when I lead the horses out. Her eyes widen when she sees us.

"We're riding?"

"If that's okay with you? I assume you can ride."

The grin she sends me is full of mischief.

"Hell, yeah."

"This is Moonbeam." I hand her the reins to the almost entirely black mare. She has only a few spots of white on the back of her thighs. "She can have a bit of a hard mouth, but I'm sure you can handle that."

There's a reason I'm not handing her one of the easier horses. I'd like to see how she manages.

As expected, that proud, pointy chin of hers jerks up a fraction.

"You bet."

I admire the way she mounts her effortlessly, looking entirely at home in the saddle. She loosely wraps the reins around the horn and adjusts the stirrups that are too long for her.

"Ready?"

She nods sharply and I notice she's wearing that ratty old ball cap again today.

"You know, you need a proper Stetson. That cap may keep the sun out of your eyes but not off your neck." Her hand instantly goes to the bill of her cap. "You'll get burned more easily at this elevation," I finish.

"I'll think about it," she says in a way that implies she already knows the answer, and it's no.

She'll have to find out the hard way, I guess.

"By the way, I thought this was lunch. Where are we going?"

"Don't worry, I'll feed you. It's not far."

I let her take the lead, giving her directions as we go. It gives me the opportunity to observe how she does with Moonbeam.

To my surprise the reins are still very loosely looped around the horn. She's giving the mare her head and uses nothing but her knees and a soft pat of her hand on Moonbeam's left or right shoulder to indicate direction.

Of course it helps the mare has been on this trail before, but it's pretty clever nonetheless. She's not controlling or challenging the horse, she's guiding, and it seems Moonbeam is responding. I'm pretty confident in the saddle, but I'll be honest, she's doing better than I am.

Blitz doesn't like to follow, he's used to leading, so I'm having a hell of a time keeping him back. He's been bouncing around since we left the ranch.

"Oh, this is gorgeous."

Up ahead Alex has just cleared the tree line and slows down. I let Blitz pass them by and lead the way into a clearing right next to the Fisher River. The river bends here and years of erosion have widened the stream. With the winter runoff in early spring it always grows to the size of a small lake. It's one of my favorite spots on the ranch.

I bring Blitz to a halt and dismount, walking him to a small copse of trees on the edge of the water where I tie him off in the shade. When I turn, Alex is already doing the same with her mount.

"Are we fishing for our lunch?" she asks.

Her tone is lighthearted but the way she chews her bottom lip betrays her nerves.

I grab the saddle bag and hold it up.

"Nope. I brought it."

"You planned ahead," she observes.

"Yes, I did."

Alex

It really is beautiful here.

The water is so calm, it reflects the peaks of the mountains on the other side like a mirror.

"Here."

Jonas presses a warm metal mug in my hands.

"Hot chocolate," he explains, pouring a second mug from the thermos he pulled from the saddlebag. "I'd take credit for it, but this is all Ama. She wanted to know if I was nuts when I asked her if she could pack a picnic. Was afraid I'd give you hypothermia by making you eat out here."

I grin at him.

"This is perfect," I tell him honestly. Especially now I'm holding a warm drink.

I take a tentative sip, surprised to find the drink still piping hot.

Jonas unearths a bunch of containers from the bag.

"We've got sandwiches," he says, opening one of them. "Looks like some kind of soft cheese with some of that green stuff on top."

He shows me.

"You mean sprouts?"

"That what they are?" he counters with a wry grin. "Ama is always trying to get me to eat more green stuff. I'm more of a meat and potatoes kinda guy, but I don't mind the occasional greens as long as they're fried."

I snort a laugh. He'd get along famously with Jackson, who is of the same mind. Despite my attempts to introduce a large variety of fruits and vegetables into his diet, he resorted to living off hamburgers and mac and cheese when he was in college.

"You're like Jackson. I'd hide vegetables in dishes whenever I could get away with it."

He hands me one of the sandwiches wrapped in a napkin.

"Jackson?" He wants to know.

"My son. He's twenty-three."

Jonas sits down on the rock beside me with a sandwich of his own.

"I didn't realize you have children."

"Only the one," I clarify. "Although I guess, technically, he's no longer a child."

Wouldn't really fit to call a young man who is somewhere in Iraq serving his country a 'kid.'

"In college?" He wants to know as he takes a bite of his lunch.

I shake my head.

"US Army. He was deployed to Iraq six months ago."

Immediately sympathy steals over his face.

"You must be worried."

The warm tone in his voice makes swallowing the bite I just took difficult. I simply nod my response. He seems to guess I need a moment and turns his gaze to the view.

"I spent twenty years in the military. Enlisted at eighteen. I was full of piss and vinegar back then, determined to be part of something bigger than the fifteen-hundred-and-twenty-acre ranch I'd grown up on."

I glance over at him, noting he hasn't taken his eyes off the view.

"Dad was disappointed but proud. He'd always hoped I'd work the ranch with him, but couldn't fault me for serving my country." A small smile tugs at his lips. "I think he secretly hoped I'd get my fill after a few years, but that turned into twenty. My mother was heartbroken and terrified, but also proud." He turns his head to me. "I'm guessing that's about how you feel."

"Pretty much," I confess, my voice hoarse, and I quickly take another bite. "I wasn't too happy myself when he announced he was dropping out of college to follow in his father's footsteps."

"And what did he have to say about it? His father," he clarifies.

"We'll never know. He was killed in action when Jackson was a small boy."

Jonas shifts his position on the rock so he's fully facing me. Then he places a warm hand on my shoulder.

"I'm so sorry."

I shrug and inadvertently his hand falls away. I know it's ridiculous but I immediately miss its weight and warmth.

"It was a long time ago."

"But it left you to raise a young child on your own. That can't have been easy."

"It wasn't at first," I admit. "But once the sharper edges wore off, we did okay. Jackson was a pretty easy kid."

"Made for quite the shock when he announced enlisting," he observes quite astutely. "Does he know how long?"

"He told me nine months at the outset, but he warned me that could change."

As much as I avoid the news these days, I know there has been growing unrest in the entire region. Call me selfish, but I hope my baby comes home before it really heats up.

"I'm sorry I haven't been around," Jonas apologizes, abruptly changing the subject, for which I'm grateful.

"Not to worry, your dad's been great."

"I'm glad. It's good for him to stay involved, and to be honest, it gives me peace of mind to know he's keeping an eye on things."

He takes another bite and chews in silence.

"He mentioned something about you helping on a search?" Curiosity has me ask.

"Yeah. Aside from High Meadow, I also run the High Mountain Trackers. As the name implies, we specialize in mountain search and rescue. On occasion, we're contracted by law enforcement to assist. Then it becomes search and extract."

"You're looking for the escaped prisoners," I confirm.

"We are. There's reason to believe they've holed up somewhere in these mountains, which means it could take some time. This kind of search can be a bit erratic. I'll be around while Sully flies the drone, checking out possible hideouts from the air, and when he finds something worth exploring, the rest of us go in on horseback to have a closer look. You might see me in the morning, and then suddenly we disappear for up to a few days at a time."

"Okay."

I'm not entirely sure why he's telling me, but I appreciate the insight.

"I like you, Alex. I'd like to ask you out to dinner—do this properly—but there's a distinct possibility I'd have to stand you up, which I don't really want to do. So I have to take my opportunities when I can. Hence the picnic."

Oh.

Wow.

Butterflies are back in full force as I wonder how the hell to respond to that.

"It's nice."

It's nice? Oh, dear Lord, shoot me now.

I can feel my face flush. I should've just kept my damn mouth shut.

Jonas doesn't seem bothered and grins wide.

"It *is* nice, isn't it?"

I don't really taste anything when I take a huge bite of my sandwich, but at least it keeps my mouth from saying something else embarrassing.

For a couple of minutes we finish the sandwiches in companionable silence, when Jonas hands me another container and produces a fork.

"Ama made my favorite last night; cherry cheesecake. It's a miracle there was enough left this morning but she managed to pack some up for us."

"Love cheesecake," I confess, digging my fork in.

I moan when the sweet creamy flavor hits my taste buds and notice too late how his eyes are focused on my mouth.

"You said something about Blitz," I mention, eager to steer the conversation to neutral territory.

"I did," he says, dragging his gaze up to meet mine. "I was hoping you might have some time to work with him, since it looks like I might have my hands full for the foreseeable future. I'd ask Dad, but—"

"Yes!" I blurt out a little too enthusiastically. "I mean, I'd love to. He has so much potential."

I've eyed the beautiful horse, stopped by his stall, or visited him at the fence to the smaller paddock behind the barn where he'd occasionally stand, looking starved for attention.

"I agree, but he's not channeling his energy well. He's still very much a puppy. Unfortunately his previous owners barely worked him at all. He needs a firm hand."

"Are you asking if I'm up for the job?"

"Only one way to find out; I want you to ride Blitz back."

I know I'm grinning like a goof, but I'm so excited at the prospect.

"Hell, yeah."

He shakes his head, with a twitch at the corner of his mouth, before decimating half his slice of cheesecake in one bite.

I take in a deep breath of clean mountain air, trying to curb my excitement, when suddenly something occurs to me.

"You gave me Moonbeam to test me."

He takes his time answering but when he does, he's honest.

"I did, but you handled her really well."

The compliment feels good but only for a minute.

"And if I'd failed?"

"But you didn't," he counters.

"You still don't trust me," I conclude, a little sad.

"Quite the opposite, actually," he corrects me on the spot. "I wouldn't be letting you handle Phantom if I didn't. That horse is High Meadow's current livelihood. Blitz is the future and I wouldn't even have considered handing over that responsibility if I didn't trust you."

Damn, that feels good.

And a little scary.

Eight

JONAS

The ride back is silent.

This was the third run—checking another couple of places—in the past six days where we've come up empty. That is, if you don't count the hapless father and son we gave the scare of their lives about two hours ago.

We had our hopes pinned on this last cabin when we crossed two different sets of boot prints in the damp earth. We approached the last cabin on our list carefully, noting the embers in the firepit still smoking. Someone had made sure there was plenty of firewood to last a while, but there was no one around. The cabin was empty but also showed the presence of two individuals.

Then we laid in wait for five damn hours. We'd tied off the horses well back and got closer on foot, taking up positions around the cabin. Despite stiff muscles and creaking joints, we had the two men who came walking up disarmed and facedown in the dirt, hands cuffed, in seconds.

Turned out to be an accountant and his teenage son from Kalispell who'd taken a couple of weeks off to go bear hunting. Poor kid pissed his pants, he was so scared.

Definitely not our guys, but it gave us an opportunity to ask whether they'd seen anyone else up there. They hadn't seen anyone. Hadn't even been aware of the missing prisoners. I think that may have been a little more than they bargained for and they were packing up when we left. I suspect they won't be far behind us.

After that burst of adrenaline, the letdown leaves you drained. Even the horses seem to be dragging their feet. At least it feels a fuckload longer coming out than it was going in.

But it's my job to keep up morale.

"Could've just as easily been them, guys. Good practice run. We'll get them on the next one."

"Fucking hope so," Fletch, who is moody on the best of days, grumbles.

Yeah, me too.

Schroeder is breathing down my neck for results, but we're going as fast as we can if we don't want to miss anything.

"Ready for a shower and some of Ama's chili," Sully shares.

"So am I," James agrees.

"And a shot of the good bourbon," Bo suggests, receiving several confirmative grunts.

I'm looking forward to my bed—my whole fucking body is sore—but I keep that to myself. Then tomorrow morning after I've slept all the kinks out, I hope I can convince Alex to go on another ride.

Since our picnic, I've only been able to catch her once when she was working with Blitz. I enjoyed watching her too much—she really is a sight to behold—so by the time I approached her for a chat, I got called away again.

From what Dad and Ama shared, she's been busy between the rescue, my horses, and the hunt for a new truck they apparently need. I'm told Hugh Standish has inserted himself in that effort, which pisses me off. He's a decent enough guy, I guess, but that doesn't mean I have to fucking like his involvement with Alex.

I'm starting to feel the pressure.

"That dang Arabian tossed Alex today," Dad says before I even have my boots off.

The house smells amazing and my mouth was watering the moment I walked in. My plan was to wash the stench off first, but Dad was waiting for me.

"Is she all right?"

"She's fine. Before I could check her out that dang filly got right back in the saddle. She's a tough one, I tell ya. She doesn't flinch, no matter what that fancy horse of yours throws at her."

Despite my worry, I grin at him. He's right, she is made of tough stuff. I could tell when I had her ride him back to the ranch that one day, she'd be able to handle him. But I hadn't counted on the damn horse bucking her off. Not that I didn't think he'd try—heck, he's been trying to toss me since I got him—but I didn't take into account he'd have an easier job with her. She's half my size, it wouldn't be more to him than tossing a feather.

"And another thing." Dad stops me as I head for the stairs. "I think Missy's gettin' ready to drop her foal. She was pacing back and forth along the fence line, so I got her inside not twenty minutes ago. Had Dan put down clean straw in her stall and sent him to find some wrapping for her tail."

I don't waste time telling him I don't usually bother

with that. It's sometimes done to keep the tail clean and out of the way, but it's just as easy to wash up any mess after.

It's not a big surprise. I expected it sometime this week or the next. The other day when I checked her udder, she was leaking a bit. But I wish I could've gotten a good night's sleep in first. Now it looks like I'll be spending the night in the barn.

"Get some dinner first, Dad. The wrap can wait. I'm going to hop in the shower, grab a bite myself, and then I'll give you a hand in the barn."

The shower and clean clothes go a long way to feeling a bit better and, hopefully, the couple of ibuprofen I took before coming down will do the rest of it.

I'm lucky Ama put me aside some cornbread and a hearty bowl of her chili, because of course the guys left nothing but crumbs by the time I make it to the kitchen. Ama is the only one left.

"Shouldn't you be heading home to the kids?" I ask her.

"Kid," she corrects me.

That's right. JD, the eldest at twenty, is away at college. It's just Una, their sixteen-year-old who's still home.

"She's at her boyfriend's. *Studying*," she adds as she rolls her eyes.

"Bet James is having fun with that," I comment as she slides a steaming bowl in front of me, along with a healthy chunk of cornbread dripping with butter.

"I had to change the combination on the gun safe," she shares dryly, making me laugh.

I can only imagine. I think if I'd ever had a daughter, I'd have locked her up until she turned thirty. Una is a younger version of her mother, gorgeous, strong-willed, and smart as a whip. Since those were the exact qualities that had James fall for Ama some twenty-odd years ago, I'm sure he's not blind to the appeal his daughter holds for the opposite sex. It's got to be hell.

"Anyway," Ama continues. "I'm just making a thermos of coffee and a stack of sandwiches for you guys tonight. Thomas tells me Missy is getting near?"

"Yeah. I'll probably stay out in the barn. The coffee and food are appreciated."

Half an hour later, I head to the barn with a backpack and my bedroll. Dad is sitting on a hay bale outside Missy's stall. On the opposite end of the barn, Phantom sticks his head over the door, his nostrils flaring.

He knows something is going on. We may need to move him outside at some point.

"How is she?" I ask Dad as I dump my pack on the floor beside him.

"She's all right. Doesn't wanna be touched much, though. I waited for you."

He holds up a roll of bandages.

It's almost eleven when I can finally convince Dad to grab a few hours of sleep in the house. We've got Missy cleaned up and prepped. She's rustling about her stall, pawing at the straw. Her version of nesting.

I'm sure it won't be too long before she goes into active labor, so I line up a few of the hay bales, spread my bedroll on top and lie down. Exhaustion has me pass out in minutes.

What feels like a short couple of hours later, I wake up to the sound of thuds. A healthy kick of adrenaline clears my head instantly.

Phantom.

I get to my feet and a quick peek at Missy shows her in the throes of a contraction, her neck dark with sweat and the muscles of her stomach straining.

Then I head for Phantom's stall, hearing another thump as he kicks at the boards. His head jerks up when he spots me.

"How about we put you in the small paddock for a bit? Give Missy some peace and quiet."

He's restless, straining against my hold when I snap a lead onto his halter and open the door. It takes every effort to keep him from beelining it to Missy, but I finally manage to get him out of the barn and in the paddock. To my surprise the first faint sign of daylight appears at the horizon.

It's later than I thought. With another hour or so, Alex should be here.

The thought puts a smile on my face as I run up to the house to warn Dad.

∾

Alex

The first thing I notice coming up the drive is the horse trailer parked on the side of the barn. Looks like the men are back.

Jonas wasn't kidding when he said he'd be busy. I've barely seen him since he announced wanting to take me out.

I've thought about that a lot. Hell, he seems to be all I think about these days. Even when Jackson Zoom called me —a very rare occurrence—the other day, he mentioned I seemed distracted and asked if everything was all right. Ashamed of myself, I banished any thoughts of Jonas from my mind and for the rest of the conversation focused on my son.

Last night, Lucy and I finally decided on a truck. Second-hand—we can't really afford new at this time—the four-year-old Dodge Ram was the best choice. Lucy almost needs a booster seat to drive it, but it's more powerful than my F-150, and would make a safer towing truck for the trailer in these mountains. At least that's what Hugh said and since I know little to nothing about engines, I'll gladly take his word for it.

He's been awesome. Clueing in to our needs, understanding the financial limitations, and finding us a bunch of different options to look at. He claims he just felt bad because the Chevy wasn't really worth the repairs it would've required, but I suspect his interest in Lucy was the real reason he spent so much time helping us out.

I park my truck beside Doc Evans's old rusty heap. Wonder why he's here so early?

The prospect of seeing Jonas has those damn butterflies going when I get out from behind the wheel.

I spot Sully heading toward the barn. I wonder if Missy is foaling, she looked primed to go yesterday. Instead of stopping in to say hi to Ama, I rush after him. It's been a hot minute since I've been at a birth and I can't wait to meet the little foal.

As soon as I step inside, I see Doc and Jonas standing outside one of the stalls where Missy is pacing restlessly, occasionally stomping the ground with one of her hooves. Her neck is glistening with sweat and her nostrils are flaring.

I don't see Sully, but when Jonas catches sight of me, I notice the lines on his face appear deeper. He's worried. Suddenly I am too.

"What's wrong?"

"She's struggling," he says. "Getting tired, her legs are shaking but she won't stay down."

"It's her first, right?"

"Yeah. Doc just got here and checked her. She's been trying to push but the foal's legs are back."

In horse terms that's a complication. Usually the front hooves and the nose present themselves in the birth canal first, but in rare occasions one or both legs, or even the foal's head can be bent back.

As we watch, her legs start to buckle and she goes down, immediately rolling on her side as her distended stomach visibly strains.

Doc Evans immediately slips into the stall, crouching down by her tail.

"What can I do?" I ask Jonas, feeling helpless.

"Help me keep her down."

I sit down on the straw beside Missy's head. Her eyes are wild as she snorts short bursts of air.

"You're okay, pretty girl," I mumble, stroking her face gently. "Hard work, isn't it? I promise you the reward is worth it, though. Hang in there, honey, you're so close."

I listen to the mare grunt as her flank contracts with the force of her labor.

"Gonna pop her sac. See if I can reach the legs," Doc announces.

He does so during the next contraction. Sweat beads on his forehead as he struggles to get hold of the slippery foal.

"Got them," he finally announces.

This time when the mare strains, along with the gush of amniotic fluid, two small hooves and a nose become visible. Doc grabs its legs firmly and pulls. Missy's grunting turns into a higher-pitched squeal as she works to deliver her foal.

"Alex!"

I scramble to my feet and turn to the barn door where Sully is standing.

"I need you out here."

I rush out of the barn to catch Sully heading for the paddock at the rear. I'm about to follow him when I hear it, the sharp snap of hooves slamming against boards.

"Phantom," Jonas says behind me.

"I'll go. Doc will need you here," I tell him as I set off on a trot. The stallion could hurt himself; undo any recovery he's made so far.

Sully is halfway into the paddock.

"Stay back," I call out as I catch up with him. "Let me."

"Be fucking careful," Sully grunts. "That horse is out of his mind."

Just as I lower myself on the other side of the fence, Phantom kicks it just a few feet from where I'm standing.

"Easy, buddy," I coo, holding up my hands as I cautiously approach. "You're not making this any easier on your girl."

For a moment he appears to recognize me, but then he suddenly rears up, a panicked neigh escaping him as he thrashes his head. I notice the wrap on his leg has come loose, creating an added hazard.

"Easy, boy. It's just me," I continue to ramble, making sure to keep my voice steady and soothing.

Finally, he seems to calm a little, still snorting hard breaths from his flared nostrils, but his eyes appear to focus on me.

"That's my boy. Nice and easy. Let me see that leg of yours."

I edge closer, staying along the edge of the paddock, and wait for him to adjust to my presence. When I'm close enough, he extends his nose to sniff the hand I hold out. Then I carefully reach down to pull off the wrap. It's safer off than on right now.

I ball up the length of bandaging and am just about to toss it at Sully when a gut-wrenching squeal sounds from the barn. The next thing I know, Phantom swings around, kicks out his rear legs, and slams me into a post. I instinctively make myself small, feeling a sharp burning pain on my side.

"Alex! Are you okay?" Sully's head sticks over the fence.

"I'm fine, just give me a minute."

It takes a little longer than a minute to talk the horse back down, but once I feel it's safe to do so, I try climbing out.

"Shit, Alex." Sully points at my shirt. "You're bleeding."

Nine

JONAS

Christ, if I weren't gray already, Sully's yell, "Alex is hurt" would've surely done the trick.

I don't even give poor Missy and her newborn foal a second glance and take off running.

She's standing beside Sully on this side of the fence, keeping an eye on Phantom, who still looks agitated. My mouth goes dry when I notice the blood on her shirt.

"What the hell happened?"

"Knocked her into the post," Sully answers, but my eyes are on Alex.

"I'm fine," she says. "He just took me by surprise."

Of course she'd defend the horse.

"Sully, go see if Doc needs help." I turn back to Alex. "And you're coming with me."

"It's just a scratch. Really, I'm fine."

She can tell me she's fine until she's blue in the face. I call bullshit, *fine* doesn't bleed.

Not about to take no for an answer, I grip Alex's arm and hustle her into the house, straight upstairs to the master bath, where I leave her to go chase down the first aid kit.

"What's going on?" Ama asks when I storm into the kitchen. "What is wrong with Alex?"

"She got hurt. Where the hell is the first aid kit?"

"I'll get it."

She ducks into the laundry room and reappears a minute later with what looks like a tackle box, holding it up.

"You can go back to the barn, I'll check on her," she says, dismissing me as she tries to pass by me.

Like hell.

I snag the kit from her hands and head for the stairs, tossing, "I've got this," over my shoulder. I just catch a grin spreading on Ama's face before I take the steps two at a time.

When I push the bathroom door open, I catch Alex trying to get a glimpse of her injury. An angry-looking jagged tear across her ribs stands in stark contrast with creamy white skin and I stop in my tracks.

Jesus.

In the time I was gone, Alex had taken off her shirt and is sitting on the edge of my bathroom vanity in nothing more than a serviceable cotton bra. Heck, it could've been black lace and it wouldn't have been any sexier. The discovery the freckles on her face extend to the creamy skin of her cleavage already has me harder than I've been in years. I need to get this cut clean before I lose all control.

Tearing my eyes from her, I set the kit on the toilet seat and start digging through for disinfectant and gauze. Then I force myself to focus on her injury. The temptation is strong to let my fingers linger on her soft skin longer than necessary, but the woman keeps twisting, trying to get a glimpse of the tear along her ribs.

"Will you sit still?"

I ignore her annoyed sigh and focus on cleaning the three-inch cut.

"Did you catch on something?" I ask to fill the static silence in the bathroom.

"I think a nail in one of the fence boards Phantom kicked loose."

"We should have Doc take a look at it," I suggest, not sure if it needs stitches.

Her scent—fresh and subtle—wafts up my nose when I bend closer to place the small butterfly bandages, just in case. Then I cover it with sterile gauze and tape it down.

"You'll probably need a tetanus shot."

"It's fine," she says, wincing a little when she hops off the counter. "I'm up to date."

"What else hurts?" I look for other injuries, but I don't see anything.

"Don't worry about it. It's just my hip, where Phantom caught me when he spooked."

"Show me."

"Been kicked a time or ten over the years, Jonas. It's nothing."

"Show me," I insist, tugging at her jeans.

"Oh, for Pete's sake. Fine. Here."

Ticked with me, she unzips her jeans and yanks them down one side, suddenly hissing.

"Nothing, huh?" I scoff.

The blackening bruise shows a clear outline of a hoof covering her hip, the skin looking puffy and swollen.

"Get out of those and let me get you something more comfortable to wear."

I don't wait for an answer when I leave her to get some clothes for her to wear from the bedroom. I take my time, needing a moment to get hold of myself.

Instead of walking back into the bathroom, I knock on the door. "There's a T-shirt and a pair of sweats on the bed for you. I'll grab some ice for that hip."

The bathroom door is open and she's in front of the mirror, running her fingers through her hair when I get back upstairs with an ice pack. It's the second time I see her wearing my shirt and sweats and the impact is much the same this time around. There's something about the sight of her in my clothes, the hair she usually has tucked under that ball cap falling loose over her shoulders, that has me toss the bag of frozen peas on the counter beside her. Her eyes flit up, catching mine in the mirror just as my hands land on her shoulders.

She doesn't resist as I turn her around and her hands automatically come up, her palms on my chest. I half expect her to shove me away, but instead she curls her fingers in my shirt.

"Stop me," I tell her, my hands cupping her face and our noses almost touching.

"Not a chance in hell," she whispers, a heat matching mine in her eyes as she lifts up on her toes and offers me her mouth.

I don't need to think twice. Jesus, I don't need to think at all.

What I lack in practice, I make up for in voracity. Her taste is much like her scent, fresh and subtle, like early morning mountain air. Underneath her willing response there's an innocence that taunts me. My tongue lashes between her lips, groaning when hers curls around mine in response. Fuck, how long has it been?

"Jonas, Doc is..." I pull my mouth from hers abruptly and glare at Ama standing in the open door, but it was Sully right behind her who'd been speaking. "Shit...shit. Sorry, man. I'll...I'll wait out here."

He pulls Ama away from the door and slams it shut.

Alex starts chuckling and I drop my forehead to hers, groaning.

"Been a really long time since I got caught making out," she jokes.

I snort. "This wasn't the way I'd planned it," I admit.

"Planned what?"

I lift my head and look into her eyes. "Kissing you. Shit, I was gonna feed you first. Not maul you when you're hurt."

"Hear me complaining?" she asks, grinning up at me.

I shake my head, smiling back.

"How about I go check what Doc needs and you put that ice on your hip."

"Maybe I can help."

I plant a hard kiss on her.

"Ice. Hip."

∼

Alex

"I hope you weren't attached to it."

Ama looks at the ruined shirt she's holding up. "It's pretty much toast."

"Toss it."

I pull the bag of peas from the sweats I'm wearing and drop it in the sink. Then I take the last sip of coffee Ama poured me and set the cup in the sink as well.

"I should get to work. I'll grab my jeans from you when I'm done. Thanks so much for washing them. Again."

She didn't exactly give me much choice, grabbing the soiled clothes from my hands when I came down the stairs. She also insisted I have a cup of coffee while icing my hip.

Subtle, Ama is not. Her intentions were obvious and she immediately addressed the scene she and Sully walked into upstairs. Not that there was much to share.

Part of me feels maybe I should be embarrassed to get caught like that, but I'm not. It was a kiss. A very nice one, but nothing more than that. At least not yet. There was a lot of promise to that kiss and I'm sure I'll analyze the hell out of it eventually, but for now I'm simply enjoying the afterglow.

"You sure you should be working?"

I grin at her. "If I let every time I get bitten, thrown, or kicked stop me, I shouldn't be doing this work. It's par for the course."

The first place I go is the barn. I need to get a glimpse of Missy's foal.

Doc Evans and Thomas just step out as I approach.

"You okay?" Doc scans me top to toe. "Sully said Phantom nailed you?"

"More like the fence post nailed me, but I'm fine. It's just a scratch."

I add a smile to reassure him.

"If you say so," he drawls, letting me know he's not quite buying it. "How's Chief responding to the antibiotics?"

"He's good," I answer, grateful for the subject change. "Doesn't seem to have any lingering effects of either his injuries or the medication."

"Excellent. Well, you take care of yourself. I'll be in touch."

"You planning to work the horses?" Thomas wants to know.

"I am."

"Give me ten minutes. I want to grab a quick bite to eat," he says.

I'm about to object. I don't know how long he's been up with Missy, but a slight lift of his bushy eyebrow has me swallow it.

"That's fine, I was going to check on Missy first anyway."

I watch the two of them walk toward the house—age showing in both their steps—before I head into the barn.

"What did she have?" I ask Dan, one of the ranch hands I find cleaning the mare's stall. The foal is already nursing on wobbly feet. No sight of Sully or Jonas.

"Colt," he says, looking up.

"Good-looking little fellow," I comment.

"Cute enough," he mumbles.

He has all the markings of a paint but appears to be a little longer in the legs. It'll take a while before we can get an idea who he'll favor in build.

"How's your mom?" I ask him.

A few days ago, he was giving me a hand with Phantom while I was waiting for Jonas's father to show up. We got to talking and I mentioned I had a son about his age. He seemed genuinely interested when I told him Jackson was in the army and currently deployed, but when I asked whether he'd ever considered enlisting he explained he couldn't leave his mother. She was diagnosed with colorectal cancer last year and was having a hard time of it.

I instantly felt for the young man, who was forced to

give up his own dream of joining the military to look after his mother. Maybe because he reminds me so much of Jackson and I desperately miss my son.

"She finished the last round of chemo yesterday," he shares. "She was a bit rough this morning."

Poor guy, he's clearly concerned about her. He should be home looking after her but instead is here, mucking out a stall. I get it—I do—he needs the job and the benefits, but there are some things that should hold priority over everything else. Sadly I doubt he'll ask for any time off. I'm not even sure anyone knows the kind of stress he's under.

Instead of trying to convince Dan, I decide to talk to Jonas. Call me a meddler, but someone has to look out for this kid.

"I hope she feels better soon. Let me know if there's anything I can do."

He turns his head once again, giving me a tired smile, and I head out in search of the man whose taste still lingers on my tongue.

I find him mending the fence boards behind the barn, the same ones Phantom knocked me into. The horse is at the far side, munching on a clump of grass, but his head comes up the moment he hears me. Jonas turns my way as well.

"Hey."

He smiles as his eyes wander down to the gray sweats I'm swimming in, tucked into my boots. I instantly respond to his lazy perusal with an annoying blush heating my cheeks, despite the damp chill in the air.

"Do you have a minute?" I force myself to ask.

"Sure." He straightens up, tosses his tools into a toolbox at his feet, and rubs his hands on his jeans. "What's up?"

Now that I have his attention, I'm having second thoughts on how to approach this. Technically, it's none of my business, but the dark shadows and lines of concern on Dan's face propel me to want to help. I'll simply have to be diplomatic about it.

"It's Dan—"

"Oh fuck, what's he gone and done now?" he interrupts.

Not exactly the reaction I was hoping for and it instantly puts me on the defensive.

"He hasn't *done* anything," I snap in response, and all my good intentions toward diplomacy go right out the window. "Are you even aware what that boy is dealing with?"

Jonas snorts. "Hardly a boy."

"Might as well be," I return. "Did you know his mom is really sick?"

A flash of guilt crosses over his face.

"He mentioned she wasn't well. I didn't know it was serious."

"It's serious. She has cancer. That boy—*man*—" I correct myself, "carries the full responsibility of her care. There's no one else. She's home, sick from her last round of chemo, with no one to look after her because Dan is afraid to ask for a day off."

"*Fuck*," he curses, presenting me with his back as he pulls his hat off his head, slapping it against his leg. With his other hand, he jerkily brushes his bald head.

I give him a moment to process until he turns to face me.

"She's got cancer?"

"Colorectal. Sounds pretty advanced."

"He never said."

My earlier annoyance evaporates when I recognize regret on his face.

"And he probably wouldn't have voluntarily. Look, I'm sorry to butt in where I have no place to, but I felt compelled to say something."

"He talks to you?"

"More like he answers my nosy questions," I admit, "but yeah, and he's worried sick about his mom. She wasn't doing well this morning as a result of her treatment yesterday."

His eyes glance past me to the barn. Then without saying anything, he slaps his hat back on his head and sets off in that direction with long strides.

"Dan!" he calls from the door just as I catch up to him.

"Sir?"

The young man comes out of Missy's stall and walks over, shooting a quick glance at me. Then Jonas reaches out and takes the muck fork from Dan's hand.

"You're done for the day. Go home."

"Sorry?"

Poor guy looks shocked.

"Dan, go home, son. Look after your mother and I don't wanna see you back here until she's well enough."

"But, sir...I..." he stammers.

"Name's Jonas, and from now on I expect you to keep me posted on your mom's condition."

"But my job..."

"Will be here when you get back."

I have to swallow hard when Dan looks at me, eyes filled with relief. Then he darts past me out of the barn and I turn to face Jonas.

"Thank you."

Ten

JONAS

"Harvey."

I take a drag of the celebratory cigar Dad handed out.

It's something I remember him doing when I was growing up. Every time a healthy foal was born on our ranch, Dad would hand out cigars to his men to celebrate. I always suspected it was his way to get around my mother's dislike of smoking. She might have put her foot down on my father, but she'd never have had the heart to take that tradition away from the men who worked for them.

I like Dad bringing the old tradition here: cigars and good bourbon. I can live with that.

Leaning a hip against the porch railing, I blow out a stream of smoke.

"Looking for an update," Schroeder says without identifying himself.

I figured as much when his name appeared on my call display.

"Afraid there's not much to report. We're heading out again tomorrow morning. We've pinpointed a few more places we'd like to check out."

"This is taking too long."

I take a fortifying sip of my bourbon and let my eyes drift to the setting sun over the mountain tops to ground me.

No shit this is taking too long. According to Alex, we should be able to fulfill Phantom's stud schedule starting next week. His leg is getting stronger every day and, thankfully, he didn't do any more damage to himself this morning. Unfortunately, that means I'll be busy with Phantom and we'll be one man short on the searches. Not that I doubt my team's ability, but the simple fact is, more bodies cover more ground.

I hope we can track them down before then. It's not going to do our reputation any good if we can't find them or take too long.

But I don't voice any of those concerns to the FBI agent.

"I'm sure it looks that way, but every time we return from a run empty-handed our search area shrinks significantly, which should be considered progress."

"Not the kind of progress the brass is looking for," Schroeder grumbles. "They're breathing down my neck."

I'm sure they are, but that's not going to make this go any faster.

I get him off the phone with a promise to connect with him after we get back and turn to Dad and Sully, smoking their own cigars.

"We need to hire on an extra hand," I start, filling them in on Dan's situation.

"Kid never said anything," Sully mumbles.

"Not that surprising when you think about it. We've

been riding him pretty hard since the incident with Phantom," I point out.

I don't mention it was actually Alex who suggested that when we spoke after I sent the kid home. She said she felt an affinity for Dan, he reminds her of her son. Maybe he could sense that and that's why he talked to her.

Been beating myself up over it all afternoon. I like to think of myself as a fair and decent employer, even a considerate one, but I clearly missed the boat on this one.

"Guess you could hire another hand," Dad contributes. "But how's that gonna help the boy?"

He's got a point. He may be getting up there but his mind is as sharp as ever.

"Got any ideas?"

The old man shrugs as his head momentarily disappears behind a thick cloud.

"Sounds like all the kid's got is his mom and his pride, so make it possible for him to work without turning him into a charity case."

"And how do you propose I do that?"

"You've got Fletch and Sully living in the old staff cabins out back. My last count I saw four, only two of them occupied. Offer the boy and his mom one."

The four cabins were here when I bought the place. Not much to them, just an open living space with kitchen, dining, and sitting areas, two bedrooms, and a bathroom. Basic but functional. I offered every member of my team one when I hired them on, but only Fletch and Sully took me up on it. The cabins would've been too small for James and his family, so he got a place a few miles south of here, and Bo opted for a rental closer to Libby for reasons of his own.

It wouldn't take much to get one cleaned up for Dan

and his mom, I guess. Dan wouldn't have to worry about rent, would always be close enough to check in on his mom, and would have all the support he might need right here at the ranch. And if I explained he'd in fact be doing us a favor since we need him here, the offer might not feel too much like charity.

"That could work," I tell my dad with renewed respect.

There was a reason his hands tended to stick around for the long haul. He was a damn good employer. Turns out, even at fifty, I can learn a thing or two from the old man.

"I can check right now," Sully offers, stabbing the remainder of his cigar out in the planter we're using as an ashtray. "See which one has the better view and make sure the utilities are all still in working order. I'm sure it won't take more than a bit of elbow grease to whip one into shape."

My father and I finish our drinks and smokes in silence after Sully leaves.

"I think I'm gonna drive into town," I announce. "Have a chat with Dan in person. Maybe meet his mom."

Dad nods. "Sounds like a plan."

He moves toward the front door where he stops and swings around.

"You know, if you're going into town, you may as well stop and pay that filly a visit on your way back. I'll be watching a spot of news and plan to turn in early anyway."

With that he opens the door and disappears inside, leaving me grinning and shaking my head.

I remember his words when an hour and a half later I pass the sign for Hart's Horse Rescue. I'm tired. Today was a long fucking day and I should be hitting the sack since we're heading out early tomorrow morning, but I find myself turning into the next driveway.

I pull up to the old farmhouse I've passed hundreds of times over the years, suddenly seeing it through different eyes.

A quick glance at the clock on my dashboard shows it's just after ten at night. A little late for an impromptu visit, but I don't really want to end my day with the gaunt and emaciated face of Gemma Blakely—Dan's mother—haunting my dreams.

Before I have a chance to get out of the truck, the outside light comes on and Alex steps onto the front porch. For a moment I simply sit there staring at her, remembering the taste of her lips. One kiss drew me here. One I would've liked to repeat a few times today but never had a chance to with the constant interruptions, and tomorrow I'll be gone by the time she gets to the ranch.

Mind made up, I get out, my eyes steady on hers.

"Is everything all right?" she asks when I step onto the porch.

Instead of answering, I walk right up and, without a word, pull her in my arms and take her mouth.

Alex

"Right behind you!" Lucy hollers.

She's standing on the running board of the much too large, shiny Dodge Ram I just paid twenty-five grand for. That's a whack of money for a four-year-old vehicle, but I've been assured it's a fantastic deal for the truck.

The money hurts, I'm not gonna lie, but it's nice to have something reliable and I should be able to write it off as a business expense. Hugh mentioned a friend, who owns a paint and body shop, who'd be able to put the rescue logo on the doors for a reasonable price. An offer I'll likely take him up on.

He's been amazingly helpful and judging by the way Lucy is smiling at him when I pull out of my parking spot, he's getting his time's worth back in spades. She's clearly into him.

I chuckle to myself. *Good*. It'll give me some ammunition next time she heckles me about Jonas. She had a front-row seat to that kiss last night and had a blast torturing me after he left.

Jonas stayed only long enough, after kissing the stuffing out of me, to have a glass of wine on the porch and tell me about his visit with Dan and his mother. I could see the meeting affected him deeply and I continue to be surprised with every layer exposed under that stern and rugged exterior.

I can't believe he offered to move the Blakelys to the ranch. Oh, he told me it was his father's idea, but one Jonas clearly endorsed and ultimately ran with.

It's a good plan, one I hope will give Dan a bit of a breather. He's too young to be carrying a heavy load like this without any kind of support. Because what Dan hadn't mentioned, but what his mother shared with Jonas, Gemma Blakely's time is limited.

When I pull up to the house, I notice Chief and Scout are barking, both restlessly moving about the chicken coop where I locked them earlier. I get out of the truck and head in that direction when I notice Hope is not at the fence.

We still keep her separate from the other horses—Lucy feels she's not ready to be introduced to the band in the back field—but I think she's getting lonely. The last week or so she's been waiting by the fence when we come outside, looking for some attention.

She's not there now, and when I scan the field, I can't see her at all.

What the hell?

There's one corner in the back I can't see very well because of the way the field angles. She could be hiding out there, but before I go looking, I'd better get these dogs out. They're still barking like crazy.

The moment I release the latch on the coop's door, both dogs push out, and I just barely am able to grab them by their collars. They seem so agitated, I'm afraid if I let them go I'll never see them again.

I'm halfway to the house to grab a couple of leashes when Lucy pulls up in the new truck.

"What's going on?" she asks as soon as she has the door open.

"The dogs were going nuts and I can't see Hope."

Lucy's head snaps around right away and she scans the field.

"Any breaks in the fence?"

"Haven't had a chance to look yet. I was just gonna grab the dogs' leashes. I'm afraid to let them go loose."

She hops down from the running board.

"Let me grab the leashes. I'm coming with you."

It doesn't take long for us to find one of the top horizontal fence boards damaged. One end is still affixed to the post but the other side is resting on the ground. So instead of a five-foot barrier, Hope would've had no trouble hopping the height of the bottom board.

Shit.

"What now?" Lucy wants to know.

"Now we go find her." I hand her the dogs' leashes.

"Secure them inside the house and meet me in the barn. I'll go get Sarge and Ellie."

Sarge has been with me for almost seven years. Malnourished and chained to a post when I found him, he was very leery of people, so it took a long time and a lot of patience to build trust. I've adopted out a fair number of animals over the years but I was never quite able to let go of Sarge.

Ellie used to be a barrel horse and belongs to Lucy. She's already by the gate along with Daisy, our resident donkey, when I get to the back field. All it takes is a sharp whistle on my fingers to have Sarge come trotting toward me.

"Daisy, you stay," I admonish the donkey, who tries to slip out after Ellie.

She voices her discontent by braying loudly when I close the gate on her.

Lucy is already waiting in the barn, stuffing a halter and lead in a saddlebag.

"I've got flashlights and a couple of bottles of water," she says when I tie up the horses so we can saddle them. "What's the game plan?"

Beats me. We got here in the winter and haven't had a chance to explore much of the land. All I know is what I remember from the aerial shots that were part of the real estate package and that isn't much. Except perhaps that a creek runs along the northern property boundary. Less densely treed on that side as well.

"We start where she got out and look for a logical trail she might follow. My guess is she'll stick as close as possible to water."

If I wasn't so worried about Hope, I'd enjoy this ride a whole lot better. It's so quiet. No road noises, all I hear is the rustling of leaves, the occasional animal noise, and the steady thud of the horses' hooves.

We've been going for almost an hour through fairly dense woods when I finally hear the sound of water, telling me we're getting close to the creek. In front of me the trees thin and the late afternoon sun is brighter in the clearing I can make out up ahead.

The moment I clear the tree line, I see the creek. The water is moving rapidly, probably still propelled by winter runoff. The view is amazing, the rolling landscape framed by the higher peaks of the mountains around us.

"Wow," Lucy exclaims behind me. "I had no idea this was back here."

Me neither but I make a mental note to come back here one day with a lunch. A perfect picnic spot. Sarge suddenly stops and lowers his head to munch on a juicy clump of grass, jarring me back to reality. I lightly kick his sides to get him to keep moving.

It's getting later and there's still no sign of Hope. I'm starting to wonder if I made the wrong call heading this way.

"That looks like a trail up there."

Lucy pulls up alongside me and indicates a widening between the trees on the far side of the clearing.

"Let's have a look."

To my surprise the trail consists of two distinct tracks, wide enough for a four-wheeler or even a vehicle. Weird that it seems to start in the middle of nowhere. Or perhaps this is where it ends, but if so, where is it coming from?

The trail takes us up a fairly steep climb through the trees, but once at the top we hit a second clearing, this one a lot smaller. Right there, maybe twenty feet from the creek bed, is Hope.

I let Lucy take the lead approaching her since she's built trust with the horse. I didn't have to worry because the moment Hope spots the horses, she neighs softly and starts moving toward us.

"You been on a little adventure, girl?" Lucy coos at the mare as she calmly dismounts Ellie, the extra halter in hand.

Hope doesn't give her any trouble as she slips on the halter. I slide off Sarge's back and approach cautiously, wanting to make sure the horse is not hurt. She allows me to check her legs and stroke her flank.

"She looks fine. Let's get going. I'd like to get back before we're stuck out here in the dark," I suggest.

I wait for Lucy to mount first and hand her Hope's lead before I go to collect Sarge, who is grazing a few yards away. I shove my boot in a stirrup and am just about to swing my leg over when I see something moving in the trees behind us.

There it is again. Definite movement.

Plenty of wildlife around here. Some of which I'd much prefer to steer clear of.

I quickly settle in the saddle and urge Sarge to catch up with Lucy, who has just reached the trees up ahead.

The next moment a sharp crack pierces the peaceful night.

Eleven

ALEX

"What the hell was that?"

Lucy yells over her shoulder as she struggles to get both Ellie and Hope under control.

The horses took off like a bat out of hell, tearing blindly through the trees. Branches whipped my face and I narrowly escaped getting tossed from the saddle after a close encounter between a tree trunk and my knee. I had to use my full body weight on the reins to get Sarge in hand, but I can feel the tension still ripple through his body.

The horses are spooked and they're not alone, I'm pretty damned rattled myself.

"Sounded like a gunshot."

I catch up with her and using Sarge's big body, help box in Hope. Wedged between the other two horses she settles down a bit.

"Isn't this still your land?" Lucy asks.

She looks as shaken as I feel. A piece of a branch is stuck

in her hair and a deep scratch mars her forehead. I imagine I look much the same.

"I'm pretty sure, but it's not like there's a clear delineation. Someone may have inadvertently wandered across property lines without realizing."

"And start shooting at us?"

"Could've been a hunter. I thought I saw something move up on the ridge but I couldn't make out what it was. They may have thought they were shooting at a bear or something. Who the hell knows?"

"Well, whoever it was, I don't plan to wait around and find out," Lucy announces. "Let's get out of here."

My thoughts exactly.

It's almost dark by the time we make our way back to the barn. My heart rate is finally back to normal, but my face stings and my knee is throbbing. My body has taken a beating these past few days. I'd like to think of myself as in good shape, but right now I'm feeling every single one of my forty-five years. And then some.

"Let's stable them for tonight," I suggest, swinging my good leg over the saddle. I follow it immediately by a sharp hiss and a mouthful of curses when my feet hit the ground.

Sonofabitch, that hurts.

Unable to do much more than hobble, I unsaddle Sarge, rub down his back with a handful of straw, and lead him into one of the stalls.

"You look rough," Lucy comments.

"I feel it," I admit.

"Why don't you head up to the house, I'll finish in here. Maybe let the dogs out."

Right. I'd all but forgotten about the dogs. I'm sure they'll want to check on their buddy Hope.

As I limp from the barn, I make a mental note to do a

little research tomorrow. I'd like to find out whose land might be bordering mine.

Maybe Jonas would know.

I'm still limping this morning.

The bath I took last night to try and soothe my aching body helped get me to sleep, but it still took me a good half hour to get out of bed. Lucy saved the day when she knocked on my door with a bag of frozen corn. Ten minutes with the ice pack on my knee and I was able to move.

A little.

"What happened to you?"

Thomas comes down the porch and walks toward me, his eyes squinting at my hobbled gait before they focus on my face.

"Close encounter with a tree," I volunteer airily.

"Looks like the tree won," he comments dryly. "Shoulda stayed home in bed."

"Nah. I'll use the lunge rope today."

I already decided there's no way I'll be able to get into any saddle in my current state.

"Not letting you get close to Blitz in this condition," the old man decrees. "I'm expecting the boys back sometime this morning. Jonas can handle him."

I suppress a grin at his use of the word 'boys' to describe Jonas's team. All well over forty and every one of them solidly built, there's no mistaking them for anything but men. Rugged mountain men at that. It's even funnier coming from the mouth of the frail-looking old man before me.

"How are *you* doing today?" I ask, suddenly concerned

with Thomas's rather gray pallor and stooped shoulders as we slowly make our way to the barn.

"Me? I'm just fine. Don't you worry about me," he grumbles, clearly not welcoming my concern.

I shrug my shoulders. "I'm just asking because you look like you could keel over any minute, and I'm not sure I'll be able to pick you up in my state."

In my peripheral vision I catch him glaring in my direction.

"Rough night is all," he finally volunteers grudgingly. "I'll be fine."

"Guess we'll make it a light day for both of us then."

I spot Dan hanging over Missy's stall door.

"How are they?" I ask, moving up beside him.

"Good, I think. Little guy sure eats a lot."

The pretty little colt is latched on to its mother again.

"Pretty much all they'll do when they're this young. Lots of energy goes into growing." I reach for the latch. "Okay if I go in?"

Dan seems surprised I'm asking him. He darts a quick glance at Thomas behind me, before answering.

"Sure."

Missy turns her head and focuses those big, liquid brown eyes on me when I slip into the stall.

"Hey, momma. How are you holding up?"

She lets me lightly rub the swirl on her forehead, and seems to lean into my touch. Such a sweet girl.

Distracted from his meal, the colt turns around and nuzzles my sleeve.

"Okay if I touch your baby?" I mumble softly as I drop my arm to let the little one sniff.

With Missy's scent all over my hand, the colt doesn't shy away when I lightly stroke its jaw. My fingers find the hollow behind his cheekbones and scratch lightly. Immediately he stretches his graceful neck, wanting more, while the mare looks on.

"Where's Phantom?" I ask when I notice his stall is empty.

"The paddock out back," Dan answers. "The boss said to put him out there. The fence is fixed," he quickly adds.

So defensive and insecure. The kid needs a confidence boost. From what I've seen of him he's good with the horses.

"Think you could get him for me? Put him in the corral? Thomas and I are both a bit under the weather today, so we could use your help."

"Speak for yourself," the old man grumbles, but I ignore him.

"Okay."

His answer is more of a question than a confirmation, but I shoot him an encouraging smile. He hesitates for a moment before grabbing a lead from a hook on the wall by the tack room and heading outside.

"What are you up to?" Thomas asks sharply.

"Phantom needs exercise and neither of us are in any condition."

"Tell me you're not thinking of letting the kid on that horse. He barely knows the front from the back end."

"He knows how to ride and he has good instincts," I counter. "How else is he gonna learn?"

I give the little colt a last scratch and edge out of the stall, where Thomas is waiting with a scowl on his face.

"Oh relax," I add. "I'll keep a lunge line on him for now."

He grunts his skepticism but doesn't say anything else as he follows into the barnyard.

Twenty minutes later, Phantom is trotting easily around the corral without the lunge, Dan sitting proud and tall in the saddle, a barely-there grin on his face.

"Too much horse for that boy," Thomas grumbles as he leans on the fence beside me.

I poke him with my elbow.

"Bullshit. He's a natural and you know it."

∿

Jonas

Fuck, I'm tired, but it was worth it.

We only had maybe half an hour of daylight left when Bo spotted a patch of soil that looked to have been recently disturbed. Only a quarter mile from the last location to check out, it caught his interest.

It didn't take long to unearth the two pairs of prison-issue shoes and the familiar orange jumpsuits that were buried in the shallow hole. That got my heart pumping. Finally we had something concrete.

Unfortunately with night looming, we could do little more than get close to the cabin Sully had pinpointed for us to check out. We had a thermal camera aimed at the modest structure all night, but there was no evidence anyone was in there. Still, it made sense they probably had been at some point and could possibly return.

This morning at first light we searched the place. It was clear someone had been there not that long ago.

A couple of empty soup cans were tossed in a bucket beside the small propane burner on the makeshift counter, along with a few granola bar wrappers, and a bunch of empty plastic water bottles. The old wood stove held a few charred logs that didn't look like they'd been there a long time.

But what drew my interest was the old, dirty travel trunk with the shiny new padlock left open and empty in front of the threadbare couch. It held a strong scent of gun oil and the implication of that was not a good one. It was enough for me to suggest we head home and consult with Schroeder before we go any farther.

A few hours on an actual mattress, a decent meal, and supplies for more than a single day wouldn't hurt either.

"What the fuck?" Sully mutters beside me as he turns the truck toward the barn.

When I follow the direction of his gaze, I add my own handful of choice words. As soon as the truck comes to a stop, I scramble out of the cab and hustle to the edge of the corral.

"What do you think you're doing?" I bark, my eyes focused on the kid riding my prize stallion.

"Calm down, Son."

My eyes snap in Dad's direction who is leaning against the fence, cool as a goddamn cucumber.

"Don't tell me to calm down."

"It was my idea," Alex says and my gaze moves to her.

The first thing I notice are the scratches and bruising on her face and the horse and rider are instantly forgotten.

"Jesus, Alex. What happened to you?"

"A mishap with a tree," she quickly dismisses, brushing my hand aside when I try to touch her. "Don't worry about it."

Then she turns her attention to Dan, who has brought Phantom to a stop and starts dismounting.

"Don't stop," she calls out to him. "You were doing so well." To me she says, "Just watch."

I open my mouth to object but Dad jumps in.

"Trust me. I didn't like it either, but she called this one. The kid's good with him."

Dan is back in the saddle, softly clucking at the horse, who resumes his easy trot around the enclosure. Behind me the second truck and trailer carrying Fletch, James, Bo, and the horses rumbles down the drive. I watch Phantom's head come up as his ears flit back and forth. A spirited animal, he doesn't like the big trailer and starts bucking.

To my surprise Dan sticks to the saddle like glue, not looking the least bit scared. I can't hear what he says but he's mumbling something. He's not overcorrecting or even attempting to manage Phantom, and yet the horse appears to calm down.

Well, I'll be damned.

The whole thing lasted maybe a few minutes and already Dan looks to have the situation back in hand.

"He's a natural," I mumble.

I hate to admit it, but I'm a bit envious. I'm no slouch with horses, but that didn't exactly come easy. I had to work hard at it.

"He is," Alex agrees, smiling proudly like you'd expect a mother would. "And I bet he'd do well with Blitz as well. He's nonthreatening," she explains when she catches my reaction. "He doesn't challenge Phantom—there's no battle for dominance—but he still manages to guide him."

"You ask me, that boy's wasted on the grunt work," Dad contributes.

Damn. This is going to require some thinking but I'll need a clearer head first.

"We'll talk about it later," I tell Dad before turning to Alex. "You, I'd like to have a word with."

I put a hand on her arm and guide her away from the pen and my father's interference, when I notice she's limping.

"I know what you're going to say," she starts.

"No you don't."

"And you're right, I should've checked with you first." She stops abruptly and snaps her head around. "Wait...what?"

"Why does your face look like someone took a few swings at it, and why the fuck are you limping?"

Irritation and exhaustion—and the fact I really don't fucking like to see Alex hurt—have me snapping.

"I told you," she says with a roll of her eyes. "I went for a ride, my horse got spooked and he took off through the trees." She points at her face. "A tree branch did that and I hit my knee on a trunk. That's all."

I rub a hand over my face.

"What spooked the horse?"

"I don't know," she says, but when she averts her eyes, I know she's lying.

"Alexandra..."

"It's...I thought I saw someone up the ridge. Next thing I know there was a loud bang."

"A loud bang like a gunshot?"

The hair on my neck stands on end.

"Can't be sure. I guess it's possible," she says casually.

Way too fucking casual if you ask me.

"Who the hell shot at you?"

That came out a little too forcefully, which is instantly evident from the pissed-off look on Alex's face.

"For real? I wasn't about to wait around and ask for his number, Jonas. Besides, it was probably a hunter."

"On your land?"

"Yes…no… I don't know, okay? I think it was still on my property but I can't be sure."

Can't be sure? It either was or wasn't, that hardly seems an ambiguous question. But before I can say anything, Sully taps me on the shoulder.

"Sorry to interrupt, Boss, but Schroeder's on the line."

"I'll be right there," I tell him before turning back to Alex. "What are you doing tonight?"

"Me? Why?"

"Because right now I can barely see straight I'm so tired, I have the FBI waiting on the phone for an update, I need some food and sleep, but I really want a chance to talk to you. We're likely back out there tomorrow morning, and this time we probably won't be back until we find them. Have dinner with me tonight."

She seems to be torn with indecision as she stares at a spot beyond me.

"Alex?"

Her eyes snap to mine.

"Fine. I'll cook. Lucy has a date tonight and I don't feel like going out."

She doesn't seem too excited at the prospect, but I'll take what I can get.

Twelve

ALEX

I've reconsidered half a dozen times since leaving High Meadow.

After all the different layers to his character Jonas showed me these past few weeks, I'd almost forgotten I thought he was an asshole the first time we met.

I remember now, although I suspect his overbearing attitude was more out of concern this time.

"I'm off!"

Lucy comes flying into the kitchen, stealing a piece of the cucumber I'm slicing.

"Hugh's not picking you up?"

"Are you kidding? He's a nice guy and all, and he can make me laugh, but I don't know if I'd want to date him. Or anyone else for that matter."

I notice she looks much the same as she always does. Not even a hint of lip gloss but she did put on a pair of jeans without rips and a clean shirt.

"Does he know that?"

"He should. I told him the same thing. He still wanted to take me to dinner."

I hope Hugh took her at her word, because I know Lucy and she doesn't play games. She says what she means and means what she says.

"What time is Jonas coming over?"

She shrugs into a jacket. Despite the fairly mild temperatures during the day this time of the year, the nights and mornings can still hold a chill.

"He mentioned around six thirty."

Lucy grins wide.

"Then I'd better get out of here, and don't worry, I've got my earplugs ready in case he's still here when I come home," she teases, as she steals another slice of cucumber from the salad bowl.

"Go already." I wave her off.

She sticks out her tongue and heads for the door.

"The lasagna smells good!" she yells, before slamming the door behind her.

It better. I'm a mediocre cook in comparison to Lucy, who has mad cooking skills, but I can do a pretty decent lasagna. My go-to dish when I want to make a good impression.

Such is the level of my hypocrisy. On the one hand I'm talking myself out of liking Jonas, while at the same time trying to impress him with my cooking abilities.

The truth is, I like Jonas—I even like his bossy bark because I've come to realize it comes from a place of concern —but he scares me all the same. Or rather, caring for him scares me. I could see myself falling to his appeal and that could leave me vulnerable in a way I haven't allowed myself to feel for a very long time.

I dump the last of the cucumber in the salad and drop the knife and cutting board in the sink. Darting a quick glance at the clock tells me he should be here any minute and a sudden surge of nerves has my hands shaking. To keep them busy I turn to the sink to hand-wash the few dishes when I catch sight of my gun.

I set it next to the phone when I came in the house to start dinner, but I had it on me all afternoon working outside.

Jonas urged me to do that before he went in to take his call. I had no argument with that. It's normally in the glovebox in my truck because some of the rescue calls we go out on can get hairy. I've never actually carried a gun on my body but after yesterday's events, I have to admit, I felt better for having it on me.

What I didn't do, however, was report the incident to the police like he suggested. For all I know it was a hunter who ventured a little close to my property lines. I'm new here trying to build a reputation. I haven't even had a chance to meet all my neighbors yet, so the last thing I want to do is run the risk of alienating them.

Still, when Lucy and I ventured out behind the back field after lunch, I made sure I carried. We made a start on the cleanup of the discarded barbed wire coils, rotting fence posts with old nails sticking out, and a bunch of other crap the previous owner or owners dumped in the trees. We uncovered a few rusted barrels, a broken wheelbarrow, half a dozen old tires, and a couple of concrete cinderblocks, all of which were overgrown with weeds and vines.

It took us about three hours to haul a substantial pile next to my truck. When it became clear it would take us at least three separate runs to the dump to get rid of what we'd pulled out at that point, I called a garbage removal service.

Unfortunately, they weren't able to send a truck until next week, but it'll give us time to clear out some more.

My muscles ache and my knee throbs like a sonofabitch. Mountain life certainly isn't for the faint of heart. Since moving here, I've done more physical work and incurred more injuries than in all my years running the rescue in Billings.

I'm just putting away the cutting board when I hear the crunch of gravel outside.

"Wow."

It's all I manage when I open the door.

His hat and a bottle of wine in one hand and a bouquet of wildflowers in the other, Jonas stands grinning on my doorstep. A far cry from the tired-looking, grumpy man I saw this morning.

He looks *fine* wearing a dark chambray shirt, dark jeans, and that silver facial hair freshly groomed. Smells amazing too. I'm painfully aware I may have misjudged this dinner date. In my defense, he was pretty irritated at the time he mentioned dinner, and I wasn't too sure whether he considered this an actual date or just the quick sharing of a meal.

It looks like a proper date. Hell, one look at him tells me that, and I feel bad I didn't put more effort into my appearance.

"Something smells good," he says, snapping me back to the present.

"Come in." I quickly step aside to let him enter.

He immediately deposits his hat on the coatrack. The only times I've seen him without were momentary glimpses. I have to say he makes an impression both with and without.

"Boots on or off?" he asks, checking out my socked feet.

"Oh...uh...you can keep them on. We usually do, but I had a shower and changed earlier and..."

My voice trails off when his eyes snap to mine, darker and definitely more intense than a moment ago. *Yikes.* Maybe mentioning the shower wasn't such a good idea. One thing is clear though, my lack of effort in my appearance doesn't seem to bother him much.

He clears his throat and shoves the flowers at me.

"Ama said I should bring these. She picked them."

I shove my face in the bouquet to hide the smile that forms on my lips. The fact he seems to be as out of practice when it comes to dating as I am is endearing.

"They're beautiful. Thank you."

The sound of the oven timer going off has me hurry to the kitchen, indicating for him to follow me. I lay the flowers on the counter and grab my oven mitts.

The lasagna is bubbling nicely and the cheese is perfectly browned, just the way I like it. I quickly slide it on top of the stove where it can cool for a few minutes.

Jonas eyes the massive pan.

"Wow. You made a lot of lasagna." He makes a point of looking around. "Expecting anyone else?"

"Leftovers," I explain. "Lucy made me promise to make enough and it'll be even better tomorrow."

He grins and casually leans a hip against the counter, not two feet from where I'm standing. Still, he makes an imposing figure and my roomy kitchen suddenly feels small.

"I just need to toss the salad and then we can eat," I announce in an attempt to cut the charged atmosphere. Then I dive into the fridge for the dressing I made earlier. "Did you want something to drink?"

"I can take care of that. Where can I find a corkscrew?"

"Uhm, right..."

I point at the drawer which is partially obscured by his hips. It takes him a second to clue in.

By the time we sit down at my small dining table, my nerves are shot and my normally healthy appetite gone. I almost spill the wine he pours me when I try to take a fortifying sip.

The next moment he's on his feet, reaching for my hand and pulling me up from my chair.

"What's wrong?"

"Get ready," he warns, sliding his hands on either side of my neck and using his thumbs to tip up my chin. "I'm about to kill the elephant in the room."

Before I can decipher the cryptic words, his head bends down and his mouth takes mine.

Holy shit.

≈

Jonas

She was jumpy as fuck from the moment she opened the door.

The kiss seems to work though. Her hands are no longer trembling but firmly clasped at the back of my neck as I try to break away.

"Hold on, Sweets," I mumble against her eager mouth. "Let's save some of that for dessert."

Her mouth tastes way too good and if I keep sampling, I won't be able to stop. Despite the condom I slipped into my wallet on a whim, it hadn't been my intention to end up in bed with her tonight. Not that I don't want to—fuck, it's all I've been thinking about, especially with her taste on my lips

—but she isn't some quick itch I'm trying to scratch. I have a feeling she could be a lot more than that.

When she takes her seat, her cheeks are prettily flushed and the small smile dancing on her lips is better than the tense line they formed earlier.

The lasagna is amazing. Better than Ama's, and that's saying something.

"This is great," I mumble around a full bite.

"It's my signature dish," she tells me before modifying her statement. "Well, actually, lasagna is the only thing I do well. Lucy is the real cook in this household. My cooking is mostly just edible."

"That's more than I can say. I can fry an egg and grill a steak. That's about the extent of my culinary capabilities," I admit. "No one wants me in the kitchen, except to do dishes."

She smiles graciously. "I'm sure it's not that bad."

"It is. You can ask the guys tomorrow."

"Aren't you heading out again?"

Shit. That's right, we'll be out of there at first light.

"Dawn tomorrow," I confirm. "We may have found a trail."

"The missing prisoners? That's amazing."

"Let's not celebrate yet. We found a cabin they may have stopped at. Looks like someone collected some supplies but we haven't found where they went after that. We've got two FBI agents coming with us tomorrow to check it out."

"Can they ride?" she wants to know.

"If not, they're gonna learn fast," I point out. "We're packing to stay out there a couple of days. Hopefully long enough for us to locate them and bring them out. At least, that's the plan."

"I hope you'll be careful; it sounds dangerous."

I read the concern on her face and I try to remember the last time anyone other than Dad and maybe Ama were worried about me. It feels damn good. I don't think even my ex ever showed much concern.

Which reminds me, I should probably share I was married straight out of high school. It lasted only a couple of years and barely even registers for me anymore, but Alex should know.

"We're fine. My team has done this a time or two," I explain. "We've been doing this kind of work for over twenty years, although initially it was for Uncle Sam."

"That's right, you were in the military."

I hesitate for a fraction. Sharing this kind of information is not something I do easily but in the short time I've known Alex, I've learned trust is as important to her as it is to me. It's not like she's a stranger to military life.

"Army at first. I was young, married straight out of high school before I joined." I notice a hint of surprise register on her face. "Megan wasn't a fan of life as an army wife," I continue. "And I had divorce papers waiting for me when I returned from my first deployment. I turned around and worked my way into Special Ops. My guys and I were a tracking team then, and we're not just a team, but family now."

If there's any chance of us ending up together, it's best she knows right off the bat how important these men are in my life.

"That explains a lot. I thought you acted more like brothers than boss and employees," she observes.

"It's because at the end of the day we are."

She nods her understanding and reaches for the serving spoon in the lasagna.

"More?"

I look up at her and don't bother to hide I want her. "I think I'm ready for dessert."

She sucks in a breath and stares at me slack-mouthed.

"Unless that offer is off the table?" I check.

"Let me clear these off first."

I know she's buying time when she stacks the dishes and carries them to the kitchen. Did I scare her off? She seemed heavily invested in that kiss earlier and I wonder what suddenly has her jittery again. It's pretty obvious, from the way she kissed me back, the idea wasn't offensive to her.

I follow to the kitchen carrying the big pan. Her back is turned as she runs hot water in the sink, I assume to wash the dishes. Yet she has a perfectly good dishwasher right beside her.

Definitely buying time.

I slide the pan onto the stove and step close behind her. I can feel the tension coming from her body.

"What did I say?" I ask softly by her ear.

I figured that was the safest assumption. My understanding is clearly limited when it comes to the opposite sex. At least outside of the bedroom it is.

"Nothing," she responds far too brightly. "Why would you think that?"

I wait for her to slide the dishes in the water before I put my hands on her shoulders and turn her to face me.

"Because you seemed to shut down on me when you were eagerly participating in a bout of tonsil hockey earlier."

Her demeanor changes on a dime as her eyes shoot flames.

"Crass," she snaps.

"Maybe. I call it straightforward. Am I misreading things here?"

Fuck. Am I?

I instantly drop my hands from her shoulders.

"No. I'm sorry...it's not you. It's me."

Great, the words every guy wants to hear. *Not*.

But she follows it up with a hand on my arm and the look on her face is sincere.

"Wait. That didn't come out right."

"Give it to me straight, Alex. I'm a big boy, I can handle it."

At least for as long as it takes me to chase down those damn terrorists. Once that's off my plate, I plan to pursue her until she admits she's as attracted to me as I am to her.

One thing the woman doesn't know about me yet; I don't give up.

"Look. I lost a husband to the military. I go through my days terrified one day those officers will be back with the same news about my son. I can't—"

"Sweets...I retired a decade ago. I work for myself, not Uncle Sam," I interrupt.

"But you're doing the same work. Dangerous work. If I let myself get attached..."

She lets the statement trail off as she shakes her head

Gun-shy, that's what she is. I see it—hell, I even understand it—but I'm not gonna let it stop me.

"It's not the same, and if you give yourself a moment to think, you'll recognize that."

I pull her into my arms and am relieved when she comes willingly, resting her cheek against my chest.

"Do you think whether or not you kiss me again is going to make a difference?"

She tilts her head back and rolls her eyes.

"You're pushy."

I tighten my hold on her.

"Get used to it."

Then I bend down and brush her lips to test her. When she doesn't shy back, I do it again to make sure. Then as her hands slide up around my neck, I lick at the seam of her mouth and she opens willingly.

Thank fuck.

Her mouth is liquid heat and I groan as her blunt fingernails scrape my scalp. I back her into the counter and give her some of my weight. Our bodies are plastered together, but just as I let my hands explore, a door slams.

"Shit. I'm so sorry."

Thirteen

ALEX

I survived the morning on ibuprofen, but barely.

Some of the trucks and the big horse trailer were gone when I arrived at High Meadow, a stark reminder Jonas was out in the mountains somewhere, facing possible danger. It didn't help settle my nerves after an already restless night.

He'd left shortly after Lucy walked in, full of apologies, but first kissed me again on the front porch when I showed him out.

"We'll pick this up when I get back in a few days," he promised before getting in his truck.

I stood there watching until his taillights disappeared.

By the time I got back inside, Lucy had retreated to her room, but I noticed a healthy serving of lasagna missing from the pan. I cleaned up a little, putzing around the kitchen before finally heading upstairs as well.

Unfortunately, sleep was for the most part elusive—every time I closed my eyes my mind would start churning with all my conflicting thoughts and feelings around Jonas —and I finally gave up when the sun started coming up.

When Lucy dragged herself into the kitchen to grab a coffee, she apologized again, mentioning Hugh had been called away because one of his tow trucks broke down, which was why she'd been home earlier than expected.

She's not a morning person so I was spared an interrogation, but I'm sure she's just saving it for later.

Thomas had been waiting for me, but Dan was at home, packing up his and his mom's belongings since they'd be moving to High Meadow over the weekend. That meant my sore butt was on both stallions this morning. Phantom didn't give me too much trouble, but Blitz was a pain in my ass.

Apparently, Missy and the foal were moved to the small paddock behind the main barn. Blitz—who is normally kept closer to the breeding barn with the other stallions and away from the mares—must've caught a whiff of her because I had a hell of a time settling him down.

By the time Thomas suggested I call it a day, I felt every inch of my body.

The worst part is, I have an entire afternoon of more physical labor waiting for me.

Lucy is in the kitchen when I drag my ass inside the house. Both Chief and Scout come greet me when I kick off my boots and dump my coat in the hallway.

"Chilly, isn't it?" she remarks when I walk into the kitchen. "I'm making us soup for lunch."

She's at the stove stirring a pot and the smell makes my stomach instantly respond with a loud rumble.

"We're supposed to have a cold front move through later this afternoon and tonight," I repeat what Thomas mentioned this morning as I take a seat at the kitchen table.

"According to Thomas there's a chance of freezing overnight."

"We should get Hope inside," she suggests.

Sarge and his posse have a shelter in the back field, they'll be fine and keep each other warm, but Hope is by herself and there's no shelter in the front paddock. She'll be better off in the warm barn.

"How about we get Daisy in the barn as well? Put her in a stall beside Hope. Give them a chance to get acquainted."

We've held off putting Hope with the others, but the donkey doesn't have a mean bone in her body and gets along with everyone. She could be a good buffer when we transition the newest rescue to the rest.

"Yeah. I like that idea," Lucy says, setting the bulk-sized bottle of ibuprofen and a glass on the table in front of me. "You look rough."

I shake out two pills and wash them down with the water. I am normally not one for popping pills but I need them today.

"By the way, Hugh called apologizing for bailing on me last night, but he offered to come give us a hand this afternoon. I'd mentioned it last night. I didn't say no, we could use the extra pair of hands."

Thank God. The cleanup turned out to be a much bigger job than I'd initially thought. We could use all the help we can get if we want it done before the garbage truck comes.

"How was dinner?" I ask when she slides a steaming bowl in front of me and takes a seat across the table.

"What little there was of it was fine. No romantic pings on my radar, but he seems a good guy."

"What about him? He's okay being friend zoned?"

She shrugs. "I think so. He gave me a friendly kiss on the cheek before he took off but that was it."

Or maybe he's patient and persistent, like someone else I know.

"Talking about kissing..." she drawls, an eyebrow drawn up. "That did not look like a friendly smooch I barged in on last night."

I almost choke on the mouthful of hearty black bean soup. Should've known it would come up eventually.

"It's complicated," I mutter after clearing my windpipe.

"No, it's not. He's hot, he's available, and he's clearly into you. What's so difficult about that?"

"I'm a widow."

It's hardly a valid excuse for my reluctance, I know that, but it's the only one I have.

"So? Your husband died, you didn't."

Trust Lucy to put things in the simplest possible perspective. Not that she's wrong. She knows my history, even if I don't know all of hers. She was there when I struggled to manage a teenage boy single-handedly, when I was still angry and railing against fate leaving me to handle life by myself.

It's also not that I've never dated since Bruce's death, or stayed celibate, but there was little risk involved. No entanglements, no expectations, and no real emotional connection.

It's different with Jonas, and I suspect Lucy knows that, which is why she's playing devil's advocate.

"I like him."

"I know," she returns calmly, her eyes steady on mine. "And I get what that means, but I never took you for a coward."

Ouch.

Is that what I am? Afraid to take a chance? Scared because with Jonas it almost feels like I'm betraying the memory of my dead husband?

"I can hear your wheels turning. I never knew Bruce, but if he loved you at all, he wouldn't want you to deny yourself a chance to find happiness again."

"I *am* happy," I protest instantly.

Mostly that's true, I love my son, have a passion I've been able to turn into a business, and live in one of the most beautiful places I know. What's not to be happy about?

At least that's what I tell myself.

"I call bullshit. You're content, yes, but that's a conscious choice that involves the brain and not the heart. You've limited your expectations to things you can control. You've moderated a satisfying existence..." She waves her spoon at me for emphasis. "...But you're not embracing life."

A sharp rap has the dogs run barking to the front.

"I'll get it."

Lucy gets up to open the door, leaving me to process her words. She's right, of course. The irony is, she's much the same. We've both found ways to keep our hearts well-guarded. Only difference is I know why I feel the need to, but Lucy's motivations are still a mystery. I'm hoping one day she'll feel comfortable enough to share.

Hugh ends up eating a bowl of soup with us while we discuss what needs to be done, and I'm glad for the change of subject.

"You know, if you have a truck coming to haul stuff away anyway, you should make use of it," he suggests. "Have any other piles of trash? Retired appliances? Maybe furniture you want to get rid of? Old boxes? Now would be the time."

That got me thinking about the junk we discovered up in the attic when I was looking for a place to store our Christmas stuff. The farmhouse doesn't have a basement—only a crawlspace—so the attic is the only extra storage space we have in the house. I guess it served as such for the previous owner as well, but it was never cleared out. I meant to go up there and go through the stuff at some point.

"That's a good idea, actually. I may have some things up in the attic. Why don't you guys go ahead outside and I'll have a quick look around up there."

I sneeze at the dust flying up when I flip back another one of the sheets covering an old piece of furniture. This one is a five-foot high dresser and in surprisingly good shape compared to most of the other stuff up here.

I found three old kitchen chairs that appeared beyond repair, the base of a heavy round table but no top, standing lamps that have seen better days, boxes of junk and old magazines, and a couple of trunks and worn suitcases stuffed with clothes that looked to be from a different era.

Nothing worth keeping other than perhaps this dresser.

It's not a fine piece of furniture. It's rustic and utilitarian—probably hand-hewn—but it suits the farm. It actually suits me. I can envision it in my bedroom in place of the cheap particle-board drawers storing my clothes. Maybe I'll start bringing it down now so I can move my stuff in here and toss out the old dresser.

I pull open the doors above the three wide drawers to find two generous shelves someone lined with old newspaper. I easily lift them out and study the paper more closely. I

146

can just make out a date; July 27, 1953. Technically an antique, that's pretty cool.

I haul them down the narrow stairs to my bedroom and while there, start emptying my dresser, dumping the clothes on my bed for now. This is always how it goes; I start on one thing, get distracted, and end up doing something else. When the dresser is empty, I manage to drag it to the top of the stairs going down.

This one isn't too heavy, but I have a feeling I won't be able to move the old solid wood one in the attic by myself. Those stairs are pretty narrow but someone got it up, which means we should be able to get it down too. Maybe I can get Hugh to give me a hand before he leaves. I can do the drawers by myself.

To my surprise someone upgraded those with metal sliders over the years and they glide smoothly. The bottom drawer is the only one that isn't empty. A few rolls of what look like blueprints and an old metal lockbox. That's the first thing I look at but, unfortunately, it's actually locked.

The temptation is great to look at the drawings and try to open the box, but I can see myself getting lost for hours when I should be tackling the stack of boxes I just noticed in the far corner.

Maybe tonight I can have a peek. I'll put them safely in my room for now.

Jonas

"His ass is sore," Bo mumbles beside me.

We're behind Schroeder, watching him shift uncomfort-

147

ably in his saddle. I'm sure he's been on a horse a time or two before, but not often and not for long. Even a few hours on horseback when you're not used to it can be tough, let alone eight hours with only a quick break for lunch when we got to the cabin we think the men holed up in.

"He's lucky I gave him Star," I point out, grinning.

Star is one of my older mares, who rides more like a lazy couch, but can still manage the rough terrain. Felix, Agent Wolff's mount, has a little more fire which the younger man appears to handle just fine. He looks like he belongs in the saddle.

While the agents went inside to take some pictures, we scanned the perimeter of the cabin a few hundred yards into the woods. James found their track pretty quickly. It had been obvious they'd been dragging something behind them they tried to obscure.

What's left of the markings could have been a land sled, a contraption hunters use to pull larger game out of the woods. Not a bad plan, since it would've allowed them to haul more supplies than if they had to carry them. The downside is it would've slowed them down and, as is evident, it leaves deep grooves that are difficult to hide completely.

Having said that, they unfortunately have a head start of at least a week. I'm sure they got wherever they were heading a while ago and have had time to dig in. That could prove a problem when we find them because there's no doubt they're armed, and it's entirely possible they've set traps along the way.

But my biggest concern right now is that the trail appears to be leading us south.

"Hold up!"

Sully's voice carries from up ahead.

"Stick with the agents," I tell Bo.

Then I press my heels in Sugar's flanks, easing her forward. I pass the feds, motioning them to stay, and I head up the rocky path. Sully is standing beside his horse and holding on to James's mount, looking at something on the other side of the ridge.

I hop off Sugar and grab her reins before stepping up beside him.

"Don't go farther," he says, pointing at something James is looking at, crouched down about fifty feet in front of us.

"What've we got?"

When Sully turns his head, his expression is dead serious.

"Trip wire."

Fourteen

JONAS

"Early warning system."

James joins us at the top of the ridge.

"What do you make of it?"

He shrugs, holding up a black plastic box slightly bigger than a deck of cards. "Rudimentary, but effective. It's a Minimore."

He's talking about an MM-1, a small directional fragmentation mine manufactured in Arizona. They're quite common in the Special Ops community, so we're very familiar with them, although seeing them in the hands of militants on home soil is disturbing.

The MM-1 is the smallest of that particular type, with a blast range of only fifteen yards or so, but it still would've at least taken a couple of us out. I can see the appeal; the unit only weighs about a pound and is easy to pack. Heck, you could pack a dozen and barely notice the added weight.

"How the hell would they've gotten those?" Sully questions.

"Black market," I suggest, but James brings up something I'd forgotten about.

"Remember that armory heist near Bozeman two years ago? What do you wanna bet this little guy can be traced back there?"

A list of stolen items was never made public, but I remember hearing through the grapevine that it was substantial. If that cache ended up in the hands of this Montana Sovereign Posse group, we're facing a bigger threat than we thought.

"I'm thinking it's time to get the Department of Homeland Security involved," Sully puts out there.

"It is," I agree. "But that's up to the feds. I get the sense Schroeder won't be too happy about it, he wants this collar for himself."

I turn and look back to where Bo, Fletch, and both agents are waiting. I can tell from Schroeder's body language he's already getting impatient.

"Let's mount up and get back to the others. The light's going so I'm gonna suggest we fill those guys in, set up camp for the night, and figure out what to do from there."

I was right, the older agent had been ready to dismiss the idea of notifying Homeland Security but this time his partner put his foot down.

"Not about to risk my career—or God forbid, my life or that of a handful of civilians—because you don't like sharing credit," Wolff snapped sharply after the older man stated we could handle this ourselves.

Schroeder scanned around the group, probably hoping for an ally, but he would've been hard-pressed to find one among my men.

He didn't give up easily, though, and after we tended to the horses and set up camp under the cover of trees—nothing more than individual bivy tents and sleeping bags—he tried again, suggesting we do a little more reconnaissance before we call it in.

I didn't sleep very much so had most of the night to think on that, and over breakfast—instant coffee and a protein bar—I make a suggestion.

"Wolff is right," I tell Schroeder, who doesn't look pleased. "And I'm not willing to put my men at that kind of risk. But...Sully packed the drone, just in case. We could send it up, do some low altitude surveillance in the immediate vicinity to see if something pops up. This model's only got about forty-five minutes of flight time, though, so we're limited."

"Sounds good to me," Wolff agrees and looks pointedly at his partner.

"Fine."

Less than a gracious agreement, but it'll have to do.

It takes Fletch and Sully twenty minutes to put the drone together, by which time the rest of us have packed up camp. We all head up the ridge where Sully launches the Matrice 210 RTK.

At first everyone tries to crowd around Sully, who is holding the controller with the small screen, until I tell all but James to give him some space. Having grown up here, James knows the area better than anyone.

I catch Schroeder walking off and trying his satellite phone again, but like I told him yesterday, he's not likely to get a signal with this thick cloud cover. We're lucky it stayed dry.

"Are we that close to Fisher River?" I hear Sully ask, pointing at something on the screen.

"That's not Fisher," James corrects him. "I think that's Swamp Creek. Hang on." He pulls a map from his pack and folds it open. "Yup. Swamp Creek. See where it sharply turns west?"

He's just showing Sully the map when I approach.

"What've you got?"

"Looks like we're less than a mile from Swamp Creek."

The creek branches off Fisher about twenty-five miles north of High Meadow's east property line. The river slightly curves toward the highway, and finally flows underneath at the bridge just south of the ranch. Swamp Creek runs a similar path, except west of the river until it suddenly curves toward US-2. It runs parallel to the highway for maybe a couple of miles, and then dips under to the other side, only to reconnect with Fisher River south of the bridge.

By my calculation, we're only about ten or so miles from the northern edge of the ranch. Still a ways from the house, the ranch is just under sixteen hundred acres in total but only a couple of hundred of those are being actively used, but closer than I thought.

"Here. Look at this."

Sully holds up the small screen and points at what looks like part of an old forestry road.

"Where does that run?" Schroeder—who's crowding me from behind—wants to know.

James checks the map.

"Nothing showing on the map."

"It's definitely a trail," Sully notes.

The two parallel tracks appear to follow along the creek, but only for a small section when it curves under the cover of the trees. For the next fifteen minutes Sully tries to find where it leads or where it originates, without any luck, before he needs to turn the drone back or the battery will run out mid-flight.

"Maybe we'll have better luck pulling up satellite imaging. Should be easier to spot," Wolff suggests.

If we leave now and aim straight for the trail where we left the trucks, we can be home mid-afternoon.

"Sounds like a plan. Let's head back."

Then maybe I can see what Alex is up to tonight.

Alex

This has turned out to be a huge job.

I take off my work gloves and rub my sweaty palms on my jeans while stretching my back.

Lucy walks up, her arms full of lengths of rusted rebar. We discovered a pile hidden by overgrown underbrush.

"This is the last of the rebar," she says, tossing her load on the substantial pile of junk we've been accumulating.

"I'm starting to think one truck won't cut it," I observe. "Any guess what this might weigh?"

"That's a math question." Lucy groans as she does her own version of a back stretch. "You know me and math don't get along."

The company sending out a truck on Monday charges based on weight, and I'm afraid this cleanup project is going to cost a shitload more than just a sore back and aching muscles.

I do a mental review of the state of our financial reserves, which have already been dinged hard by the purchase of the new truck. At this rate, those house renovations I was hoping to start this summer will have to wait another year.

The one bit of good news was the phone call I received earlier today from a dude ranch along the Kootenay River, close to Ripley, which is about half an hour from here. Sam Deere, the owner, is a friend of James and Ama and mentioned I came highly recommended.

One of his horses was attacked by a mountain lion last week and although the horse got off with relatively minor injuries, the animal was seriously spooked. Sam admitted that normally he'd simply get rid of the horse, but it's his teenage daughter's favorite.

I agreed to drive up there Monday afternoon to have a look.

After a very slow startup, it looks like we have a bit of business coming in. Good. We need it.

"I'm gonna check on the dogs, get cleaned up, and get dinner started," Lucy announces.

We left Scout and Chief safely inside. Too risky for them to roam around back here. At least until this pile is gone.

"I won't be far behind you. I'm just going to do a quick walk around the area we tackled today for anything we may have missed."

It was Hugh who suggested yesterday it would be easier to do the cleanup in sections to avoid missing stuff. He did a lot of work, ended up lugging some of the big junk from the attic, and helped me move the dresser to my bedroom.

He offered to come back Sunday—tomorrow—but

Lucy told him we had it handled. Hardly, but I get she doesn't want to send the guy the wrong message.

Every step hurts, but I drag my ass back into the woods. Just a quick walk-through, making sure we got all the junk out before we move to the next section tomorrow. I don't think we'll get this entire woodlot cleared by Monday, but we'll get most of it.

I still don't get why someone would turn their own backyard into a dump, but you see it all over the place. Not sure if it's laziness or lack of care. Personally, I get a little stabby when I see a property surrounded by rusted out cars, old furniture, building materials, and God knows what else.

I'm about to turn back when my foot catches on something and I land face-first in the undergrowth. A sharp pain stabbing my knee has me cry out.

Damn. That's my bad knee too.

Before I have a chance to catch my breath, I'm suddenly grabbed under my arms from behind. Panicked I reach out for the first thing my hand encounters as I'm hauled to my feet.

Jonas is barely able to avoid the arc of the empty paint can I'm wielding as I swing it around. The movement landing me right back on my ass on the ground.

"Christ, Alex...don't take my fucking head off," he grumbles.

Then he reaches down to grab my hand, tossing the rusty can aside before pulling me up.

"You scared the shit out of me."

I bend down to rub my knee, twisting my neck so I can look up at him.

"Same," he says. "Lucy pointed me here when I saw you hit the deck. For a second there I though you got shot."

"I tripped. I think on that damn paint can."

He shakes his head and grins. "Don't think I know anyone as accident prone as you are."

"I'm not," I protest.

Jonas clearly doesn't buy it, cocking an eyebrow.

"Could'a fooled me. I'm gonna have to stock up on ice packs with you around."

I decide to ignore the comment. Mainly because he has a point. Apparently, I've become an accident waiting for a place to happen.

"What are you doing here anyway?" I ask, tentatively putting some weight on that leg. "Aren't you supposed to be out searching?"

He bends down to grab the paint can, slips his other arm around my waist, and starts walking us out of the trees.

"Got back early."

"Did you find them?"

I hiss at the strain on my knee and he tightens his hold on me.

"We found some evidence that caused us to call off the search."

"Like what?"

He tosses the can with the rest of the garbage as we make our way to the house.

"A tripwire attached to a bomb."

"A bomb?" I stop in my tracks and turn to face him. "Up there?" I indicate the mountains behind us. "Why?"

"Sweets, if I knew that we'd be a hell of a lot farther along," he comments with a sardonic chuckle. "As it is, I left my guys with a federal agent foaming at the mouth at my office back at the ranch because I was this close to putting a bullet between his eyes. Dan and his poor mother just moved into the cabin this afternoon, wondering what the hell they've gotten themselves into.

Tomorrow Homeland Security is showing up. And while all this is going on, I somehow have to figure out a way to get Phantom to Elk River, Idaho by nine o'clock Monday morning."

I heard everything he said but am stuck on one thing.

"Homeland Security?"

He sighs as he helps me up the porch steps.

"Long story."

I stop him with a hand on his chest before he can open the door.

"Jonas? Why are you here?"

He covers my hand with his and leans down so his nose is almost touching mine. This close up, I notice the fatigue around his eyes and tension in the lines around his mouth.

"Because I needed this."

He takes my lips in a sweet, languid kiss, slowly crowding out every twinge, ache, and pain in my body.

"That's a really good reason," I tell him when he ends the kiss.

"It is. Your mouth is the only thing standing between me and a capital murder charge," he jokes.

I lightly punch his shoulder.

"That's not funny."

"Wasn't meant to be."

I lean back a little and glance up at him. The fatigue is still there but his mouth is relaxed, slightly tilted up at the corners, and his eyes are warm.

"Can you stay for dinner? Lucy is making coq au vin. You can tell me all about your day," I suggest lightheartedly.

"No clue what you're offering me for dinner, but if it tastes anything like what I can smell even out here, I'm game."

I grin up at him. "A fancy title for chicken stew, but it's

soaked in wine, served over mashed potatoes, and Lucy makes lots."

He smiles back. "Sold."

It's close to nine when I walk Jonas out on the porch.

"Come here," he mumbles, pulling me into his arms.

I could get used to this. He smells of soap and horse and I feel completely at home in his embrace, like I used to when Bruce would return home and sweep me up in his arms.

Not that they're anything alike, other than perhaps their height. Bruce had been all lean lines and hard muscle. Jonas is fit and strong but bulkier, and age has softened the edges with a hint of padding. It's like being hugged by a bear— soft and powerful at the same time.

He told us about the mine they found and how it might have been part of a cache of arms stolen from a military armory. That's why they'd decided to call in Homeland Security. I shiver when I think what damage that thing could've inflicted, and I'm glad they didn't push to go after them by themselves.

"You cold?" he mutters in my neck.

"No. Just grateful no one got hurt."

He sets me back and brushes my lips lightly. "Promise me you'll be careful."

"Been carrying my gun everywhere."

"Keep your eyes open at all times and if you see something off, call right away. It looks like these guys could be a lot closer than we thought."

Another shiver runs down my spine.

"I will. We'll keep the dogs with us tomorrow. They'll alert if anyone comes close."

"Good. Depending on what happens tomorrow, maybe Tuesday I can bring Sugar over and we can take a ride around your property."

"I'd like that."

He tucks me close again, resting his chin on top of my head.

"Good. Cause I'd really like to have you to myself at some point."

This time the shiver skirting over my skin is one of anticipation.

Fifteen

JONAS

"You're fucking welcome!"

Fletch flips the bird, as the three nondescript black Escalades leave a trail of dust speeding down the driveway toward the road.

"Fucking bastards," he adds, voicing what the rest of us are thinking.

Almost four hours ago, those same SUVs had come rolling up to the house like the cavalry arriving. I noticed Schroeder blanch when a rotund man around my age stepped out of one of them.

I understood why when the man introduced himself as an FBI Executive Assistant Director. He's their boss. The other four men were DHS and from the moment the ranking agent—a mousy-looking guy with the unfortunate last name Limpkin—opened his mouth, it was clear the DHS was not happy with our involvement.

In fact, over the next hours we were being grilled as if we

were somehow involved with either the armory heist, the disappearance of the prisoners, or both. They seemed suspicious of our knowledge of weaponry, weren't satisfied when I explained we were ex-special forces, and then scoffed when I wouldn't elaborate on any specific missions we'd been involved in.

Finally they asked to search the house and premises, something I told them they could do as soon as they showed me a warrant, which didn't earn me any friends.

When they left, they specifically instructed me to stick close to home in case they thought of something else to ask me.

More of a *fuck you* than a thank you for your assistance.

That's fine, this is why I had Schroeder sign a contract, for which we've already received the substantial deposit. If they try to back out of paying the remainder, they have another thing coming. I have a few friends in high places I've never had to call on yet, but wouldn't hesitate to if my hand was forced.

"Fuck," I mutter as we walk back to the house. "Now how am I gonna get Phantom to Elk River?"

"I'll do it," Sully volunteers. "That is if we can switch trucks so I can tow the trailer."

"Yeah. That's not a problem, thanks. Dad's gonna want to go, though."

Sully grins. "Got no problem with that. Maybe the old man's got some more interesting stories he's willing to share with me."

Oh shit.

Last weekend Dad was invited to play poker—he was tickled pink—and the guys plied him with bourbon and got him to spill a few stories dating back to my teenage years.

That's all I need, more ammo for Bo and Sully to torture me with.

"Don't get him drunk again," I warn him.

Dad looked miserable for a few days after that little escapade.

"I'm just kidding. I do prefer driving tonight as opposed to getting up at three tomorrow morning."

"Fine by me. Check to see if that works for my father."

Sully heads inside. I'm not sure where the others went but I'm left alone on the porch. James probably already left for home. We normally keep Sunday for family unless we have an active case. I'm not sure what the hell Bo does with his spare time, but I don't see his wheels around anymore either. Fletch is probably in his cabin sulking, the moody bastard.

That basically leaves me to fend for myself. Unless...

She answers on the second ring.

"Hey."

I can hear the smile in her voice. Feels damn good to know I have the same impact on her as she does on me. I was already smiling before she even answered.

"What are your plans for tonight?"

"Tonight?" she echoes.

"Yeah. The house is empty. I know I already told you what a shit cook I am, but I can grill steaks and I'm sure we've got plenty of makings for salad. Maybe even some baking potatoes."

It's silent for a beat before she comes back with, "I can handle those."

"Perfect. Come whenever you're ready."

"Did you know that?"

I'm leaning over Sully's shoulder, who has a satellite image pulled up on the screen. The same one we'd studied yesterday afternoon when we got back.

"What am I looking at?"

He points at a slightly darker line in all the green.

"That's Swamp Creek." Next, he indicates a red marker. "That's where we found the trip wire. And there is Fisher River. Now focus on the triangle of land bordered by the river, the creek, and the highway."

He pans out, hits a key, and the red flag disappears but a grid of white lines superimposes over the map.

"Property lines," I conclude, recognizing the elongated shape of the ranch, which follows the flow of Fisher River on the southeast side. "That's High Meadow."

"Yeah, but look here."

He points to a section where the creek meets US-2.

A smaller, wedge-shaped parcel of land is marked off. Wide on the west side where it starts at the highway, but narrowing to the east. The creek runs along the north side of the property line.

I know where that is.

"That's the rescue. Alex's place."

The point of the wedge of land stretches much farther into the mountains than I expected.

"Right. Now watch this."

Sully hits a key and the red marker appears back on the screen, way too close to the tip of the rescue's boundaries.

"That was no hunter," I mumble under my breath.

Sully swings around. "What?"

"Last week when Alex went for a ride, her horse got spooked by a loud gunshot. She says she noticed movement up on a ridge before she heard it. Thought it might have been a hunter wandering onto her land."

He turns back to the screen and asks, "Whereabouts was it?"

"I have no clue," I grudgingly admit.

I should've taken it more seriously and asked her. *Dammit.*

"We're supposed to take a ride around her property this week, she can show me then. Could you send me a set of coordinates based on those boundary lines?"

It's still on my mind a few hours later when I close the back of the trailer, locking Phantom safely inside. I give it a few bangs to let Sully know it's secure and I take a step back when he starts pulling out.

I turn to the house to grab a quick shower before Alex shows up, when my phone rings. It's Dan.

"What's up?"

"Sorry to bug you, sir. I cleaned out Phantom's stall like you asked."

I don't bother correcting him again. If the kid feels better calling me sir, so be it. I've been called worse.

"Good. Was that it?"

"Uhh, no. There's a problem with the shit bin."

What we call the shit bin is a thirty cubic yard container we use to dump the horse manure. Every month or month and a half a truck comes to haul the container to a commercial facility where the horseshit is turned into compost.

"What problem?"

"Looks like the door wasn't latched properly."

I drop my head and rub a hand over my face. It's my own fault, I probably should've told Ama to call for a pickup last week but it slipped my mind. We probably overloaded the damn thing.

Sounds like I'm about to shovel some shit.

~

Alex

I catch wind of him when I'm still steps from the porch where he's watching my approach.

Horseshit.

He looks and smells like he rolled in it.

A grin forms on my lips, but he looks far from amused.

"Did you trip and fall in the manure pile?" I tease, keeping about six feet between us.

"Fucking latch popped on the bin," he grumbles. "Thing was busting at the seams and spilled all over the damn place."

I'd been a nervous wreck all afternoon. When he'd made a point of mentioning nobody would be at the house, I recognized it for more than just an invitation to dinner. I'm pretty sure this time there's going to be *dessert* and as much as I'd like there to be, I'm scared shitless as well.

I've always been quite comfortable in my skin. My love life when Bruce was alive was loving, healthy, and active, and my husband never failed to make me feel desired. After he passed away, it took me a while to think of having sex again, but I found that without that emotional connection, I didn't much care what my partner thought of me.

Selfish?

Probably, but I figured as long as both of us got a physical release out of it there was no harm done.

It's not quite as simple with Jonas. I already feel a deeper

168

connection, which means I care a lot about his perception of me.

Seeing him standing in front of me covered in manure helps a great deal to settle those nerves. He's a little less imposing this way.

"You're smiling. I just spent half an hour trying to stuff shit back into a bin that was already overflowing, and you're getting a kick out of it," he accuses.

"I'm sorry."

The words are automatic and a total lie, which doesn't seem to escape Jonas.

"No, you're not." The corner of his mouth twitches as he takes a threatening step closer. "I think I deserve a kiss."

A laugh bubbles free as I hold up my hands defensively.

"Not while you smell like that, thank you very much."

"Is that so?"

His eyes sparkle and he bites his lip as he suddenly shrugs off his jacket, letting it drop on the porch.

"Maybe I should have a shower."

Next, he pulls the shirt he's wearing underneath over his head, and drops it on top of his coat. His chest is broad and lightly covered with the same silver he has in his beard. His stomach isn't flat, but his waist still well defined. *Damn.* I notice his nipples pucker against the cold chill in the air.

"You're gonna catch a cold," I warn him, sounding a little breathless, even to my own ears.

"Can't wear these inside or I'll stink up the house."

Then he kicks off his boots, strips of his socks, and loosens the buckle on his belt. With his eyes boring into mine, he finally drops his jeans, standing only in his boxer briefs in front of me.

The more I try to avoid looking at his crotch, the stronger my eyes are drawn there.

Well, hello.

"Feel free to follow me in. I'm just gonna get this cleaned up for ya," he taunts, pulling open the storm door before he disappears inside.

He looks as fine going as he does coming. For a fifty-year-old man he has a remarkably tight ass. Guess a lifetime spent in the saddle will do that.

Yowza.

It takes me a few seconds before I follow him in.

My momma didn't raise a fool. I recognize those words for the promise they hold.

I feel like we may be leaping ahead, but I'm surprisingly okay with that. So okay, I'm actually contemplating whether I should get a head start.

I hang up my coat and kick off my own boots in the hallway before closing the front door. Then I make my way to the base of the stairs where I hear the water turn on upstairs.

Should I?

I only hesitate for a moment before I grab the bannister.

Upstairs I pass by the bathroom door, which is open a crack, and head for his bedroom where I stop on the threshold. I was only here the one time before but never really looked around. The decor is rustic like the rest of the ranch; lots of wood, natural fabrics, and masculine colors. Other than a huge black-and-white print of fog rising up from a mountain meadow, the room is sparse, its main feature the large king-sized bed with a tan leather-tufted headboard.

Am I overstepping? Is this moving too fast?

Uncertainty starts creeping in, but then I catch a glimpse of myself in the full-length mirror on the back of the closet door. Even though I put more thought into my appearance than I normally do, I'm still just me. But my eyes are bright, my cheeks are flushed, and I'm wearing my best underwear.

We're both well into adulthood, there's no one to answer to, so why not?

By the time the shower turns off, twilight shines in through the blinds and I'm in his bed in only my fancy lingerie, reconsidering my decision yet again.

"Fucking dream, walking in here finding you in my bed."

Too late.

Jonas's green eyes are intense when I turn my head to face him.

"I wasn't sure," I admit.

Instead of answering, he lumbers over—unapologetically naked—and bends over the bed until his eyes are just inches from mine. Then he lowers his mouth to mine, kissing any doubt from my mind. When he releases my lips and straightens up, I have a chance to peruse him in his entirety. There's a lot to admire.

"Only complaint I have is you're wearing too many clothes."

I snort, the frilly bits of fabric barely covering me can hardly be called clothes.

But my laughter fades quickly when the rough pad of his index finger snags on the lace of my bra, sending prickles over my skin.

"You can fix that," I suggest, too aware of his eyes skimming every inch of my body.

For a moment I'm startled when he takes my hand and

pulls me up and off the bed, but then he takes my place and arranges himself with his back against the headboard.

"I'd rather watch you do it."

Oh shit.

I'm already feeling a little exposed and God knows I'm far from a seductress, so a sexy striptease is out of my wheelhouse. Then I catch the blatant appreciation in his eyes and realize the man isn't expecting a show, all he wants is for me not to hold back and give myself voluntarily.

That I can do.

It takes me one point two seconds to take off my bra, like I do every night in my own bedroom. My panties I shimmy down my hips and step out of, kicking them aside. When my eyes return to his, he's not even looking at the parts I exposed, but are focused on my face.

Then he holds out his hand.

"Come here, Sweets."

He is clear where he wants me so I climb on his lap, straddling him.

"Gorgeous," he whispers, cupping my breasts with his hands and rubbing his rough thumbs over my nipples.

In turn I explore his chest with my fingers, loving the light abrasion of his chest hair.

I hiss when his lips close over a nipple, and my back arches as he draws me into his mouth.

"So goddamn sweet," he mumbles against my skin.

Sixteen

JONAS

Dear God in heaven.

I'd hoped we'd end up naked but I figured I'd have to work for it. Finding her already in my bed threw me for a loop, but only for a second.

Her skin is so fucking soft I'm almost afraid I'll leave marks, but I can't stop touching her. Gorgeous, and she doesn't even realize it. There is no guise with this woman, no effort to appear anything other than who she is, and that in itself makes her irresistible.

I find her wet when I trace her spine to the curve of her ass and dip my hand between her legs. She moans into my mouth as liquid heat coats my fingers. Already my cock is weeping, craving her touch.

It's not long before she is rocking against me, riding my hand.

"Jonas..."

Her plea is soft but her nails digging into my shoulder

are leaving marks. Her other hand trails down and finds my cock, wrapping firmly around the hot steel.

I hiss sharply. "You're gonna undo me, Alexandra. Be gentle."

She raises her head and grins at me, lifting her hips as she slides the tip along her slick folds. A natural temptress, drawing a tortured groan from my lips, and it's all I can do to keep from burying myself in her heat.

Grabbing her firmly around the waist, I abruptly flip her off me and onto the mattress, following with the weight of my body.

"Protection," I mumble, bracing myself above her as I try to reach the drawer of my nightstand where I tucked the box of condoms I bought last week.

"Boy Scout," she teases, but her body squirms restlessly.

My hand is shaking with anticipation as I try to roll the damn thing on.

"Let me."

Her hands are steady and sure, and the moment I drop my hips in the cradle of hers, she guides my cock in place. I brace myself on my arms and look down at her, her brown eyes brazenly hungry as she grabs a firm hold of my ass.

Christ have mercy.

I'm trying to go slow as I push inside her, but the moment I feel the heat of her body close around me I lose all control.

"Fuck," I grind out as I bury myself to the root.

Despite the slight wince on her face, she instantly clamps her legs firmly around my hips, anchoring me in place. I close my eyes and lower my forehead to hers, giving her time to adjust.

"You feel good," she whispers, tilting her hips to allow me deeper.

I take my cue and slowly start moving inside her.

"You have no idea," I return, my lips already seeking out her mouth.

Too soon I feel a telltale tingle at the base of my spine. Alex is moaning down my throat as her fingers dig into my ass cheeks, urging me deeper. She's close, but so am I.

The air is thick with our scents and the sounds of exertion as I power inside her, quickly gliding a hand down to where we are connected. I find her clit and roll it under the pad of my thumb until I feel the walls of her pussy contract around me. As she keens her release, I grunt out my own, my body jerking with the force.

My heart thunders in my chest when I collapse my full weight on top of her and bury my face in her hair. Realizing I'm too heavy, I try to lift myself up on trembling arms but she wraps me up in her limbs, holding me tightly.

"I'm too heavy," I tell her breathlessly, but she disagrees.

"No. You feel perfect."

"Great steak."

I sit back in my chair and grin at Alex.

"Told you the only thing I've been able to master is the grill."

The corner of her mouth twitches. "I'd say you've mastered a few other things along the way as well."

I still carry her scent on me and even though she's sitting across from me—dressed in one of my shirts—all I see is her freckled, sweat-slicked skin, and those sated brown eyes smiling up at me. I would've been happy staying in bed and forfeiting dinner, but her stomach had rumbled reminding me of my promise to feed her.

She's cute when she's playful like this, showing me another side of her, which only adds to the appeal.

"Glad to know I haven't disappointed you."

"Far from it," she assures me as she gets up and starts collecting dishes.

"Leave those. Ama will take care of it in the morning."

Wrong thing to say.

She turns and throws me a pointedly raised eyebrow over her shoulder.

"I will do no such thing. I'm sure Ama has better things to do than clean up after us."

Damn, I must be falling harder than I thought: even the way she puts me in my place turns me on.

Maybe I've become a little too accustomed to the luxury of having someone pick up after me. I'm trying to remember the last time I made my own bed.

She's right. Ama not only has her hands full with her own family, but also my house, the business, my father, and now I've also asked her to keep an eye on Dan's mother during the day. I'm a grown-ass man, she shouldn't have to look after me as well.

I walk over to where Alex is standing in front of the sink, the hem of my shirt almost coming down to the back of her knees. Knowing she has nothing but a pair of flimsy panties on underneath is a little distracting. It would be so easy to slip them aside and plunge into her from behind.

The sudden sound of running water in the sink snaps me out of it, and I grab for a dish towel. Somehow, I get the feeling me showing her I heard and understood will gain me more credit than bending her over the sink.

Besides, I never got around to telling her about the property map Sully showed me.

~

Alex

I think I was twenty-one, and still in college, the last time I had to execute a walk of shame.

The clock on my dashboard says it's only five thirty and I would've expected Lucy to still be sound asleep, but all the downstairs lights are on.

Before I left last night, I did tell her not to wait up for me, but hadn't intended to stay the night. I'd fallen asleep after Jonas decided to introduce me to a few other skills he'd clearly mastered.

That was after he informed me the mine they'd discovered on their search had been found near the creek bordering my property. At first, the idea they might be close made me a little uneasy, but Jonas told me my land reached much farther up into the mountains than I'd realized, which made me feel better. Besides, they'd hardly bother us if their objective is to stay hidden.

Still, arriving to a house ablaze with lights at five thirty in the morning makes me wonder if perhaps I should've come home right away. I slip the gun I'd kept in my glovebox at the ranch in my pocket and exit the truck. The front door opens when I put a foot on the first porch step.

"What's wrong?" I ask Lucy, who steps out on the porch.

"Nothing wrong," she answers, shrugging her shoulders. "I saw your truck pull up, that's all."

I can smell the lie even from where I'm standing. I'm about to call her on it when she pivots and heads back inside. I follow her in.

"I'm guessing you had a good time?" she says, heading for the kitchen as I kick off my boots and toss my jacket.

"Yeah. I dozed off, sorry."

I bend down to greet the dogs, who have fast become part of the family, before I follow after Lucy.

She's already pouring coffee in my favorite mug and hands it over.

"No need to apologize."

The chattiness along with the obviously fake smile this early in the morning cranks my suspicions even higher.

"All right. Out with it. Why are you up, and why is the house lit like Lumen Field at the Seahawks opening game, at this time of morning?"

She turns her back to pour herself a cup while I—not so patiently—wait.

"Fine," she mumbles when she finally turns around. "I got a little freaked out and imagined I was hearing things."

"Like what? Where?"

"A noise up in the attic. Anyway, it's a moot point because I got up, went to check it out, and there was nothing up there. Every door in the house was locked and the dogs didn't alert," she says, tapping a finger to her head. "All in my mind."

"And yet here you are before the sun's even up, with every light on," I point out.

"Yeah, well, it brought up some stuff I'd just as soon forget." She sets her mug on the counter and dives into the fridge. "Feel like an omelet?"

I don't need to be a mind reader to know Lucy doesn't plan to elaborate on that comment, but I'm not willing to let it go that easily.

"I'd love an omelet, but Lucy?" I wait until she looks at me, albeit reluctantly. "Any time you want to talk, I'm here to listen. No judgment, no expectations, no strings attached. Just a caring ear. Okay?"

Her lips press together and I catch her swallowing hard, but she nods her agreement. Then she turns her attention back to the contents of the fridge.

Whether she'll ever take me up on it or not, I don't know, but at least the offer is out there. I get the unsettling feeling her story won't be a pretty one.

"Do I have time for a quick shower?"

"Please do. I don't want the olfactory reminder of your date night's activities to spoil my appetite."

There's the Lucy I know and love; direct, snarky, and completely irreverent. With a headshake and a grin, I walk out of the kitchen and head up the stairs.

Ten minutes later I feel a bit more presentable, although I miss smelling Jonas on my skin. I can smell bacon and frying onions waft upstairs and quickly get dressed. As I walk across the landing to the top of the stairs, I notice the door to the attic open a crack. Lucy probably left it open.

I'm about to close it when I decide to have a quick look. It's entirely possible we have some critters who made their home up there, but if that's the case I should probably get pest control in here. I don't mind a mouse or two, it's par for the course living in the country, but I'm not a fan of possums and I've heard of colonies of bats found in attics. That's where I draw the line.

Apparently, Lucy had been sufficiently spooked to leave the light on as well. The single bulb dangling from the low beams shines a harsh light through the now mostly empty space. There's a small dormer with a window on either side of the rectangular space and I check both. There are no windowpanes broken and neither one budges when I try.

When I head back to the stairs, I notice one of the boxes

of junk in the corner I haven't gotten around to has toppled over, dumping part of the contents on the floor. That's probably what she heard. It's likely I hit the stack when I pulled that old rolled up carpet out of the attic, and gravity finally toppled it over. I hope it'll put Lucy's mind at ease.

Picking up the contents of mostly old newspapers and magazines, I stuff them back in the box and flick off the light as I head downstairs.

"It's not in your mind," I tell her when I walk into the kitchen. "One of the boxes stacked in the corner had fallen. It was still on top of the stack when I took that rug out yesterday. I must've knocked it, shifted that box."

"So you're telling me I have you to thank for barely three hours of sleep?" She glares at me, pulling back the omelet she was about to slide in front of me. "I'm having second thoughts about feeding you."

I snatch the plate from her hand and sit down at the table, shoving a forkful in my mouth.

She waves a spatula in my direction.

"You know, you could be a bit more remorseful. Next time I might consider putting something in your food."

I grin with my mouth full.

"You wouldn't. You love me too much."

She ignores me and sits down across the table, digging into her own omelet. But when five minutes later I pick up my plate and head for the sink, I hear her teasing voice behind me.

"You will never know."

Seventeen

ALEX

"Is Buster going to be okay?"

I smile at the teenage girl sitting on the fence.

"I sure hope so. He's such a handsome boy."

I watch as Sam—the girl's father—leads a good-looking palomino from the stable. The horse is clearly difficult to manage, even for the sturdy rancher who quickly unclips his lead as soon as they reach the exercise ring. I asked him to just give the horse his legs for a bit so I could observe.

Buster doesn't seem to be bothered much by his injury as he kicks out his hind quarters and takes off bucking to the far end. There he slides to a halt, his head high, nostrils flaring as his ears twitch in all directions.

The horse is definitely spooked.

"Is he usually spirited?" I ask when Sam walks over.

"Not really. I mean, he'll blow off steam when we put him out after a long ride, but never when saddled or on a lead. Wouldn't let Mickey handle him otherwise."

He must be referring to his daughter, who snorts audibly.

I clap my hands a few times and watch the horse's muscles bunch as he startles at the sound. Then he launches into a canter, his head still high as he restlessly circles the exercise ring, making sure to steer clear of the side we're standing.

I wait until he slows down and finally stops, again on the far side, his eyes and ears now focused on us. Now that I have his attention, I hold my hands out by my hips, palms out, and slowly start moving toward him. I pay close attention to his body language. When I reach the center of the ring, I can tell he's ready to bolt and I abruptly stop. Keeping my hands in the same position, I turn around and start walking back the other way.

I go through this exercise a few times, each time able to get a little closer. At some point he lets me get close enough to see puffs of breath coming from his nostrils. Then I start talking in a soft voice—mostly nonsense but in a soothing tone—as I inch my way even closer until I've pushed it about as far as he'll let me come.

This time when I stop and turn my back, I hear him snort behind me and wait. Then I hear it, the faint thud of a hoof on the packed dirt in the ring. It's followed by another, and when I hear a third, I start walking back toward Sam and his daughter. A quick glance over my shoulder tells me Buster follows at a safe distance, but the closer I get, the farther he falls behind, coming to a complete stop in the center of the ring.

"That was awesome!" Mickey says enthusiastically when I reach them. "That was good, right?"

"It was a hopeful start."

I weigh my words carefully, because this is not like throwing a switch. Building trust takes time—a lot of it—and inevitably there'll be setbacks. I convey as much to father and daughter. The girl is clearly disappointed but Sam looks pleased.

"So how long do you figure?"

"If only I had a crystal ball," I tell him with a chuckle. "It would help if I could work with him every day."

Sam shrugs. "I don't have a problem with that."

"Thing is," I admit. "I'm afraid I wouldn't have time to make it out here every day. Unless, of course, you stabled Buster with me. That would make it a lot easier."

By the time I drive away from the dude ranch, I'm high-fiving myself. Sam is bringing Buster over tomorrow night.

The idea of boarding had come up before as a source of revenue for the rescue, but by combining it with my behavioral work it had the potential to grow both sides of the business while maximizing my time.

My head is full of ideas as I make my way back home and I narrowly avoid a head-on collision when I pull into my drive. I almost run into a large dump truck pulling out. I hold up my hand and mouth an apology at the guy behind the wheel, who merely shakes his head before turning onto the highway.

I'm so relieved that junk is gone. That wouldn't have been a good look if my new client pulled up here tomorrow seeing a pile of rusted garbage.

"It's gone!" I yell at Lucy who comes walking toward the house, the dogs at her feet.

"And so is my good mood," she grumbles when she catches up with me.

"How's that?"

She waves an agitated arm in the direction of the highway. "That idiot truck driver. I'm sick of misogynistic assholes. Men!" she spits before stomping up the porch steps.

By the time I say hello to Chief and Scout, and head inside, she's already disappeared upstairs. Not sure what happened, but I know better than to try and get it out of her until she's ready.

When she surfaces forty-five minutes later, I am just putting the finishing touches on the meal it was my turn to make. Spaghetti, meatballs, and a green salad. Quick and easy, just the way I like it.

"So how did it go at the dude ranch?" she asks as she grabs the bowl of salad off the counter and carries it to the table.

"First thing tomorrow morning, I plan to put the stable in order and give that big stall a good cleaning. We've got a guest coming."

"Oh?"

I tell her about the beautiful palomino who seemed scared of his own shadow and my plans for him.

"And the owner went for it?"

"Hook, line, and sinker. After I explained I'd be able to work with the horse more effectively if I had free access to him, of course. He agreed to a weekly boarding amount and I reduced my treatment fee by the travel time and fuel. It's a win-win for everyone."

The first real smile of the day blooms on Lucy's face.

"Very clever. You think it's going to catch on?"

I pull up my shoulders. "Time will tell. Word of mouth is alive and well in these regions so as long as I do good work, I'm sure business will be picking up."

"How are Hope and Daisy getting along?" I ask, sliding a plate in front of Lucy before sitting down myself.

"Good. I had both of them outside today. They're not bosom buddies yet, but they were grazing close together. When I called for them when that truck showed up earlier, Daisy came trotting up right away and Hope stuck close behind her. I think Daisy will be good for boosting the mare's confidence."

Things are looking up all around. Aside from Sarge and Ellie—our horses—the others are all permanent guests due to age, or injury, or attitude. Hope, however, could be marketable. Doc Evans guessed her at about six years old and now that she's looking healthier, and Lucy is making headway, she could make someone a good horse.

Lucy's mention of the truck hasn't escaped me so I dive in.

"What happened?"

She knows exactly what I'm referring to.

"Pretty little thing like you all alone on a ranch like this?" she mocks.

"Is that what he said?"

"First thing out of his mouth."

Yikes. That wouldn't have gone over well with me either, but Lucy seems really upset.

"Guy gave me the creeps. Suggested I put the dogs in the house," she scoffs. "Like I was going to. If not for those two getting all protective of me, I'm not sure he'd have kept his distance. Then I would've had to pull my gun on him and that could've been messy."

"We should report him to the company. As soon as the office opens tomorrow morning, I'm calling."

"Don't," she says sharply. "Seriously, guys like that are a

dime a dozen wherever you go. There's really nothing to report and it would only make things uncomfortable."

She has a point, but it doesn't sit right with me to let it go. Maybe I'll mention it to Jonas when he comes by tomorrow, get his take on it. It's a pretty small world up here, maybe he even knows the guy enough to know whether that was supposed to be an innocent comment or if the man is someone to be concerned about.

"Fair enough," I concede.

$\sim$

Jonas

"Are you for real?"

I almost laugh out loud at the look on Dan's face as he holds the artificial vagina, or AV, far away from his body. It's basically a tube with a sturdy handle, which is lined with a bladder attached to a plastic collection bottle.

I figured we'd get Blitz used to the collection process. Who knows, humping a breeding dummy—a construction on two height adjustable legs bracing a bolstered body mimicking a mare—might help him get rid of some of that fire. It also seemed a good opportunity to get the kid a little more *closely* involved with the stallion.

Yesterday we did a 'dry' run with just the dummy, but today Blitz is getting the full treatment.

Fletch, who is giving me a hand in the breeding barn, barks out a rare laugh.

"Would you wanna stick your dick in a dry pussy, kid?" he teases.

Dan glowers at him before snatching the bottle of lube from his hand. He squirts some in the sleeve he's holding.

"Gotta do him too." Fletch points at the horse I'm holding.

Blitz already can't stand still, his body primed to go.

"Awww, Jesus," the kid mumbles.

"Steady hand and don't fumble," I warn him. "After, you wanna get into position right away and don't spill. This stuff is worth gold."

I catch Fletch's eye, who is grinning at me.

He knows whatever we manage to collect won't count for much. Not yet anyway. But it's fun to rattle the new guy. We've all had to endure the same at some point in time. Be the butt of jokes, get the dirty jobs. It's a rite of passage. The truth is, during breeding season we collect every other day. It becomes just like any other chore that needs to get done on a ranch.

Artificial insemination has taken over a large chunk of the breeding industry. It's easier, safer, and cheaper. Despite that, there are still some breeders out there who prefer *live cover*: stud services the old-fashioned way.

Dan holds up well. Despite his awkward start with the mechanics, he does have a way with the animals and I let him lead Blitz back to his stall.

"Not bad for a greenhorn," Fletch mutters beside me as we make our way to the house for a bite of lunch.

Probably some of the highest praise anyone could get from him. Fletch was the last to join us here at the ranch. Sully finally tracked him down in Canada. He was living as a virtual recluse in the mountains near Fernie, British Columbia, and would occasionally freelance as a hunting guide to make some money. It had taken a bit of convincing to get him to come.

"Nope, and Alex was right; he does have a natural instinct with the horses."

Fletch's only response is a grunt.

Sully and Dad are already at the kitchen table when we walk in. They got back from Elk River well after midnight last night.

I put a hand on Dad's shoulder. "Did you get any rest?"

"Some."

He still looks pretty wiped, although he'd seemed a little gaunt already last week. I wonder if he's coming down with something.

"You know what I was thinking?" I take the empty seat next to him. "We've been so busy you haven't had a chance to find a new doctor here yet. Maybe Ama can set up an appointment at the medical clinic in Libby for you. Doc Sansome is a good guy. You'll like him."

He shoots me a glare.

"Nothing wrong with me."

Ama gives me a little encouraging nudge as she slides a bowl of beans and a thick slab of bread in front of me.

"Shit, Dad. Nothing wrong with me either, but I still go yearly for my physical. When's the last time you've been?"

It took some doing, but by the time I give Alex a call to let her know I'm on my way with Sugar, my father has conceded to see the doc.

I find her in the stable, saddling a good-looking buckskin.

"Hey," she greets me with a smile.

I slip a hand behind her neck and pull her to me, covering her mouth with mine.

"Mmmm. I think I like your hello better," she mumbles

when I let her go. Then she leans to the side to look behind me. "Where's your horse?"

"Left her tied to the trailer. I wasn't sure if you were ready. Lucy sent me this way."

She turns to her horse and rubs his muzzle.

"Ready, Sarge?"

"Sugar's easygoing," I let her know as we walk out. "Gets along with everyone."

"So is this guy."

She throws me a questioning look when I grab a rifle from the cab and slip it in the saddle holster.

"Standard gear," I explain. "Insurance against wildlife up here."

She produces a bear can and pats her coat pocket, where I assume she keeps her gun.

"I've got my own measures."

I won't burst her bubble and tell her the spray may slow a bear or mountain lion down, but won't stop them, and she'd need to have perfect aim to be any more lucky with that gun. Doesn't mean I won't bring it up at a later time. If she plans to head into the mountains she needs to be prepared.

"Which way?" she asks when we mount up.

"North side."

I'm most interested in checking out the area along the creek where she heard the shot. It's been a while, but if someone was up there, I may still be able to find tracks.

The horses do well side by side, but the narrow trail heading into the trees is only wide enough for one. I slip ahead of her. If we encounter anything, I'll be in the line of fire instead of Alex.

But we don't get far when I hear a cell phone ring and

my hand immediately goes to my pocket as I bring Sugar to a halt with my other.

"It's mine," Alex says behind me.

I turn in my saddle and watch as she puts her phone to her ear.

"Luce, we just left."

I'm too far to hear Lucy's side of the conversation and Alex seems to do all the listening. Her eyes snap up to mine and I read the regret.

"He wasn't supposed to be here until tomorrow night. Okay. I'll be right there. No, I should probably be there."

"Problem?" I ask when she hangs up and stuffs her phone in her pocket.

"Minor emergency. A client showed up with his horse earlier than he was supposed to. I'm afraid I'm gonna have to turn back."

I start turning Sugar when she stops me.

"You don't have to come back with me. It's not hard to find, the creek, that is. Just follow this trail. It'll take you to the first clearing, and then maybe fifteen minutes farther along the trail you'll hit the second, smaller, one. You'll be able to see the ridge from there."

I'm almost relieved but I'm not about to tell her that. If there is anyone hiding on her property, I'd rather not have to worry about Alex.

"Sure you don't mind?" I ask to make sure. "I wouldn't mind getting a lay of the land. Maybe see if I can find any evidence someone was up there."

"Not at all. Maybe I can make it up to you with dinner after?"

I maneuver Sugar alongside Sarge and lean over to press a hard kiss on her lips.

"I'll bring my appetite."

Despite heading out on my own, the ride is nice. Crisp mountain air, clear skies overhead, and pretty views. Prettier still when I get to the first clearing next to the creek. I notice the water is pretty high and running fast and I'm thinking this would be a great spot to bring a couple of fly rods and a cooler of beer, and spend the day.

But I'm not here to admire the scenery. I cluck and press my heels into Sugar's flanks, guiding her to the trail that picks up ahead.

The second clearing Alex mentioned is not that far. As a precaution, I stop my horse at the edge of the tree line and scan the ridge rising up on the other side, where the cover is not quite as thick. The first thing I notice is that what was a narrow trail coming up here, looks to suddenly change into a clear two-wheel track heading farther up the mountain.

Weird. Why would tracks like that start or end in the middle of nowhere?

But then I remember Sully picked up similar tracks with the drone. I wonder if these could be from the same trail.

Curious, I cross the clearing, keeping a close eye on the ridge. I'm feeling a little exposed and breathe a sigh of relief when I'm under the cover of trees again. Here the path turns steep, leading me almost straight up. Luckily that's no problem for Sugar, she's tackled worse.

When we reach the ridge, I dismount and take a look around. I have a good view of the clearing below. A very good view. I can easily make out the spot where I was standing earlier, looking up here.

I pull out my phone and check the coordinates. I'm not that far from the most eastern point of Alex's property, which means I'm also not that far from where James found that trip wire.

My eyes scan the ground, looking for tracks or footprints, but it's hard to see when most of the ground is rock and gravel. I'm about to give up and get back on my horse when the light reflects off something metallic. I crouch down and brush aside some weeds to uncover a rifle shell.

Bingo.

When I reach to pick it up, I hear the crunch of a footstep behind me.

Eighteen

ALEX

That's weird.

I'd expected to see a second trailer parked next to Jonas's rig, but instead there's an unfamiliar silver SUV sitting in front of the house.

Maybe Sam's gone and left already, but then why didn't Lucy call me back to tell me? I could've stayed with Jonas. It's annoying. I'd really been looking forward to the ride with him. For a moment I consider trying to catch up with him, but by now he has at least a half-hour lead.

By the time I bring Sarge to a halt outside the barn and dismount, I'm actually getting a little pissed off until I catch sight of the SUV again, and a sense of unease starts creeping in. Whose car is that?

I lead Sarge into his stall and quickly remove his saddle and bridle. I'll have to put him out after I see what's going on. I throw his bridle over my shoulder, hook my arms under his saddle, and walk toward the small tack room next to the barn doors.

Sliding the saddle onto the rack, I sense movement near me but before I can turn around two arms wrap tightly around me from behind.

I'm pretty sure I screamed as I struggle to get free. My arms are trapped uselessly against my body so I use my legs, trying to do as much damage as I can kicking back. A deep grunt tells me I made contact, but then I hear a deep chuckle by my ear and freeze.

I recognize it. The sound of it as familiar to me as my own reflection.

"Jesus, Mom. You're more dangerous than some of the insurgents we encounter."

The arms release me and I whip around, tears already blurring my vision and I furiously wipe at them. I need to see it's really him.

My God, *my baby*.

So handsome and grown-up, he looks like an adult version of the boy I saw off what feels like ages ago. Six months, two weeks, and three days ago, to be exact. An eternity when you know your child is on the other side of the world, facing all kinds of danger you have no way of protecting them against.

"Jackson."

His name slips out on a sob as I fling myself back in his arms.

"Missed you, Momma," he mumbles, his face pressed into the crook of my neck.

"Missed you more."

A loud sniff has me lift my head to find Lucy standing in the doorway, her eyes suspiciously shiny.

"You knew?"

The question is more of an accusation but she quickly shakes her head.

"Trust me, I was just as surprised when I found him on our doorstep."

"Luce cried," Jackson contributes, straightening up as he throws her a grin.

"Did not," she fires back defiantly, sticking her chin up stubbornly. "I never cry."

"Bullshit." My son tries—and fails—to cover his comment with a cough, but Lucy hears and narrows her eyes at him.

"I *was* going to make you stuffed French toast for breakfast tomorrow, but you can forget about that now."

"Awww, Luce. Don't be that way." He walks over and pulls her reluctant body into a hug.

My boy, the charmer. That much at least hasn't changed.

I can't say the same for his body, which has somehow filled out from the long-limbed, scrawny kid I shipped off. He's not wearing his uniform but a pair of jeans and a navy sweatshirt that looks molded around wide shoulders and muscular arms.

Neither has the almost sibling-like banter between my friend and my son. They can bicker like sister and brother but underneath they absolutely adore each other.

He looks so much like his father now.

Blinking off a second wave of tears, I grab Jackson's arm and slip mine through.

"Help me set Sarge out and you can tell me how you got here."

"I'll take care of Sarge," Lucy says. "You guys head inside and let the dogs out for me. There's fresh coffee in the kitchen."

"How did you get here? Why didn't you tell me you were coming? We spoke only a few days ago. How long are you home for?" I start firing off questions as soon as we start walking toward the house, my arm firmly hooked in his and my eyes fixed on his face.

"In a rental car and I wanted to surprise you," he answers, grinning down on me.

"Wiseass," I accuse him, noting he didn't answer the last question. "I thought you'd be gone for nine months at least."

"That's what they told us at the onset, but things change all the time."

The dogs are going nuts inside when they hear us coming up the porch steps and I quickly open the door.

"I see you've expanded the rescue," he comments, bending down to give Chief a little attention while I endure Scout's excited welcome.

"They came with Hope, our latest equestrian rescue."

"She the one chumming up with Daisy out there?"

"That's her. She was in bad shape. The dogs too," I share. "They've gotten attached to us."

He straightens up and grins at me.

"More like you two got attached to them."

Touché.

The dogs—having gotten their fill of attention—bound off toward the barn.

"Whose trailer is that?" Jackson asks as I step through the door.

I'm not sure why the question feels so loaded, or maybe it's just the way I hear it.

"Jonas Harvey. He's a neighbor," I hurry to explain as I lead the way to the kitchen. "He was helping me check the property line."

Guilt immediately overwhelms me. Although, whether it's for passing Jonas off as just a neighbor, or hiding my involvement with him from my son, I'm not sure. Maybe both. I'm just not sure how Jackson would react if he found out I was developing feelings for someone other than his father.

I pour us coffee and hand him a mug. Some of my thoughts must've shown on my face because Jackson looks at me from under his eyebrows.

"A neighbor?"

"Uh-huh." I step around him and take a seat at the kitchen table. "Come sit. You never answered me how long you'll be home."

"Two weeks."

He pulls out the chair across from me and sits down.

"Only two weeks?"

I'm not sure what I was thinking. Maybe I'd hoped he'd be home for good? Decided military life wasn't for him after all?

"And then what? Back to Iraq?"

He shakes his head, his eyes intently watching me.

"Fort Bragg."

That's North Carolina. Not next door, but at least on US soil and not all the way in the Middle East.

"What will you be doing there?"

His eyes drop down to the mug in his hands.

Uh oh. Why do I get the feeling I won't like what he has to say?

"Some more training."

I almost grin. His father used to be a master at feeding me information he didn't want to share piecemeal. The apple does not fall far.

"Training for what?"

"A special unit."

I close my eyes and take a deep breath. It's like pulling teeth.

"What kind of special unit?"

Then his eyes come up.

"You're not gonna like it."

Well, if that isn't reassuring.

"Jackson…" I threaten.

"Special Ops. I've trained my ass off these past months."

I glance at his new wider shoulders and muscled chest, and swallow hard.

So that's why.

"Look, it's not as bad as it sounds," he hurries to add. "I'd be based stateside."

"But you could be gone in a flash, and I wouldn't know where you are or how long you'll be gone," I counter, a lump forming in my throat.

He hears it and leans over the table, grabbing my hand.

"I probably won't even make it through training. Few do."

Bless him for trying, but I know my kid. If he sets his mind to something he'll make it happen.

Pride battles with the stark fear.

"But you will," I tell him, my voice thick with emotion.

The front door slams open and the dogs barge in, followed by Lucy.

"Is Jonas in here?"

I twist around in my seat.

"Jonas? No, he's still on the trail, why?"

"Because his horse is out there by his trailer."

～

"Hold up! Where are you going?"

Jackson catches up with me halfway down the porch steps.

"I'm gonna look for him."

As Lucy had said, Sugar is standing next to the trailer, the saddle still on her back and the reins dragging on the ground. To top it off, Jonas's rifle was still sticking from the saddle holster.

Jonas is nowhere in sight.

I walk up to the horse, putting a hand on her butt as I circle her. Reaching down, I pick up the reins so she can't take off, but as I straighten, I notice blood running down her front leg from a cut low on her shoulder. More like a groove.

"She's cut."

"What? Let me see."

Jackson pushes me out of the way and bends down to see better.

"That doesn't look like a cut, Mom. It looks like a bullet graze."

I look at my son dubiously. "How would you know?"

He doesn't say a word, but his eyes speak volumes and for a moment my heart squeezes hard. For innocence lost. For the things my child has witnessed in these short past six months that have him recognize the graze of a bullet.

What if Jonas was shot as well? He obviously never had a chance to grab his rifle. What if he's out there somewhere —hurt?

I won't allow my mind to go any further than that as I quickly tie Sugar's reins to the trailer and march toward the barn.

"*Fuck*. Mom, stop!"

"Where is she off to?" I hear Lucy ask behind me as the dogs run past me.

I ignore them both, but when I step out of the tack room a minute later carrying Sarge's tack, both Jackson and Lucy are blocking my way.

"Listen to me," Jackson pleads, holding his hands out in front of him. "You can't go off half-cocked without knowing what you're walking into."

"Well, I can't leave him out there," I protest, trying to push past him.

"Let me call High Meadow. If anyone is equipped to find him it's those guys," Lucy suggests.

"Call them, but don't expect me to wait around for them. It'll take them valuable time to get here. Time Jonas may not have."

"What's High Meadow?" my son wants to know.

I leave Lucy to explain while I grab the opportunity to rush to the back meadow and whistle for Sarge.

There's no way I'm gonna sit around and wait when I could be out there doing something.

I'm just about to mount Sarge when Jackson comes running up, carrying tack with a rifle slung over his shoulder.

"What do you think you're doing?" I snap as I swing my leg in the saddle.

"If I can't stop you, I'm coming with you.

"Jackson—"

"Mom, no," he says, firmly tossing his gear to the ground.

When he slips inside the gate, he still has the rifle over his shoulder. It looks like the one from Jonas's holster. Ellie —who just tried to sneak out behind Sarge—is easily caught.

"You're gonna hurt yourself with that thing," I try in a last-ditch effort to deter him.

But my son snorts as he quickly saddles Lucy's mount.

"Hardly. I can do more damage with this rifle at five hundred yards than you can with your peashooter in a crowded room."

I open my mouth to protest, then snap it shut again when I realize I have no hope of winning this argument.

The box of plaques in the spare bedroom for first place in the Quigley Buffalo Rifle Match since he turned eighteen is proof of that.

Dammit.

Nineteen

JONAS

Dirt.

I smell damp earth.

My head feels like it's going to explode and I'm not sure where I am, but I recognize the scent of dirt and decaying vegetation.

I'm lying on it. Curled on my side with an arm wedged underneath me, on hard soil. My entire body hurts like I've been hit by a truck. I try to move my hands, only to discover them tied behind my back. The movement has whatever they used cut into my wrists.

Wire?

Shit. This isn't good.

Then I try moving my legs. The top leg, my right side, seems okay, but when I try to wiggle my left foot, I'm rewarded with a searing hot pain.

Fuck.

I try to remember what happened. Last thing I recall I

was on top of the ridge looking down at the clearing below. Everything after that is a blank.

I carefully crank an eye open, bracing for light, but there is none. It's dark. Is it nighttime? Where the hell am I?

"You did what?"

The sound of a raised voice comes from above, startling me. I jerk my head up only to drop it right back to the ground. It hits hard. Not just dirt, but rock underneath. My head feels like it's stuck in a vise and someone just stabbed an icepick in my skull.

I swallow a groan and carefully turn my head. Then I open my other eye too. I squint, looking up at a small circle of night sky too far above me. I'm in a hole. Quite literally.

A cave?

Fragments of a conversation filter down. Two voices.

I strain to hear what is being said but it's hard with one ear pressed to the ground. My six-pack may no longer be evident but I still have decent core strength and manage to sit up, leaning my back against the solid rock wall. It takes a few seconds for the nauseating pain in my head and my ankle—as well as the ringing in my ears—to recede.

"...would've found the compound."

"You didn't figure the guy would be missed? What the hell were you thinking? First you shoot at that woman–"

"She saw me! She would've—"

"Your job—your only job—was to keep an eye out. You may as well have set off a fucking flare to point the damn pigs our way, Terry."

I have no doubt this Terry is Terrence Adams, one of the escaped terrorists. Holy fuck. The pissed-off guy must be Wright.

"I'll kill him. Toss him off a cliff. Make it look like he had an accident and they won't have to look for him."

I straighten my back. To do that they'd have to get me out of this hole and I like my chances a lot better up there than down here.

"That might've worked if you hadn't shot the damn horse, fucking moron," Wright points out.

Sugar. My heart sinks, she was a fine horse. Steady and loyal.

"And then you missed!" he continues.

"I didn't miss."

"Dead horses don't run off. Jesus fucking Christ, after the incident with that woman you'll be lucky if the general doesn't shoot you on the spot. He wasn't supposed to be back until next week with supplies, but what do you wanna bet he's gonna be up here as soon as he finds out about this last stunt? We were supposed to lay low."

The general?

They have someone on the outside. Jesus.

"So what do we do with him?" Adams asks.

Suddenly there's a sound of dirt falling down. I narrowly manage to let my body slump back to the floor and turn my face in the dirt before the beam of a flashlight shines down.

"He's still out but breathing." Wright's voice is clear now, bouncing off the hard surface of the walls. "We'll keep him alive, let the general decide. You better hope he has some use for him."

I wait until darkness returns and I no longer hear anything. Then I slowly lift my head, letting my eyes adjust to the lack of light. With the few glimpses I got of my surroundings in the beam of the flashlight locked in my mind, it doesn't take long to figure out my makeshift cell.

It's no more than a hole in the ground, at the bottom maybe six-and-a-half feet in diameter. Most of the rock is covered with a layer of damp dirt and leaves, I'd barely have enough room to stretch out in. Unfortunately the cave is at least double that deep. If I stood up and reached my arms above my head, my fingertips would still be about four feet shy of the edge. The opening at the top is narrower, the walls leaning in the farther up you get.

All of those are moot points, though, since my hands are tied and my left ankle is fucked up.

I can't do anything about my ankle, but I can try and work on loosening my bindings.

Hopefully when daylight breaks, I can better assess my options.

∾

Alex

"Are you sure he came this way?"

I turn in the saddle to look at Jackson.

"Positive. He wanted to check out…"

Shit. I haven't had a chance to fill Jackson in on recent events. I'd kept both the shooting incident and the escaped prisoners to myself in our chats. No need to have him worried about me when he should be worried about himself.

"The ridge," I finish reluctantly.

"What ridge?"

I slow down as soon as Sarge steps into the clearing, allowing Jackson to pull up beside me. Then I point at the ridge rising up from the trees on the far side.

"That ridge. Maybe a week ago, I thought I saw

someone up there just a moment before we heard a shot. Sarge spooked and took off the other—"

"A shot? At you?"

"Well, I don't know about that. Could've been a hunter shooting at wildlife. There's no way to know."

It sounds flimsy, even to my own ears, and especially now that someone seems to have taken a potshot at Jonas's horse. Oh well, in for a penny, in for a pound. I should probably tell him about the escaped prisoners and the mine Jonas found not too far from here.

"*Jesus*, Mom. That's it, I'm taking the lead," Jackson announces when I finish.

I'm not sure if I like that but he's not waiting for my okay before he urges Ellie past Sarge, taking the rifle off his shoulder and resting the barrel on his thighs.

My eyes are glued to the ridge as we approach it. Would Jonas have gotten this far? We haven't seen any sign of him. I'm sure if he saw the dual tracks heading into the trees, he would've gone to investigate those.

I'm about to tell Jackson but he's already steering Ellie in that direction.

A high-pitched buzzing noise overhead has me turn around and look up at the sky. I spot a small black dot in the sky heading straight for us.

"Mom! Get over here!"

I turn back to see Jackson has led his horse into the trees and is gesturing wildly. With one last look over my shoulder at that thing coming toward us, I dig my heels in Sarge's sides and lean forward.

"What the hell is that?" I ask when reach him.

"Drone."

He urges me up the ridge and, while still under tree

cover, dismounts and hands Ellie's reins to me. "Hold on to her and stay here."

Then he takes the rifle and starts climbing even higher on foot,

"Where are you going? Jackson..."

He swings around and presses his forefinger to his lips.

I almost don't recognize him. No easy smiles, mischievous sparkle in his eyes, or relaxed swagger, instead he looks intense, focused, and *hard*.

The next moment he's gone from sight, and a cold shiver runs down my spine.

Am I really just going to sit here and let my kid go off alone?

No fucking way.

I've never been one to wait at the sidelines and I'm not about to now.

Slipping out of the saddle, I quickly loop Sarge and Ellie's reins around a tree. Then I pull what Jackson calls my *peashooter* from my pocket and start climbing after him.

"What are you doing?" he hisses when he spots me, his face angry.

He's crouched behind a large boulder at the edge of the trees, the barrel of his rifle resting on top, aimed at the clearing which is visible below.

Ignoring his angry tone, I duck low and make my way over.

"I should ask you the same thing," I return, crouching beside him.

He tries to stare me down but I have a few more years of practice on him. He finally turns his attention back to the clearing, shaking his head.

"Insurgents use those things for surveillance. They pinpoint troop locations before launching attacks," he finally shares. "You see or hear a drone, it's always bad news."

First word that comes to mind is paranoia. I'm dumbfounded. What happened to my boy in those short six months over there?

I'm not sure how to respond for fear of saying something wrong.

"Jackson, we're in the US—this is Montana. People here use drones for fun. For taking pictures or shooting video."

As he slowly turns his head, I see his lips twitch and his eyes have that fun-loving sparkle back.

"I'm aware, Momma," he drawls.

Relief has me blowing out a breath, but then his expression turns serious.

"But this drone is flying over your land, after a couple of domestic terrorists went missing in the area, a trip wire was found, you were shot at, a horse got grazed by a bullet, and your boyfriend went missing."

Okay, when you put it like that, a little extra caution is probably warranted. Then my mind registers the last thing he said.

"He's not my boyfriend."

One of Jackson's eyebrows draws up to disappear under the heavy lock of the auburn hair he inherited from me.

"Twenty-three, Momma. Not three. You wanna tell me you tore out of there like a bat out of hell to go look for a neighbor? Puleeze," he adds for good measure, a grin forming on his handsome face. "It's about damn time too."

I huff but can't hide the smile slipping out.

"Fine, maybe—"

"Shhh," he cuts me off as his eyes snap back to the clearing.

On the other side I see two—no, three—forms

215

appearing from the narrower trail on the other side. Three horses, three men.

Jackson shifts slightly, lining up his rifle sight on the front rider. I can't see his face from this distance but the black Stetson on his head stands out, as does the horse he's riding.

"Wait..." I put a hand on my son's shoulder. "I know them."

"You sure?"

He tries to hold me back when I get to my feet. From this angle I'm also able to recognize the other two riders.

"Positive. That's Sully up front, followed by Fletch, and the last guy is Bo. These are Jonas's men."

By the time the three men make their way up to us, Jackson reluctantly stands beside me, the rifle held loosely at his side, the barrel aimed at the ground. Still, as Sully dismounts, his eyes never leave the weapon.

"This is my son, Jackson," I quickly explain, feeling the level of testosterone ratchet up as each of the guys approach.

"Jackson," Sully mutters, nudging toward the rifle. "I believe that belongs to Jonas."

"Emergency," Jackson responds. "My gear is on its way to Fort Bragg."

I have no idea why but that random statement seems enough to have the three relax visibly.

"Tell me exactly what happened," Sully instructs me.

The man I've gotten to know as easygoing and jovial has turned dead serious, assuming an air of authority I would normally associate with Jonas. No need to question who is in charge now.

He listens carefully until I get to the part where I noticed the drone.

"That was ours. James is running it from your place and has been in contact with us via radio. He pointed us here."

I turn to Jackson. "Good thing you didn't shoot it down."

Bo, who is standing behind Sully with the horses, coughs.

"That is a good thing, since it's roughly twenty grand to replace," he comments dryly.

"Sully!"

We all turn to Fletch, who is crouched down next to a rock about twenty feet farther up, his back turned. Sully starts climbing in his direction and I automatically follow.

"Fuck," I hear Sully mutter under his breath when he leans over the other man's shoulder.

Curious, I try to catch a peek over his other shoulder. First thing I notice is a shell casing Fletch drops in Sully's upturned hand. Then I suck in a sharp breath when I see what's on the ground.

"Is that blood?" I manage through a tight throat, staring at the dark stain soaked into the dirt and stone.

"Could it be from the horse?" Jackson, who apparently stuck close behind me, asks.

"He'd have left the horse back there," Fletch responds, cocking his thumb over his shoulder to where they left their horses. "Too easy for them to lose their footing up here."

Sully straightens and turns around to face me with a sympathetic look.

"Could he have fallen? Hit his head? Maybe he wandered off confused?" I'm desperately trying to hang onto scenarios that don't involve bullets or escaped prisoners.

"Mom, that was a bullet wound on the horse," Jackson softly reminds me.

"We don't know that for sure."

Panic is setting in with a burning feeling in my chest, like I can't breathe.

Sully grabs me by the upper arms but when he speaks, he does so over my shoulder, addressing Jackson.

"I want you to take your mom back to the house." He wraps the shell in a tissue he pulls from his pocket, handing it to my son. "Give that to our man back at the rescue." Then he turns to me. "I need you to tell James to get Max out here and to contact DHS, he'll know who to get hold of."

"I'm not going anywhere," I object stubbornly. "If he's hurt, he'll need my help. I have some medical training."

I don't clarify I'm referring to veterinary skills, but even those might come in handy.

"Bo was a surgical nurse in a previous life and is a trained field medic," Sully returns.

I turn my head to glance at the bulky, bald-headed black guy and have a hard time imagining him in scrubs, but I have no doubt he's very capable.

"Come, Momma." Jackson grabs my arm. "We're just going to get in the way up here."

I let him pull me with him, but I'm not an idiot. They're worried things may not have turned out so well for Jonas and I wouldn't be able to handle it. I can see it in the way they look at me.

The thing is, I'm not so sure myself.

Twenty

ALEX

It's dark before we're even halfway back.

A bit tricky for the horses to find their footing but every so often the moon peeks through the clouds, which helps. Still, I let out a breath of relief when I spot the lights in the distance.

Jackson and I have been mostly riding in silence. A cacophony of thoughts tumble through my mind as I struggle to process everything. That and the overwhelming concern for Jonas—making me sick to my stomach—have left me numb.

It took me a few minutes after we rode off to realize the message Sully asked me to pass on to James was only to give me a purpose. By his own admission, they were in radio contact so I'm sure by the time I see James he'll have already received word.

As we get closer, I notice Lucy has the place lit up like a

Christmas tree. Every possible light is on, illuminating the barn, the corral, and the house. A number of trucks are parked out front, the trailers from the High Meadow Ranch, along with a couple of vehicles I don't readily recognize.

The two dogs are the first to spot us, barking as they jump off the porch and run to greet us. Lucy isn't far behind and meets us at the barn.

"Brace," she says, taking Sarge's reins from my hands when I swing myself out of the saddle. "We've got the sheriff in the house, and a few neighbors showed up wanting to help with the search. Word travels fast here."

Great. I already dread having to sit around and wait, and now I'll have to do it surrounded by a bunch of strangers.

Jackson leads Ellie into the barn and Lucy follows with Sarge, leaving me to bring up the rear. By rote I loosen the cinch and slide the saddle off Sarge's back. When I carry it into the tack room, Lucy is right behind me with his bridle.

"How are you holding up?"

I've been able to keep myself together in front of Jonas's teammates, in front of my son, but when my bristly and blunt friend uses the soft tone normally reserved for the animals, my resolve crumbles.

Lucy takes one look at my face, wraps me in her arms, and I let go.

"Ms. Hart? I need to ask you some questions."

I stiffen at the sound of the man's voice behind me but Lucy's arms lock me in place.

"Give us a fucking moment, will you?" she snaps at whoever it is.

"I can tell you whatever you need to know," I hear Jackson say just before someone closes the door.

I indulge a few more minutes before resolutely stepping out of her hold and wiping at my face.

"Guess I needed that. Thanks," I tell Lucy.

She grunts and points at the small sink in the corner. "Wash your face."

When we come out of the tack room, I notice Jackson has led the sheriff—guess that's who had questions—outside the barn.

"Go." Lucy gives me a little shove in the back. "I'll put the horses out back."

"Thanks, but leave them inside. We may need them later. If you wouldn't mind tossing some hay in their stalls."

I walk up to the sheriff at the same time James does. His soulful eyes focus on my face.

"Hangin' in there, Alex?"

"Yup," I answer, popping my P.

Then I remember my manners and introduce myself to Sheriff Ewing and my son to James.

Jackson immediately pulls the tissue Sully handed him from his pocket and shows it to James. The sheriff looks on as James unwraps the shell.

"That's a .223 shell," Ewing announces.

"Nope, not a Remington. This shell is heavier." James turns it over and shows the tiny inscriptions on the bottom. "See? If this were a .223 it would be inscribed on the bottom of the shell. This one just has a date and a symbol."

"It's a 5.56 NATO," Jackson identifies. "Military issue."

"*Shit*," Sheriff Ewing mutters. "That plays into the suspicion these guys were involved with the robbery of that armory. *Goddamn*, I already have feds trampling all over my county, last thing I need is a bunch of yahoos with access to a cache of military weapons to start playing war."

He flips off his hat and scratches his sparse gray hair

before adding, "Old man Jenkins would'a gotten a kick out of this."

"Who's that?" The name sounds familiar.

It's James who answers me.

"Clive Jenkins, this property was in his family for generations before the bank foreclosed on it last year. Old goat defied authority as a sport, one of those sovereign citizen types. He died last November."

"Here?" Lucy blurts out, making James chuckle.

"No. Nursing home in Libby where he ended up."

Jenkins. Now I remember where I saw the name—on an address label on a magazine in one of the boxes up in the attic.

"And there's the feds," the sheriff announces when headlights come up the driveway.

Looks like my rescue has become the center of this investigation.

So much for moving to the quiet countryside.

If not for Lucy forcing me to eat something, I might've collapsed hours ago.

It's past midnight when I finally manage to excuse myself and head up for a shower and change. I desperately crave a few minutes of peace and quiet. The house has had a revolving door all night. Even Hugh Standish and Esther Grimshaw showed up with offers of help, but Sheriff Ewing told them—like he told any others who dropped by—there was nothing they could do right now and to go back home.

The federal agents, both FBI and Homeland Security, brought in maps and satellite images. Both Jackson and I fielded questions about location, terrain, what we saw and where. Questions about what Jonas was doing up there in the first place, did I get the impression he knew where he was going.

I got the sense quite quickly this guy from DHS had a real hard-on for Jonas, implying he somehow had a part in this. That didn't enamor him to anyone here, not even to the sheriff or the young FBI agent who both voiced a protest.

Then it became a battle for authority when the DHS guy told James to recall the High Mountain Tracker team, and James in turn told him to go to hell. When Ama showed up with Thomas and Max, a few minutes later, and her husband prepared to take the dog up the mountain, the agent threatened to put him in cuffs. Ama intervened in that disagreement, pulling James aside and after some intense gesturing on her part, James conceded that battle.

Ama left half an hour ago, taking Thomas home to get some rest, but she did tell me on the way out not to worry should James and Max be missing in the morning. It wasn't long after the young FBI agent and DHS Agent Limpkin left, the latter taking the shell Fletch had found, and announcing he'd be back in the morning with his own team.

The taillights were still visible going down the driveway when James clipped a long lead on Max and took his horse from the trailer. He was going up to the ridge where his teammates apparently set up a base camp. Ten minutes later he was heading after his team, his horse loaded up with gear, and the assurances he'd be fine in the dark with his night-vision goggles.

The only person who hasn't left is the sheriff, who was handed a radio by James so he'd be able to stay in touch.

Needless to say the tension has been high and my nerves

are worn to the quick. All this bickering is not doing Jonas any good.

The hot water soothes and for the longest time I just stand there, letting the forceful stream beat on me until I can feel my muscles relax.

"Are you okay in there?"

"Yeah, I'll be right out, Luce."

I quickly finish my shower and get dressed before joining the others downstairs.

"I thought you'd try to get some sleep."

Jackson is on the couch, his feet on the coffee table and some twenty-four-hour news station playing on TV. He's leaning back, his head twisted my way.

The sheriff is nodding off in the chair on the other side.

"Wouldn't be able to sleep," I say softly as I walk to the back of the couch, lean over, and kiss my son's cheek.

"Come sit by me, Momma."

"I will in a minute. I just want a quick word with Lucy."

The truth is, the idea of sitting still for any length of time feels impossible. I'm itching to do something useful instead of waiting for things to happen.

Lucy's in the kitchen—which looks like a bomb exploded—and is kneading dough. My eyes slide to the kitchen clock.

"It's one fifteen," I point out.

"I know," she says, using the back of her hand to brush a hank of hair from her face. She leaves a streak of flour in its place. "I have to do something. I know this place'll be overrun again in the morning so I thought I'd be prepared."

The fresh dough smell makes me nostalgic. Childhood memories of my mother baking fresh bread every Saturday for the week ahead. The bittersweet reminder brings emotions back to the surface that burn behind my eyelids.

Determined I've already allowed myself enough tears, I blink them back. I'm going to go crazy if I don't do something. I need some fresh air.

"I'm going to check on the horses."

Lucy lifts her head and eyes me carefully. "You're not thinking of heading back out there, are you?"

"Of course not."

Actually, it's crossed my mind, but I don't have night-vision gear and would probably get lost in the dark.

"Uh-huh."

She doesn't bother hiding her skepticism, but doesn't stop me when I head for the front door.

"Hey, buddy."

Sarge whinnies softly when I walk to his stall. He sticks his head over the door and lets me nuzzle him. In the stall next to his, Ellie snorts, but when I check on her, she's against the back wall, one of her rear legs slightly cocked and she's dozing.

When I turn to the stall on the other side of the aisle where Lucy put Jonas's horse, Sugar, I notice she's not resting. She's staring right back at me.

"You're worried too, aren't you, sweetheart?"

Jonas

I lean my head against the rock wall for a moment and close my eyes.

Great idea, but now my head and ankle are not the only things throbbing. My wrists are torn to shit.

The wire they tied me up with is cutting my skin open. I

figured wire is prone to metal fatigue so if I twisted my wrists in opposite directions, back and forth, eventually it would snap. Unfortunately, it also creates a sawing motion digging the ties deeper into my skin, which is why my hands are now slick with blood.

Those guys haven't been back, although I swear I could hear some movement above earlier. Probably nocturnal wildlife foraging for a meal. Other than that it's been silent, there's not a lot of noise that penetrates down here. It's the kind of silence that could drive you crazy over time. Unless the lack of food and water kills you first.

I don't plan to wait around for either of those to happen. I want to get out of here, preferably before dawn, because there's a third guy out there they call the general. Someone who is close enough to bring supplies and no stranger to these mountains. My guess would be someone local and *that* makes me very uneasy. Especially since everything that's happened so far has been on or close to Alex's land.

She's not safe.

Bracing myself for the burn, I lean forward and resume working on my bindings.

I clench my jaw against the pain and it doesn't take long for sweat to start dripping down my face. Determined, I push through until I finally feel the first strands of the twisted wire snap. Encouraged, I double my efforts, keeping my eyes on the sliver of sky I can see above me.

I'm so focused, it startles me when the last wires break and my hands suddenly move independently.

Using my numb and slick fingers, I try to unwind the wire wrapped around each wrist. When I've accomplished that, I shrug out of my coat, take off my shirt, and slip the coat back on. With the help of a piece of wire, I rip off the sleeves of my shirt and use them to bandage my wrists as best I can. The rest of my shirt I tear in long strips, wrapping them tightly around my foot and ankle like a brace.

Lack of sleep and nutrition, combined with the pain of my injuries, has completely zapped my energy. Before I even attempt going up that wall I need to recharge. I rest my back and head against the rock wall so I can catch my breath.

I must've dozed off because when I blink my eyes open, I see the first signs of daylight above me. *Fuck*. I was hoping to be out of here already.

I groan at the protest my body launches when I struggle to my feet. I carefully test my ankle, putting some weight on it. It hurts like a sonofabitch, but it feels steady. I can handle pain but I need both feet and both hands if I have any chance getting out of this hole.

Standing up, it's evident the walls start narrowing about halfway up. If I can pull myself up high enough, I'll be able to brace my legs on either side of the pit, and hopefully get myself out. At least that's the plan.

Stretching my arms as high as I can, I feel around for any hand holds. When my fingers find purchase, I take in a deep breath, blow it out, and propel myself up.

Only to feel my fingers slip and I land my full weight on my bad ankle.

"*Fuck!*"

I bend over, gasping for air as the sharp pain has my stomach revolt.

After a few moments I straighten up, wipe my slick fingers dry on my jeans, grind my teeth, and reach up again.

I find my hand holds and steel my resolve.

Wait.

What was that?

I swear I heard something and wait to see if it comes again.

There it is again, the faint sound of a dog barking, and I know that bark.

I fill my lungs and yell.

"Max!"

Twenty-One

JONAS

My throat is dry and raw from yelling and the only sound I manage to produce now is no more than a croak.

Not that I think I was heard before, there have been no more barks since I started calling out.

Maybe it was my imagination playing tricks on me. I haven't had as much as a sip of water since lunch yesterday, before I loaded up Sugar and headed to Alex's. The lack of hydration is giving me a throbbing headache, or perhaps that's still the aftermath from the hit to my head.

I now vaguely recall finding a rifle shell up on the ridge and hearing someone approach, but everything after is still a blank. I assume I was clocked good, knocking me right out, and I suspect I have a concussion.

Haven't been down here even twelve hours and already I'm weak as a kitten. Fucking old age. I let myself sink down on my ass and close my eyes, but they snap back open when

I hear a noise. Rustling, and then a soft metal clanging sound, much like the tags on a dog collar.

I try calling out but nothing more than a rasp comes out.

More clanging, followed by the sound of a voice.

"Good boy, Max. Find him."

James.

I can hear the horse's footfalls now too.

Frantically looking around I try to find something I can throw, when I spot the pieces of wire. With trembling fingers I twist them together in a ball, while listening to the sounds moving away again. Then I scramble to my feet and, shooting up a prayer they'll be able to hear it, I toss the makeshift ball up and out of the hole.

The impact is disappointing, barely loud enough for me to make out. Still, I wait and strain to listen.

Then I hear sniffing. *Max.*

I stick a hand up as far as I can, hoping he'll pick up my scent. Max isn't a trained search and rescue dog, but he has a good nose.

"Max," I croak.

The next moment his muzzle sticks over the edge, sniffs a few times, and then he starts barking.

"Sight for sore eyes, my friend."

Bo is crouched beside me, tending to my wrists, while Sully leans over, tilting a water bottle to my lips.

I grunt my agreement. I sure as fuck was happy to see my guys.

James managed to haul me out of the hole. He'd apparently been searching with Max since first light.

Turns out the team has been up here all night at a base camp on the ridge just a ten-minute ride from where Max found me.

"Find any tracks? There were two guys," I rasp.

"Yup. Two sets. We were able to track them leading away from the ridge, until we hit the sharp turn the creek makes about a mile east of here. We lost them there."

Sully hands me a protein bar and I bite off half of it.

"It was pretty dark last night so we decided to try again this morning. Maybe do a low flyover with the drone."

I swallow my bite.

"We should head down as soon as possible," I share, clearly taking Sully by surprise.

"James and Bo were gonna take you and Max down."

I shake my head. "I think we should all go back. Pretty sure these two are Adams and Wright, but that's not all, they mentioned the involvement of at least one other person. Someone they called *the general*, who's been keeping them supplied. I think it's someone local."

"Makes sense," Fletch says, walking up. "These guys obviously didn't stumble on this area randomly and they've been successfully hiding for weeks now, that would've been near impossible without local support."

But who?

No one I know has ever presented as particularly radical. Then again, that probably wouldn't be something they'd advertise, which in turn makes everyone a suspect.

Suddenly I'm in a rush to get down the mountain and see Alex. She must be worried.

"By the way," James comments. "DHS was at the rescue last night and tried to get me to call back the guys. Limpkin was gonna pull together a team and planned to return first thing this morning."

"Fletch and I can stay up here and wait for those guys. At least to show them what we found," Sully offers.

It sounds reasonable but I'd rather we stick together. United we stand, and all that. Especially after what happened to me yesterday. Besides, right now I don't know who to trust, and my pounding head makes it impossible to think clearly.

"We all go," I order.

"You bet," Sully concedes. "Ewing stayed at the house last night, he's got the radio, want me to give him a heads-up?"

"No. Let's just get down there."

I don't want to announce to anyone that we're on our way.

Safer to trust no one.

∼

Alex

"Mom, coffee."

I blink my eyes until Jackson's face takes shape.

I'm on the couch where I must've fallen asleep at some point. I'd been exhausted, especially after losing my shit in the barn last night.

The memory has me shoot upright.

"Any word?"

"Nothing yet," Jackson says, taking my hand to pull me to my feet.

Beyond him I see the sheriff sitting at the kitchen table, his hands wrapped around a steaming mug and looking a little the worse for wear.

Judging by the amount of light coming from outside, it's still fairly early as I follow my son to the kitchen. Guilt suddenly wracks me. The poor guy comes home to surprise me and lands in the middle of this drama.

"I'm sorry," I feel compelled to tell him when he pours me a coffee. "I'm sure this isn't the kind of homecoming you were expecting."

"Momma..." He turns around and folds me in a hug. I'm still getting used to the size of the chest and arms surrounding me, but they sure make me feel cared for. "I'm just glad I could be here."

Before I end up bawling again, I ease from his hold and aim for my coffee.

A moment later Lucy comes down the stairs, looking fresh from the shower but with blue circles under her eyes. She mumbles something unintelligible as she makes a beeline for the coffeepot.

Scout and Chief, who were sleeping curled up on the dog bed by the back door come ambling over, looking for some attention.

"Need to go out, boys?" I reach down and ruffle their heads. "Let's go."

The moment I open the door both of them shoot outside. I'm still sliding it shut when the dogs start barking furiously and run off like a bat out of hell.

"Probably a rabbit or something," Lucy—who stepped up beside me—concludes.

It's possible, but I can still hear them going at it and the door is now closed. I haven't forgotten the injuries on Sam's horse, Buster. There is wildlife out there I don't want near my animals.

"Probably, but I'm just gonna make sure the horses are okay. By the way," I add as I make my way to the front door to get my boots on. "Sam Deere ever show up with his palomino, Buster?"

"I thought he wasn't coming until tonight?" she points out as she follows me down the hallway.

"What day is it?"

"Tuesday, and yesterday was Monday, when you went to the dude ranch," she adds.

I'm losing the plot. The dude ranch feels like it was days ago, not yesterday morning. So much has happened.

"If you like, I can give him a call and tell him we're dealing with an emergency and that we'll connect soon to set up a new time."

"Yes, that would be good." One less thing to worry about. I shove my feet into my boots and shrug my oilskin jacket on. "I'll be right back."

I can still hear the dogs. Sounds like they're heading toward the back field. I have visions of some predator stalking the horses back there and I start running as I dig around my pocket for my gun.

Rounding the barn, I catch sight of the horses clustered around the shelter and I do a quick mental count. All there.

The dogs are nowhere in sight, but I can hear them in the woods on the other side. When I reach the tree line the barking suddenly stops. I do too.

"Scout! Chief!" I put my thumb and forefinger in my mouth and whistle loud.

At first there's no response, but then I hear movement in the underbrush.

First Chief, and then Scout come charging out of the trees, closely followed by...*Max?* Then James appears, on foot and leading his horse. Finally I catch sight of Jonas, riding James's mount, clearly alive and apparently in one piece, or close enough.

My knees buckle but I force myself to stay standing and jut up my chin.

I will not come apart.

His blue eyes lock on me as he approaches. Now I can make out the dried blood coating his ear and staining the rim of his hat. He has bloodstains on his coat as well, and both hands, resting on the saddle horn, look stained as well.

"Go on ahead," he tells his men in a hoarse voice. "We'll be right behind you."

James grins and hands me the horse's reins. The other three men ride past, tipping their hats to me. Then I glance up at Jonas, who is still looking at me.

"Are..." I clear my throat and start again. "Are you okay? You've been hurt. There's blood..." I tap my own ear.

"Rock is harder than my head after all," he says dryly.

I nod stupidly, afraid to speak.

"Sweets, it's not easy for me to get off or I'd already be down there kissing you. Do an old man a favor...get your ass up here and kiss me."

The quarter-draft horse is sturdy enough and I slip my left foot in the stirrup Jonas vacates and pull myself up to face level with him. This close I can see the deep grooves lining his face. Whatever happened to him, he's been through the wringer.

"I'll tell you everything later," he promises, sensing my curiosity. "For now give me your mouth. Wasn't sure I'd get to taste it again."

When I press my lips to his I'm sure he can taste my tears.

"That's too bad. You're going to have to wait."

Bo's booming voice carries all the way up here.

I have a mental image of Jonas's guys blocking the stairs for that DHS agent and grin.

James and Sully helped Jonas inside earlier. The stubborn man refused to be taken to the hospital and wouldn't let us call EMTs, but finally conceded to having Bo give him a proper once-over after he had a chance to clean up.

However, he didn't voice an objection when I offered to help him with that.

"You know, this would be much easier if you got in here with me," he grumbles, sitting in my tub while I rinse the blood off his head and face with the handheld shower.

The cut on his scalp isn't big but it sure bled a lot, and I can barely look at his wrists, they look like they've been through a meat grinder. Yet none of it seems to be a deterrent for him to try and get me naked.

"You're delusional if you think I'm starting anything with you now. You're hurt."

"So? The important parts are still fine and functioning."

I shake my head but can't maintain a stern face.

"And I'm grateful they are. However, we have federal agents frothing at the bit to talk to you, a houseful of people, and more importantly, you haven't had a proper meal since yesterday."

The agents arrived fifteen minutes ago. I watched them roll up from the bathroom window, two SUVs and a large van. I have a sneaky suspicion they're here to stay, at least for the foreseeable future.

Jonas doesn't push anymore and I'm pretty sure he's more exhausted, and probably in more pain, than he's willing to admit. We finish up his 'assisted' shower in silence until I hear a soft knock. I leave Jonas to finish drying off to open the door a crack.

"Got some clean gear for Jonas," Jackson says, holding out a stack of clothes.

"That's great. Thanks, honey."

"Need anything else?"

I smile at my kid in a moment of pride I allow myself. I did okay raising him.

"See if you can get a fresh pot of coffee going. He's gonna need it. Oh, and let Bo know he's out of the shower."

Jackson gives me a two-fingered salute and heads back for the stairs.

I turn to find Jonas studying me.

"I like your kid."

The smile on my face widens. "I'm glad. I do too." I set the clothes on the counter. "Even though he seems determined to have his mother worried sick about him."

The clothes are Jackson's, a pair of gray sweats, a T-shirt, and some socks. Luckily, they stretch because as much as my son has filled out, Jonas is definitely bulkier.

"How so?" he asks when I kneel in front of him and carefully ease the sweatpants over his bum ankle.

"He announced he's heading for Fort Bragg next." I look up at him and roll my eyes. "For Special Ops training."

Jonas widens his eyes in surprise.

"That training is no picnic."

I help him to his feet, so he can pull up the pants, and try not to get distracted by the way his attributes are clearly outlined against the soft material.

"I know. Is it bad I have this little niggle of hope he won't make it through?"

"No. I don't blame you. I think if I had a son I'd feel the same way," he agrees.

His comment shocks me. "Really? I would've thought you'd be in support."

"Don't get me wrong, I am. And I commend him for choosing that path, but it's not for the faint of heart."

He bends down so I can slip the T-shirt over his head.

"It's funny, six months ago when I sent off my boy, I would've been convinced he wasn't built for it. Not physically or emotionally. But from what I've seen these past not-quite-twenty-four hours I'm not so sure anymore. Doesn't mean I like it."

Jonas lifts a hand to my cheek. "I can have a word with him, if you like."

I turn my head and press a kiss in his palm.

"That's sweet of you, but I think you've got other, more pressing, things to worry about."

As if to underscore my point, Bo walks into the bathroom.

"Oops. Didn't mean to interrupt, your boy said—"

"It's fine," I tell him quickly. "I'll leave you guys to it."

I slip past Bo and out the door, but I can just catch his muted words.

"You're a lucky bastard."

It's followed by Jonas's deep chuckle.

Twenty-Two

JONAS

"So you're telling me you didn't catch a glimpse of them?"

I take in a deep breath.

What I'd really like to do is plant my fist in Limpkin's smug face, but I doubt that's going to further my case. Best thing I can do is keep my cool, answer the man's questions, and other than that, keep my mouth shut. He's clearly looking for something to pin on me, although for the life of me I can't figure why. I don't even know the guy.

"I did not. As I mentioned the past four times you asked me, I had my back turned when I heard a footstep and didn't even have a chance to turn around. No, I don't know what they hit me with. And when I woke up in the cave, I heard them but never saw them. The only time they could've been visible, I had a flashlight aimed at me."

I've been over this a few times and can't quite keep the irritation out of my voice.

He's already talked to my men and gotten their account.

James showed him exactly where the cave he pulled me from was on a satellite image. Yet he keeps returning to this.

"You know what I'm struggling with?" he starts, that superior smirk on his face. "If you've never met either Mr. Adams or Mr. Wright before, and you were never able to see either of their faces, how can you be so sure it was them? Unless of course, you know more than you're willing to admit."

"Because, like I mentioned, the one who got pissed off called the other guy Terry. Would be a tremendous coincidence for two guys named Terry to be hiding out in these mountains."

He shrugs. "It's a fairly common name, if that's even the one you heard. You admitted yourself, you were out like a light and had just woken up with a pounding head. Could be you misheard it? Maybe you were confused or hallucinating."

I bite my tongue, not giving him the satisfaction of knowing he's getting under my skin.

He flips through his small notebook before he focuses on me.

"You were Special Forces—any chance you suffer from PTSD, Mr. Harvey?"

I'm halfway out of my chair when Wolff—who has sat by quietly this whole time—suddenly speaks up, checking something on his phone.

"Helicopter is en route."

"About bloody time," Limpkin mutters as he gets up and walks out without so much as a glance my way.

"Don't mind him," the young FBI agent tries to reassure me. "He's in charge of the task force and therefore in the hot seat. The brass isn't happy this is taking so long, so he's getting it from all sides. I'm sure he was hoping for a quick resolution."

Right. At whose expense?

"He's barking up the wrong tree," I tell him. "And I'm worried in his eagerness to discredit me, he's dismissing a potentially important lead."

"The general," Wolff concludes correctly.

Thank God. At least one of them has been paying attention.

"Sounds like he could be local. At least very familiar with the area and close enough to drop off supplies without people noticing."

"I'll look into it," he says. "I'll get in touch with my office."

It's better than nothing, I guess.

I don't like the uneasy feeling I get not knowing all the players. It makes me suspicious of everyone.

After Wolff leaves, I hobble to the window and glance outside. Alex's farm looks to have been turned into a staging area for a battle.

I catch sight of her outside, trying to calm down the mare in the front paddock, spooked by the sudden flurry of activity.

Moving out of the small office and down the hall, I join Bo and Alex's boy in the kitchen, where Lucy appears to be holding court.

"They done with you?" Bo asks.

"For now. The others gone back to the ranch?"

"Yeah, about fifteen minutes ago. Took the horses, including Sugar."

"Good. I'm gonna need your phone. The assholes took mine."

I know Sully already spoke with him when they found me, but I want to give Dad a quick call myself.

Bo hands it over and I'm about to dial the ranch.

"We haven't officially met."

I turn to look at Alex's son getting up from the table and offering his hand. He pulls it back at the last second.

"Shit, I'm sorry, I wasn't thinking."

I look down and notice the bandages Bo reapplied after my shower. I feel my head and my ankle, but I barely feel the injuries to my wrist.

"It's just a scrape," I assure him, tucking the phone in my pocket. Then I hold out my own hand, which he grabs tentatively. "Jonas Harvey. I understand I owe you gratitude."

The kid looks a little taken aback. "Jackson Hart, sir. I... uh...didn't really do anything."

"I wouldn't say that," I disagree. "You took your mom's back, pointed my guys in the right direction, but most importantly...you didn't shoot down my drone," I tease.

The guys told me how the kid faced off with three of my men—and they're not choirboys—but right now he's looking like he's about to shit his pants. I suspect Bo may have had something to do with that.

Bo confirms it by chuckling in the background, and I swear I hear Lucy snort as I clap Jackson on the shoulder.

"Yanking your chain, my man. I'm not sure what Bo has been feeding you, but I suggest you take it all with a grain of salt. We're not in the military here, at ease."

"You're bad." Lucy wags her finger at Bo, who unsurprisingly takes it as a compliment. "But you—" She turns to Jackson, snickering. "—you should've seen your face. Damn, I should've thought to take a video. I will never let you live that down."

Jackson, who seems to have recovered somewhat, grins back sportingly.

"Bring it on," he retorts. "I've waited a long time to use that juicy little clip I've been sitting on for three years now."

"You wouldn't dare," Lucy warns him.

"This is getting interesting," Bo mumbles, rubbing his hands together.

"Are you guys at it again?" Alex comes walking into the kitchen with a sharp look at Lucy and then her son. She turns to me and shakes her head. "Let me apologize on their behalf. I swear they're both of legal age, but sometimes it's hard to tell."

"Hey, I take offense to that."

"Me too," Jackson says as he moves over to Lucy and drapes an arm around her shoulders.

"Are the agents done with you?" Alex asks, ignoring those two.

"For now they're distracted with a helicopter that's apparently coming in."

Her eyes grow large. "What? Here? They can't bring it here."

She bolts out of the kitchen, Lucy right behind her. The rest of us follow at a more modest pace

"Some of the horses will go apeshit," Jackson clarifies as he slows down to let me catch up with him on the porch.

Alex is standing next to the van, gesticulating wildly as she faces off with Limpkin, while Lucy is already heading for the paddock housing the mare and the donkey. Bo is right behind her.

Jackson stays beside me as I approach the van, an idea forming in mind.

∾

Alex

My head feels like it'll explode, the man is insufferable.

"Ms. Hart, this is a matter of national security. There are strong indications to suggest you are harboring suspected domestic terrorists, along with a stolen cache of weaponry, on your land. I'm shocked you wouldn't think that deserves priority over a handful of horses."

Harboring? Is he seriously suggesting I have anything to do with this?

"Excuse me, Agent Limpkin? A word?"

I turn around to find Jonas standing a few feet away, my son by his side. Both are wearing expressions of steel as they stare down the agent.

"I have no time for this," the idiot says, threatening to walk away.

"I suggest you make time," Jonas says harshly. "Or you'll leave me no choice but to put in a call to my friend, Bob Dickson."

I have no idea who he's talking about, but it's clear Limpkin does. The man blanches at the mention of the name.

"You have one minute," he says, straightening his spine in an attempt to look unaffected, but it's clear he is.

"That's all I'll need," Jonas replies, already walking to the front of the van.

The agent follows and Jackson comes to stand next to me.

"You okay, Momma?"

"That man is a boil on the ass of society," I mutter.

It really takes no longer than a minute of Jonas towering

over the agent and speaking to him in a low voice. Whatever he's saying seems to make an impact because Limpkin—whose tight mouth only becomes tighter during the course of the one-sided conversation—ends up giving Jonas a tight nod before he disappears around the other side of the van.

"We have two hours," Jonas announces when he joins us.

"What am I supposed to do in two hours?" I ask, exasperated.

"We're moving the animals to High Meadow."

That takes me by surprise so I react from the gut.

"No. Absolutely not."

"Mom..."

My eyes snap to my son. "No, Jackson. Some of these horses are so traumatized, it's taken them months to settle in here. Now he's suggesting I disrupt them again? No. This is their home."

"Sweets..." Jonas starts in a reconciliatory tone that feels more like a pat on the head.

"And how do you propose I do that? I have a trailer that carries only two. Do you know how long it took me to get Flint and Ladybug in the trailer last time? Three-and-a-half hours, Jonas! Besides, why should I—"

His hands land on my shoulders and he bends low, his blue eyes boring in mine.

"Because the agent may be an ass, but he's right; this is a matter of national security. These guys are out there, potentially plotting their next attack, Alex. It sucks that the rescue seems to be at the center of all this, but that's not Limpkin's fault."

He's right, of course, but I don't have to like it.

"Two hours, though?"

He gives my shoulders a light shake before continuing.

"We can do it. Sully and James can drive over the large rig and my double. Between those two and your trailer we can take all of your animals in one run."

"Provided we can get them in the trailers," I grumble stubbornly.

Jonas slides his hands to my neck and before I can stop him, drops a firm kiss on my mouth.

Right in front of my boy.

I can't bring myself to look his way and stare at the toes of my boots instead.

"We now have an hour and fifty-seven minutes left," Jackson announces. "You may wanna save that mushy stuff for later."

Lucy and Bo already have Daisy and Hope in the barn by the time I get there. In a few words I explain what we hope to accomplish.

Jackson followed me, but Jonas stayed behind talking on the phone. Presumably organizing the transportation.

I look around the barn. We have four stalls, three of which are occupied—Lucy stuck Daisy and Hope together —only one stall left and five horses to go. The idea is to get them all in the barn first, back the trailer up to the entrance using the doors as a barrier and herd them in as best we can.

But first we've got to get the other five in here.

"Let's try and round up the others. We can put Flint in the empty stall—he doesn't always play nice with others— but the others we'll have to tie in the aisle until the big trailer gets here."

"It's gonna be tight," Lucy observes.

"Mmm," Bo mumbles in agreement and turns to me. "If you don't mind me making a suggestion; if I can borrow your buckskin over there." He points at Sarge. "I can round up those five in the back field real quick. Block 'em in by the gate and someone can lead them to the barn's back door one by one."

"Got any experience, cowboy?" Lucy taunts.

It's like a shutter comes down over the man's face as he glances at her, suddenly without any emotion whatsoever.

"Grew up on a ranch with three-hundred head of beef cattle. I've done my bit in the saddle."

"I stand corrected," Lucy mumbles, her hands up defensively, but Bo has already dismissed her as he continues to outline his plan.

"In the meantime, we've got your trailer already out there. You can start loading these guys up, make room for the others coming in."

"Works for me," I agree. "Lucy, if you wanna go with him?" I ignore her wide-eyed look. "Jackson, keys are on the hook by the front door. If you get the trailer, I'll start getting supplies and tack together."

When Lucy leads the first horse in the back door, we already have Ellie in the trailer. She'd better be nice to Hope, because she's up next.

"Why don't you get Daisy in there?" Lucy suggests. "It's not a long trip and she's small, she'll fit up front."

Good idea, because once the donkey is in the trailer, Hope follows easily.

With my trailer parked off to the side, I stand in the open doors and watch as Jonas directs his big rig backing up to the barn. Then he hobbles over to me.

"Why don't you and Lucy go pack a bag? We've got it from here."

"Pack? For what?"

"You wanna stay here while this place is overrun by law enforcement? Makes more sense to camp out at the ranch where you can be close to your animals, and you can still work."

Dammit. He makes it sound so reasonable.

"What about Jackson?" I want to know.

If I only have him home for two weeks—minus a couple of days already—I want him close.

"Him too," Jonas agrees easily.

"You have the room?"

"Sure. There's a one-room cabin sitting empty Lucy can have, and a pullout couch in my office for Jackson."

"What about me?"

The curved eyebrow and faint smirk on his lips sends a little shiver down my spine.

"You'll be bunking with me."

I'm still tingling from my head down to my toes as I dart into my bathroom to grab some toiletries. I packed enough clothes to last me a couple of days and try to focus on what else I might need. Maybe I should bring a sweater or two, the nights can still get chilly.

"Are you done?"

Lucy sticks her head around the door.

"Almost."

"I'm gonna quickly pack up a few things from the fridge that are gonna spoil otherwise."

"I'll be down in a few," I tell her.

When I turn back to my closet to grab a sweater, I knock my shampoo off the mattress and watch it roll under the bed. I get down on all fours and reach under to retrieve it when I catch sight of something I'd almost forgotten about.

Might as well bring those too.

Twenty-Three

JONAS

I crashed early last night.

It had been a long couple of days and I was zapped of energy.

We had to clear the paddock behind the barn to make room for Alex's horses for the time being. All but the mare and the donkey, they're sharing one of the bigger stalls in the barn.

I'd talked to Ama earlier, who already had the bed in the cottage and the pullout couch in my office made by the time we got to the house.

Dad looked like he'd aged years in one day and, despite talking to him on the phone earlier, he was clearly relieved to see me in one piece. He's never been particularly demonstrative, so it threw me when he wrapped me in a hug. I can't remember the last time that happened. I'm starting to wonder if he's as healthy as he claims to be.

After a rowdy dinner—Ama made enough stew to feed

our unexpected guests as well—and I popped a few Tylenol for the pain, I started dozing off on the couch.

Not how I'd envisioned the night to end.

I roll over in bed and take in Alex's sleeping form. She's curled up in a tight ball and almost falling off the edge of the mattress. Her hair is a tangled mass, evidence of a restless night.

I never even noticed her getting into bed last night, I was dead to the world. But I'm well aware of her now. She must've had a shower before coming to bed, I can smell her shampoo.

Reaching out, I hook a finger around a strand of hair, bringing it to my nose. A subtle herb scent with a hint of citrus. Fresh, earthy, like the woman herself. I can't resist pulling the quilt down a few inches, exposing her naked shoulder.

Christ, is she naked under there?

My body instantly responds.

It's only the second time she's sharing my bed, but I already know I don't ever want her to leave it. She's firmly burrowed under my skin.

Feeling like a bit of a pervert, I slide down the cover a little farther, finding a narrow, silky strap across her upper arm. Not naked, then, but no less enticing. I stroke a finger over her soft skin but pull it back when she stirs.

Her head lifts off the pillow as she turns to look over her exposed shoulder. Her sleepy brown eyes sparkle.

"Morning," she mumbles, barely moving her mouth.

I grin down at her. "Morning, Sweets."

She slowly rolls on her back and darts a glance at the window.

"It's still early."

My eyes are drawn down to the silky nightie barely

covering the slope of her breasts. Even in the sparse light, I easily make out her puckered nipples pressing up against the flimsy material.

"I know. You could sleep a little longer," I offer, dragging my eyes back up to her face.

"Mmmm. Tempting," she says in a lazy voice as a little smile teases over her lips.

Reaching up she trails the tips of her fingers through my chest hair, sending a current straight to my cock. Her eyes carry an invitation I'm not about to turn down.

Her lips are soft, sleep-swollen, and open easily when I stroke them with my tongue. She curls her arms around my neck and pulls me down to her. I try to keep most of my weight off her by planting my elbows on either side of her head, but she makes it clear she wants all of me, hooking a leg over mine.

I groan down her throat when the sensitive head of my cock brushes the inside of her thigh. Alex instantly pulls back.

"Are you hurting?"

I chuckle as I bury my face in the crook of her neck.

"Not in the way you think. Right now there's only one part of my body I can feel."

"Oh."

Yeah.

I press a kiss on her neck and another one at the base of her throat, where her pulse beats right under the surface. Shifting slightly, I pull the edge of her nightie down, lick a trail between her breasts, and slide my body lower. Then I close my lips over one tight bead, pulling it deep into my mouth, exploring her taste and texture before moving to the other side.

"Jonas..." she moans as she shifts restlessly underneath me.

"Patience," I mumble against her skin.

No way in hell I'm going to rush this.

Her legs open in invitation as I kiss my way down her body and she lifts her hips in offering when I reach her core. No underwear in my way, I push the hem of her nightgown up her hips. The neatly trimmed patch, the same color as her hair, is also woven through with strands of silver. I run a single finger through the curls until I dip into liquid heat.

Christ, she's so ready for me.

My lazy discovery suddenly turns urgent as the first taste of her sears itself on my brain.

It doesn't take long before I have her squirming, her fingers digging into the mattress as she rocks against my mouth.

"I want you inside," she pants.

Thank fuck.

I was about to blow my load in the tangled covers.

Rising up on my knees, I reach over to grab a condom from my nightstand when she grabs hold of my wrist.

"I want to feel all of you. I'm safe," she adds breathlessly.

Hell, yeah.

"Me too," I tell her as I grab a pillow and shove it under her hips.

Then I take hold of her ankles and lift her legs up and wide. This way I can see all of her.

Perfection.

Her hand guides my cock, teasing me with her soft folds before she takes me inside her, her fingers testing our slick connection.

Getting lost in her body is like barreling down a mountain, with no way to slow things down or prevent yourself from flying off the edge.

And I go willingly.

≈

Alex

Light is streaming into the room when I blink open my eyes.

Jonas's side of the bed is empty, the sheets already cool when I touch the imprint he left behind.

I lift my arms over my head and stretch, some of my muscles tight with our early morning activities. I feel myself smile at the memory and settle back into my pillow, enjoying the afterglow a little longer.

At some point I start noticing sounds of activity filter in from outside. Guilty for being so lazy, I drag my ass out of bed and peek through the blinds. The bedroom is at the front of the house, with a view of the barn and corral. I recognize Jonas at the gate of the corral, one foot lifted onto the bottom rung as he watches Dan work Blitz in the ring. I'm so glad he's giving the guy a chance; he looks like he's in control on the feisty stallion.

I should get out there.

Wrapped in a towel after a quick shower, I head for my duffel bag at the foot of the bed to grab some clean clothes. I notice the rolled-up plans tucked on the side and pull them out. I'm not sure what had me shove the rolls I found in the attic in my bag yesterday. Other than I'd hoped to have some time to check them out. I haven't had a lot of that in recent days.

Tossing the blueprints on the bed, I quickly get

dressed and smooth out the covers. Then I spread one roll out. It's a true blueprint, with the actual drawing in white lines. It must be old, because as far as I know, those haven't been used in decades although the term still exists.

I don't pretend to understand any of the details, but I can recognize the general shape of an elongated building and the different rooms inside. I know for a fact it's not my house since the footprint of that is basically a square. This structure is longer than it is wide, with two large rooms, one behind the other, and what looks to be a hallway along the length. On either of the short ends there looks to be two smaller spaces.

I have no idea what I'm looking at so I spread out the second one over top. This one has the same outline but is covered with a grid of lines and minute writing that I don't understand.

I'm no wiser, but when I start rolling the blueprints up together, I notice yet another drawing stuck behind the first one. Same size, only this one is on white paper and looks to be a sketch.

It takes me a moment to register what I'm looking at but when I do, I shove the drawings under my arm and rush downstairs.

∼

"Those are stairs."

Jackson points out.

He, Jonas, and Sully are bent over the first blueprint I spread out on the kitchen table.

"Leading where?" Jonas remarks. "There doesn't seem to be another floor."

"Leading above," I clarify, pulling the sketch out and smoothing it on top of the blueprint.

"Is that a silo?"

"No."

I give the drawing a quarter turn so Sully—who is standing at end of the table—can see it at the proper angle.

"That looks like a bunker," Jackson observes.

"More like an underground shelter," Jonas corrects.

The image is a concept sketch of a cylindrical structure, showing stairs coming down from the surface into the long hallway. In the depiction, the two small rooms behind the stairs on that end look to be a small kitchen and bathroom. The first large room is shown as living and sleeping quarters, with bunkbeds up against the walls. The second room looks like a storage facility, and I can't make out what the two end rooms are supposed to be.

Jonas taps his index finger on that side.

"I bet that holds mechanical equipment. Water pump, air filtration, maybe a furnace."

"Where did you find these?" Jackson wants to know.

"I was cleaning out a dresser I found up in the attic and these were in one of the drawers."

Sully is studying the small writing at the edge of the blueprint.

"The drawing was done by some architect group in Helena. Dominion Architecture."

He leaves the kitchen and returns moments later with his laptop, copying the name into a search engine.

"Yup. Helena based," he confirms. "Specializing in emergency shelters. Got big during the Cold War, but went belly up in the early nineties."

"Emergency shelters were big during the Cold War. Fear of a nuclear attack had every Tom, Dick, and Harry wanting one," Jonas explains. "Cold War ended in 1989, as did the imminent threat, so any business related to these shelters wouldn't be far behind."

I remember what James said about the previous owner, which makes me wonder.

"Do you think Clive Jenkins would've built one on his property?"

"Wouldn't surprise me," Sully answers. "A lot of those sovereign types are terrified of anything that reeks of communism."

"Quite a few of them are doomsday preppers too," Jonas contributes.

From my limited understanding, preppers are survivalists. I've heard of people who have stockpiled basic necessities to last them for years in remote bunkers or cabins they can escape to in case disaster strikes. The closest I ever get to stockpiling is the occasional extra package of toilet paper I pick up.

"I should let Agent Limpkin know," I suggest, turning to Jonas.

"Not sure he'll be that receptive to anything from you, or me, for that matter. And even if he is, he'll try to find a way to turn the information against us. No," he says, pulling his phone from his pocket. "We stand a better chance if we hand this off to Wolff. Let him bring it up with Limpkin."

That makes sense. The younger agent is actually a likable guy.

By the time Wolff shows up, forty-five minutes later, we have a few possible locations identified on the satellite images Sully pulled up. All three look to be small clearings surrounded by rocks and trees. Shivers run down my spine when I notice how close they all are to the now all-too-familiar ridge and the creek, and all three within my property boundaries.

When Jonas points them out to the agent—who appears to be paying close attention—he voices his suspicion that the dual tracks may lead to a back way onto my land. A way to get in unnoticed with supplies.

"It's a stretch," Wolff indicates, but he's the one who just told us they haven't had any luck with their search yet. "You're suggesting these guys stumbled on some bunker built decades ago on private land? What are the chances of that?"

"Wouldn't be that far-fetched if this *general* Jonas heard them mention is in fact a local. Someone who might have heard of the existence from the previous owner himself," I suggest.

"That's a whole lot of ifs, Ms. Hart."

Despite his obvious misgivings, the agent collects the drawings and the printout Sully hands him of the possible locations, and promises to look into it.

"Well, that was rather anti-climactic," Jackson comments when he's gone.

"Haven't we had enough excitement?" I suggest.

"Maybe for you, but I'm still young, the more excitement the better," he teases.

If only he knew what his 'elderly' mother was up to around four thirty this morning.

"If you want some excitement, come with me," Jonas says, clapping Jackson on the shoulder. "We could use an extra pair of hands in the breeding barn."

I stifle a snort as Jonas winks at me before leading my son out the front door. Then I turn to the pile of dishes in the sink. Ama apparently was off somewhere with Thomas this morning, and I see Jonas isn't the only one who takes the woman for granted.

After I've straightened up the kitchen, I head outside to the corral where Lucy is working with Hope. The poor mare has suffered a massive setback and jumps at any sound or anything that moves. We're almost back at square one and the worst part is, once we can return to the rescue, she'll have to go through it all over again.

So much for thinking she might be one we could sell.

"How is she doing?"

Even the sound of my voice startles Hope, who almost rips the lead from Lucy's hands.

"She was okay in the stall with Daisy, but is pretty freaked out here."

"We need to find a way to build her confidence," I suggest. "What if we got Daisy into the ring with her as a grounding presence? You'd still work with Hope, but let's see if she'll respond better with her buddy around."

"How is that going to build her confidence, though? Won't that just make her dependent on Daisy?"

"At first, probably, but it would give us a good idea of her potential. When we see clear improvement, we could slowly separate the two again. Wean her off Daisy, so to speak."

"Worth a try," Lucy concedes.

I head into the barn and retrieve the donkey, who happily trots beside me as I lead her to the corral.

I've just closed the gate when I notice Ama's SUV pulling up to the house. I see her get out of the driver's side and round the hood to the passenger side. She opens the door and helps Thomas out of the vehicle. I'm shocked when I see how old and frail he suddenly looks, leaning heavily on Ama's arm.

My feet are already moving in their direction and I'm just in time to firmly grab Thomas's other arm as they start up the porch steps.

"How are you doing, Thomas?" I ask as we lead him inside.

"Tired. No breakfast before the blood work and waiting for almost an hour for the damn doctor to get to me does that," he grumbles. "Be right as rain after a nap."

Sully, who is just coming out of the office, catches that and quickly steps in.

"Come on, Thomas. Let's get you upstairs," he says.

To my surprise, Thomas doesn't object.

When they're halfway up the stairs, Ama motions me into the kitchen.

"What's wrong with him?" I ask in a low voice.

"He fainted at the lab and was weak as a kitten after. The doctor just received his medical records from his physician back in Texas and, apparently, the old man hasn't been taking his medication."

"Medication for what?"

She shakes her head. "He doesn't want me to say anything to Jonas, which is why I'm telling you."

"And you want me to tell Jonas?"

She nods.

"Tell him what?"

"His father has a heart condition."

Twenty-Four

Jonas

Heart failure.

It sounds so damn final.

Damn, I knew there was something wrong. Felt it in my gut. Now I understand why after years of brushing me off, he finally agreed to sell his place and join me up here in Montana.

Oh, I know heart failure doesn't necessarily mean imminent death, but it will be the ultimate outcome. I may be fifty years old, and lucky to have had my dad for so long, but I'm not ready to say goodbye.

Alex's footsteps sound going down the porch steps. She just left my office, giving me some time to process, and I'm grateful. There's a lot to wrap my head around.

I look at the row of pill bottles I lined up on my desk. Ama picked them up at the pharmacy in town. Medication he should've been taking all along.

Why? Why did he stop?

It's one thing not wanting to tell me he's been on medication for arrhythmia for the last ten years, I get it. He's a proud man and would hate to admit to something, which in his eyes, conveys weakness. But then at some point early last year he consciously decided to stop taking them, stopped going for his regular visits with the cardiologist I didn't know he had back in Texas. That's the part I can't make sense of.

Dad's not a stupid man by far. He may not have a college education and spent his entire life on a ranch, but he's always been well-read and smart as a whip. He must've known what he was doing to his heart muscle. The medication was intended to slow down the progressive damage, which now apparently has left his heart in sorry shape.

Goddammit, Dad.

In a surge of anger I swipe everything off the top of my desk, sending paperwork flying and those damn pill bottles clattering on the floor.

Then I get to my feet, grab my hat, and stalk out the door.

I throw the last pebble I've been lobbing into the Fisher River and sit down on the large rock. The same one Alex and I were sitting on the last time I was here.

Most of the anger has faded—washed away by the river's cool waters—leaving only a sense of sadness in its wake.

Nothing like a few solitary moments communing with nature to ground me. Oh, I still want answers, but I feel better equipped asking for them now.

Sully had come flying out of the office next door when he heard my racket earlier, but I ignored him. He followed me to the stable where Alex stopped him. Told him to leave me be as I threw a saddle on Phantom. I even ignored her, but something tells me she understands.

That's why it doesn't surprise me when I hear a soft footfall behind me and two slim arms slip around my neck from behind. I feel her lips press a kiss to the top of my head and my hands automatically grab on to hers.

"Better?"

"Mmm."

I loop her arms over my head and guide her to stand in front of me before tugging her on my lap. Then I kiss her properly.

"I am now," I say, telling her the truth. "You make everything better. Thanks for checking up on me."

She strokes a hand over my bald head and down the back of my neck, resting her forehead against mine.

"That's good, but I'm afraid there's another reason I'm here."

I pull back slightly so I can look her in the eye.

"What is it?"

"Limpkin showed up. Apparently, Agent Wolff shared our findings with him. He wants to talk to you. I think he's looking for your input."

I bark out a laugh, but it's more in disbelief than from amusement.

Only yesterday he was basically accusing me of collusion with these terrorists and now he comes looking for my help? The guy needs a serious fucking attitude adjustment if he wants my cooperation.

I lift Alex off my lap and get to my feet. Then I pick up my Stetson, slap the dust off on my thigh, and shove it on my head.

"Let's go see what Homeland Security wants."

When we ride up to the barn, a group of three—Limpkin, Wolff, and Sheriff Ewing—is waiting just outside.

"Harvey," the sheriff greets me with a tip of the hat.

"Sheriff."

I nod at Wolff, who responds in kind, but I pointedly ignore the third man.

"It's about time, we've been waiting for half an hour," the idiot says as I slide off the saddle.

"I suggest next time you try calling ahead," I observe without even looking at him.

"Need I remind you—"

That's it. I've had about enough of him.

Shoving Phantom's reins at Alex, I swing around on him.

"Agent Limpkin, I believe it's you who needs reminding that as recent as yesterday you all but accused me of being a traitor to the country I served for twenty fucking years. You tried to run roughshod all over my woman, threatening *her* with a charge of harboring fugitives. And now you're back here, trying to throw your imagined weight around. What did you expect? A fucking red-carpet welcome?"

"Now listen here—" he sputters, but I'm done.

"Jonas..." Ewing tries in a reconciliatory tone.

"No, Wayne," I tell him before turning back to Limpkin. "It's time I give Bob Dickson a call."

I turn my back and walk a few feet before pulling out my phone, punching in the number I know by heart. Alex sidles up to me and nudges me with an elbow.

"Who's this Bob Dickson?" she whispers.

"Special Forces buddy. Good friend and mentor."

Then as my call is answered on the other side, I hold the phone away from my ear so she can hear.

"Department of Homeland Security, Deputy Director Dickson's office, how may I help you?"

"Calling for Bob. Tell him it's Jonas Harvey."

I love the way her initial shock makes way for amusement. She gives me a thumbs-up before walking back to the horses.

"Fucking hell, Jonas. It's been what, two years? How the hell are ya?"

"Same old, same old."

"No woman able to get her clutches in you yet?"

He's been on my case for the past ten years, since I stood up for him when he married the high school sweetheart he reconnected with. My standard answer, *"Fat chance,"* almost slips from my tongue when my eyes catch on Alex, leading the horses into the barn.

"There may be some changes on the horizon," I respond instead.

"You're shitting me!" His boisterous laugh booms in my ear. "Tell me about this miracle worker."

"Maybe another time, I called for another reason."

Catching on to my serious tone he's suddenly all business.

"Spill."

"Can't say much more than his name is known and raises flags," he shares when I fill him in. "My office has been following developments up there, but maybe not closely enough. There is a sense of urgency to resolve this case though. And this is for your ears only: we have credible intel to suggest there may be more attacks planned like last year's. Leave Limpkin to me, and I hope his behavior won't hold you back from doing anything you can to further the investigation."

"Understood, and you have my word."

Alex

By the time I have Phantom and Sarge squared away, Jonas and the three men have disappeared, but I see Jonas's dad sitting outside on the porch.

"Don't start with me," he says the moment I set foot on the bottom step.

I fight a smile and, without saying a word, sit down next to him on the wooden bench.

It was clear Jonas was shocked when I relayed Ama's message from the doctor. I lost my folks years ago, far too soon, but there are still moments I feel their loss sharply. Moments when I miss that sense of belonging, having someone love you unconditionally like only parents can. There's something about coming to terms with your parents' death that prompts the contemplation of your own mortality and that can be unsettling.

I know Jonas lost his mother many years ago, but I can imagine his father—with his larger-than-life personality—seemed like a permanent fixture in his life. Losing his dad would leave a hole in his heart without any other family to fill it.

At least I still had Jackson.

Thomas shifts beside me, perhaps uneasy with the silence. A quick glance shows him staring out in the distance.

The view from here is just as stunning as the one from the bedroom window, but the furniture out here is sorely lacking. My ass is already going numb.

Still, patience is key, so I endure the hard slab of wood and wait for Thomas.

He doesn't make me wait long.

"Damn snot-nosed doctor," he grumbles. "Barely old enough to wipe his own ass."

This time I can't hold back the snort, earning me a scathing side-eye.

"Talking like I'm some senile old coot who doesn't know what's wrong with him. I know. I've known since he was still in diapers."

He goes silent again and this time I'm the one to break it.

"How did you find out?"

He clears his throat before he speaks.

"Was after my Mary died. I'd get short of breath, dizzy sometimes. Hadn't been eating well so I thought maybe I'd need a bit of iron, but I turned out to have tachy—whatever the hell that's called."

"Tachycardia? Irregular heartbeat?"

"Yeah. Finally saw one of them cardiologists, told me if I took the meds, changed my diet, I could manage it." He picks at a piece of dry skin at the edge of a thumbnail. "Never was one for green food. God created steak for a reason. And the pills—every time I'd see that damn doctor —he gave me more. Pills to treat side effects the other pills caused. Madness. Getting old sucks."

I can't argue with that, although I still have a few years to go before I reach his age.

"Always told my Mary we'd get old and gray together, but I'm the only one old and gray and I'm damn tired of it. Not bein' able to work the ranch, most days feeling weaker than a newborn foal, I'm tired of it all. Figured if the end was coming up anyway, I'd rather go out without those goddamn drugs, enjoying what time I've got left."

I absentmindedly wipe at my face where I find a tear slowly rolling down my cheek. With my other hand I cover Thomas's restless ones.

"I get that."

We sit like that for a few minutes, my heart going out to both the old man and his son.

"My boy is pissed," he says eventually.

"Yeah, but I get that too."

Thomas turns to me with rheumy eyes.

"Good to see he finally found someone. You'll be good for him. Too much of a loner, my son."

Then he stares back at the view.

"Miss my Mary something fierce, though. I'm ready to join her, but it'll be easier knowing I won't be leavin' Jonas all alone."

The storm door opens and Sully sticks his head out.

"I thought I heard voices. I'm sorry to interrupt but, Alex, we could use you for a minute."

I immediately look at Thomas who moves one of his hands on top of mine, giving it a squeeze.

"Go on, then. Never mind me. I'm sure Ama will come bother me soon enough."

I get up to head in after Sully but hesitate at the last moment. I return to Jonas's father, whose eyes are once again aimed at the view. Bending down, I kiss his papery cheek before rushing inside.

I'm surprised to find Ama standing in the hallway, her eyes suspiciously red.

"Go on," she echoes Thomas's words. "I've got the old coot."

I take a deep breath outside the office door before walking in.

Jonas immediately walks over and pecks me on the lips. The large desk is covered with maps of all kind.

"Ms. Hart," Limpkin calls my attention. "If you wouldn't mind a few questions. Are you aware of any other access onto your property?"

I shake my head. "No. Then again, I never really had a chance to explore all the land yet."

"Your real estate agent mention anything by chance?"

"No. His office is in Kalispell. I doubt he'd been there much before he showed me the property."

"Who was it?"

I rattle off the name and notice Agent Wolff typing it in on a laptop.

"Do you know if anyone else was interested in buying it?"

"I don't think so. I believe mine was the only offer."

He nods appearing to think for a moment.

"One more question; anyone who may have expressed an interest after you bought it? Or have you noticed anyone lurking around since you moved in? Anyone who frequently knocks on your door? Maybe hired help or contractors."

"I'm sorry, I can't think of anyone." Other than Jonas, of course. "What's going to happen now?" I ask, looking at the maps.

It's Jonas who answers. "We're looking for that suspected supply route." He points at a map. "There's a small network of logging roads running parallel to Swamp Creek, about two miles from the most eastern section of your property line. Those are the closest inroads we can find. Agent Limpkin has asked my team to help find the start of that trail ending by the small clearing. Some of those old logging roads are old and difficult to travel."

"But you're still hurt," I point out.

Jonas wraps an arm around me and leads me into his own office, closing the door. Then he pulls me against him.

"I was able to ride today without a problem. I'll be fine, but I'm not gonna lie and tell you it doesn't feel fucking great to have you concerned about me."

"Whatever. Just don't get hurt again."

He grins down at me. "Scout's honor."

Then his face turns serious.

"I watched you come up the porch steps earlier but didn't hear you coming inside until just now."

"Your dad was out there, I just kept him company for a while."

"He say anything to you?"

I lift up on my toes and kiss him lightly.

"Yes, but I think you should talk to him yourself."

"I won't be able to right now, we're heading out shortly."

I can tell he's not happy about it, but this is something they need to clear the air on without my involvement.

"It'll keep 'til you get back. Your dad's not going anywhere."

I hope not for a while.

Twenty-Five

Jonas

The search so far has only pushed the fugitives to dig in.

I learned it had been Wolff and Ewing pushing for the DHS agent to seek help from my team. Figured he wouldn't have done so voluntarily.

He'd had his helicopter circling overhead and a couple of search parties on ATVs revving their engines around the property. The noise alone would've driven the fugitives to hunker down below ground. Not a chance in hell they'll surface and risk drawing attention to themselves now. At least not during daylight.

Even back when old Jenkins would've had the shelter built, they would've needed access for large trucks. No way they would've been able to get those up there from the farmhouse, and Alex confirmed that she hasn't seen anyone on or around her property since she bought the place.

The best chance to get a bead on their location will be to

find the back route we know has to exist. It needs to be done silently and under cover of darkness.

That's where we come in.

"Everyone set?"

I get confirming responses from the rest of the team and cluck softly, urging Sugar forward.

We left the ranch in convoy: the sheriff's cruiser, two nondescript SUVs with federal agents, more agents in the black van that will serve as a command center, and our two trucks towing the horse trailers in the rear. We were able to get the trucks up to a clear-cut section on the logging road, large enough to use as a staging area, but from here it'll have to be on horseback.

Glancing over my shoulder I see Sully, James right behind him, then Bo, and closing the line is Fletch. We're all wearing our night gear, which is necessary because as soon as we ride under the cover of the trees the darkness will be almost complete.

I visualize the web of faint lines showing the old logging roads on the map to navigate. The one we're on heads west, but in a mile or so we'll hit a fork with one loop circling north and another south. When we get to the fork we'll split up; James, Bo, and Fletch are heading north, and Sully will stay with me, taking the south loop.

Our objective is to find the two-rut trail, follow it to see where it leads, and confirm the location of the shelter. We are to avoid engaging with the fugitives. That could be easier said than done, which is why I not only have my rifle in the saddle holster, but this time made sure I have a sidearm on me as well. So do my guys.

"Remember, radio silence," I reinforce in a low voice when we get to the split in the road. "Signals only."

After many years as a team, we've developed a language

all on our own to convey intel. An abbreviated version of Morse code, we use a simple touch to the transmit button on our radios to convey a message. Even with the volume turned way down, to our trained ears the faint clicks are enough to relay necessary information. To anyone else listening in, it might sound like nothing more than radio static. In the field, silence was often key to success, so our method of communication was a necessity.

In this case I have a second reason to ask for it, however. Until I know who this *general* is I won't trust anyone, and that includes any member of the group we left back at the staging area able to listen in. Wouldn't want anyone to give a bunch of militants, armed to the teeth, a heads-up we're on our way.

With a thumbs-up to the group of three going the other way, we turn south.

About five minutes down this way, I'm starting to have doubts. The deeper we go, the more the underbrush encroaches on the road and I've had to duck my head a few times for low-hanging branches.

Holding Sugar back, I let Sully catch up alongside me.

"No way a truck has come through here in the past few years," I tell him, keeping my voice low. "The ruts aren't even wide enough for a pickup anymore."

"Not a pickup," Sully agrees. "But something came through here." He points at the faint imprints of tires in the dirt a few feet ahead. "Deep tread, narrow wheelbase. Maybe ATV or quad."

"For transporting supplies?" I question.

Sully slides off Cisko and walks down the path a ways, crouching down before he retraces his steps.

"There's a thinner set too on a slightly wider axel," he reports.

"Two vehicles?"

He shakes his head as he mounts his horse. "No. My guess is a quad and a small trailer."

"Those could've been there for a while," I observe.

"Edges are sharp. Last time we had rain was six days ago. These were made after."

Damn. Finally, a lucky break.

Now all we have to do is find the trail.

We almost miss it about three quarters of a mile farther.

We would've if Sully hadn't noticed the axe marks on the trunk of a young tree lying parallel to the path. It was placed there to cover the narrow trail heading into the woods.

I'm itching to follow it, but not before I send word to the rest of my team. Only when I hear the responding radio click to confirm they're on their way, do I urge Sugar ahead.

The trail is surprisingly level and when I check my GPS, I note we're getting close to the creek. A few minutes later I can hear it and motion Sully to stop. It's better we leave the horses here and continue on foot.

I let Sully take the lead as we go off-trail to get to the water. They'll likely have a filtration system in place and it would make sense they'd use it for their water supply during the spring runoff. That means storage tanks, because come summer, the creek will dry up to little more than a trickle.

It also means they'd be running a pump and those are never silent. If we can find where they pump out the water, we should be able to follow the sound to the source.

I spot the pipe a few hundred feet downstream. The gurgling of water being sucked up is prominent. Now using only hand signals, Sully indicates he'll take the lead. His hearing is sharper than mine.

Crouching down to stay behind the cover of the lower

vegetation, he leads us away from the creek until all of a sudden, he signals me to stop. He's clearly hearing something, and after a few seconds I do too. An underlying noise like the whirring of a fan. Then he points to our right, where I just make out the top of a ventilation pipe partially hidden by underbrush. It's capped with a filter and sticks about four feet out of the ground to clear the snow.

Bingo.

I motion for Sully to follow me back to the creek where we have less chance to be heard. We move a little upstream from the pump.

"We must've been right over top," he whispers.

"Yup. Time to head back to the horses and call in the troops."

When I turn around, I catch a flash of something shiny from the corner of my eye.

The next moment I'm blown off my feet.

~

Alex

"Did you hear that?"

It's four thirty in the morning and I'm having a coffee on the front porch with Thomas.

I'd been restless last night. After I watched the taillights of the last trailer disappear down the drive, I came in to find Lucy making a mess of the kitchen. Thomas was watching the news in the living room, with half an eye on my assistant, and Jackson was in Jonas's office playing some game on his laptop.

Everyone was doing something to stay busy, we were all worried about the team going out there in the dark.

Baking is Lucy's stress relief and I thought I'd join her, figuring what works for her may work for me, but after half an hour of me being more of a hindrance than a help, I got booted from the kitchen.

Then I joined Thomas in the living room and he ended up trying to teach me to play poker to kill the time. As it turns out, I suck at that too. Jackson joined us for a bit, stealing cookies from under Lucy's nose, which of course resulted in more good-natured bickering between those two.

A little after nine Thomas headed upstairs refusing any help, but I sent Jackson after him anyway, just in case.

We watched some TV after that but I can't even remember what was on. At some point Lucy started yawning and began cleaning up the aftermath of two apple pies and enough cookies to feed the average household for a month. Eager to do something with my hands, I waved her out the door. After walking her to the cabin, Jackson disappeared into the office again and when I had the kitchen in order, I turned off the lights and headed to bed as well.

Except I barely got any sleep, constantly checking the alarm clock on the nightstand. Then half an hour ago I heard Thomas get up. Worried something might be wrong, I quickly got dressed and followed him down, to find him wrestling with the coffee machine in the kitchen.

"Probably roadwork. Blasting rock," he suggests. "They were widening the highway around Logan State Park when I drove up here."

I don't argue, but the park is east of us and I'm pretty sure the loud bang was closer and came from the north. Besides, who would be blasting rock at this hour?

It makes me a little uneasy.

"I like your son."

I turn to him, a little taken aback.

"So do I."

"Was good to have some young blood around, some laughter to fill that big house. Smell of apple pie reminded me of the old ranch. Mary liked to bake almost as much as she liked to laugh, and she did a lot of it."

I smile at him. "I would've liked to have met her."

"She'd have liked that too."

We fall into a comfortable silence, sipping coffee and staring into the darkness.

"Where is your kid stationed?" Thomas asks after a while

"He just did a tour in Iraq. He's heading for Fort Bragg next."

Thomas turns to me, raising an eyebrow.

"Fort Bragg?"

I nod. "Special Forces training."

These past days have been such a roller coaster, I haven't really had a chance yet to properly process that news.

"Ouch. I remember when Jonas left for training. Threw my Mary for a loop. Me too, to be fair. Had hopes he'd take over the ranch down the line, but he was dead set on serving his country. How can you argue with that?"

Good question. I wish I had an answer.

"His father was killed in Afghanistan by a roadside bomb eleven years ago," I blurt out. "I'd already lost both my parents in the five years prior to that. So believe me when I say I'm proud of my son—he's all I have—but I don't think I could survive losing anyone else."

I sniff hard and his arthritic hand reaches over to pat my knee.

"For now your son is asleep in the house, safe and sound."

"He is, but yours is out there somewhere, possibly risking his life." A sudden panicked feeling has me jump to my feet. "And...with all due respect, I don't think that was blasting rock."

Leaning over the railing I glance to the left—or north—and scan the dark mountain ridges. Of course I can't see a damn thing.

"You love him."

I swing around, my mouth opening but no sound comes out.

Do I?

I try to imagine my future without Jonas playing a role, and I can't seem to conjure up what that would look like. He's everywhere.

"I think I do."

Thomas nods, a faint smile lifts the corner of his mouth.

"He loves you too. Glad my son found that. A good woman who can stand shoulder to shoulder with him, a son to be proud of, a house full of life. That's what I want for him."

I sink back down on the hard bench and his hand finds my knee again.

"He'll be back."

"I hope so" I mumble.

"I know so," Thomas says with surprising conviction.

"Can we make a deal?" I ask him, turning my body to face him.

"What?"

"If I don't question Jonas coming home, can you please take your medication?"

The shutters go down immediately, but I have more to say and take his hands in mine.

"That happy life for Jonas you just painted? It may be enough for you, but even after knowing your son for a relatively short time, I can guarantee it won't be for him. Not unless he has you there to enjoy it with."

He shakes his head. "I'm old, I won't be around for long anyway."

"Maybe not, but think of all the beautiful new memories you'd have to carry with you when it's your time." I lean forward. "I betcha your Mary would agree with me."

He's silent for a long time and I'm starting to worry I pushed too hard, when he finally looks at me.

"You play dirty."

I shrug. "Maybe so, but in this case, I think the end justifies the means."

He grunts, but I'm happy to take it as a concession.

My phone starts buzzing in my pocket. Hoping it's Jonas with some news, I pull it free and check the screen. Unknown number. Who else would call me at this hour of the morning?

"Hello."

"Alex?" I recognize Bo's voice and suddenly my entire body is at full alert.

"Bo?"

"Yeah, listen. Something happened..."

Twenty-Six

ALEX

"He's fine."

Fletch stops us outside the hospital doors.

"What happened? Bo said there had been an explosion?"

"Grenade. They were lucky it was dark and the fucking bastard lobbing it probably can't hit the toilet when he takes a piss. Otherwise, things could'a been much worse."

"Jesus," Thomas hisses beside me and I grab on to his arm a little tighter.

There was no way he was going to be left at home and I've been terrified for him as well as Jonas. His color is not good. The news that bang we heard earlier was probably the explosion Bo referred to filled us both with dread. He said he needed to go but did mention Jonas got hurt but was alive and they'd be transporting him to the hospital in Libby as soon as they could get him out of there.

Not allowing myself to think, I'd rushed inside, got

Jackson up, ran to wake up Lucy, and left the ranch in their care while I drove Thomas here.

"We just got here. Jonas is being looked at now, but he was awake and talking again when the ambulance arrived."

I bend over and blow out a breath. *Thank God*.

"Sully was wheeled into surgery, though," Fletch continues. "I'm waiting for news."

He may sound gruff and all business, but when I straighten up, I notice his hands are shaking.

"Anyone else hurt?" I manage.

"No. The rest of us were just riding up when the blast went off."

I turn to Thomas, who is leaning heavily on my arm, and force more strength in my voice than I feel.

"Let's go see about your son."

What I don't say is that I want to get him in a chair, and maybe looked at.

Fletch reads the quick glance I shoot him and takes up position on the other side of Thomas, so he's braced between us. Together we shuffle inside.

We're sent to a small waiting room and told the doctor will be in to speak to us shortly.

During the wait, Fletch fills us in on what he knows. Sully and Jonas had found evidence of the underground shelter and notified the other half of the team, but their presence had been caught on one of the infrared cameras hidden around the perimeter. One of the fugitives had panicked and tossed a grenade at them just as the other three arrived.

As soon as law enforcement got to the scene, the team was able to move both injured men out to the main road to wait for first responders. Bo and James went back to assist the federal agents and Fletch followed the ambulances into Libby.

By the time a doctor walks in looking for the Harvey family, Ama has joined us. I'm guessing Lucy called her.

"Mr. Harvey was lucky," the man shares, and a few relieved sighs can be heard. "He has a ruptured eardrum, which will need to be monitored, but should heal on its own. I also suspect he has a concussion from the explosion, which is not unusual. I did note some fairly recent injuries I can't quite place. His left ankle shows swelling and some discoloration, both wrists were already bandaged, and then there's a cut on his scalp that has barely started healing."

"Those are from an incident a few days ago," I volunteer. "He probably had a concussion at that time too but didn't seek medical treatment."

The man has a disapproving look on his face when he turns to me.

"That would qualify Mr. Harvey as a very lucky man, then. Although, second impact syndrome is a real concern and can be fatal. We'll have to monitor the patient closely to make sure there is no swelling of the brain, which is more vulnerable to injury if a previous concussion has not had a chance to heal properly."

That takes the air out of the room in a hurry.

"Are we able to see him?"

"One of the nurses will come to let you know."

"What about Sully?" Fletch wants to know. "The second man who was brought in. He was taken up to surgery."

"I don't know anything about him, but I can ask for you."

The doctor's eyes narrow on Thomas.

"Sir, are you all right?"

"Fine," he croaks out, just before he slumps down in his chair.

Both Ama and I grab on at the same time to prevent him from sliding to the floor. The doctor is already yelling for a stretcher as he kneels on the tile in from of him.

"Hey."

His eyes are clear and the smile on his face warm when I walk into the room.

I've held it together, even after Thomas was rushed out of the waiting room, but a sob breaks free now.

"Sweets...come here."

He holds out his hand and I grab hold, but there's no way to hold back these tears. He pulls me closer and I sit down heavily in the chair beside the bed, hiding my face in his shoulder. With his other hand, he strokes my hair. Not saying anything, he simply lets me cry it out.

"I'm still here," he says when I get a hold on the waterworks.

Grabbing handfuls of tissues from the box beside his bed, I mop my face.

"I know. It's your father..."

He nods. "I heard. The doctor left moments before you walked in to tell me what happened. They were able to stabilize him."

I blow out a breath and some of the weight pressing on my chest is relieved. "Thank God."

"Yeah. He's awake and talking. Tried to bribe staff to do what they could to keep his ticker going a bit longer."

That news makes me so happy a new wave of tears threatens, but I blink them away.

"You need to talk to him."

Jonas brings my hand to his face and kisses my knuckles.

"I know, and I will. As soon as they'll let me go see him."
He cups my face and strokes his thumb along my cheek-
bone. "I'm sorry I scared you."

"I'm okay."

I try to smile it off but my face is stiff. Who am I
kidding? This whole thing was a horrific example of déjà vu.
I was petrified I'd lose him too.

What are the odds of losing both of the men you gave
your heart to in an explosion?

"Alexandra..."

I give my head a little shake.

"I heard the explosion, you know. Your father and I
both did. He thought it was a road crew blasting rock, but I
feared it was something else. Neither of us had been able to
sleep much and we were sitting on the porch, talking. About
him, and me, but more importantly about you."

His eyes widen a fraction.

"He's a smart man, your father. He voiced something I
hadn't quite been ready to put to words myself. And then
Bo called, and all I've been able to think since is; what if I
never get the chance?"

"Hey," he says, a sparkle in those blue eyes I wasn't sure
I'd get to see again. "I'm right here."

"I know." I lower my head and kiss him gently. "I love
you."

~

Jonas

. . .

"...took a chunk out of the back of his leg, but more worrisome was the internal bleeding from the blast injury. They had to remove a section of his colon, which had ruptured."

My head is throbbing and I can't hear with my left ear, which is bandaged up, so I have to focus on Fletch's face to catch what he's saying.

"He came through surgery well," he continues. "They cleaned him out as best they could, but he's not out of the woods. The next couple of days they'll monitor him closely for signs of sepsis."

"Did you call his sister?"

"Ama did. She's flying into Kalispell. Ama is going to pick her up this afternoon."

I drop my head back on the pillow and peek at Alex sitting on the other side of the bed. That sweet smile when she told me she loved me is gone, the strain etched on her face. I never even had a chance to tell her I feel the same way about her before Fletch came in.

Giving her hand I'm still holding a little squeeze, I turn back to my teammate.

"Heard anything from James and Bo?"

He hesitates and I catch him dart a quick glance past me at Alex.

"Yes. They're still held up."

It's clear he's holding back. Old habits die hard. For decades it was hammered into us not to share any details, but this wasn't a secret military mission.

"What's going on?" I prompt him. "Everyone in this room knows what we were doing up there."

"Feds are holding on to James."

"What? Why?"

"He took out Adams. Guy was armed to the teeth, had a

gun in his hand and was aiming it at the back of your head. James shot and killed him before either Bo or I had a chance to draw our weapons."

Alex's hand spasms in mine.

Wow. Didn't see that coming.

Granted, I can't remember anything until I woke up in the ambulance, but it's a shock to discover how close I came to ending up in a coroner's van instead.

"And the other one? Wright?"

"According to Bo, he barricaded himself in the shelter. Feds found the access hatch, blew it off, dropped a few canisters of teargas, but it turns out the guy was already dead. Found him in one of the storage rooms with half his head blown off."

Alex sharply sucks in air and Fletch turns to her.

"Sorry. Guess you could've done without the gory details."

She shakes her head. "Don't worry about it."

"So what's the hold up with James?"

"They want corroborating evidence it was a justified kill and are waiting for a forensic team to show so they can access the camera feeds."

Bastards. Or maybe I should say, bastard, because I'm pretty sure Limpkin is the one pulling these strings. He can't get to me so he picks someone I care about to harass.

"I need a phone."

"For what?"

I'm surprised Alex is challenging me.

"I need a word with Limpkin."

"You need to rest," she insists.

"Besides, James and Bo have this," Fletch adds. "Sounds like Limpkin is pissed because there's no one left to interrogate."

I can see how that would be a blow to the investigation. No one to question means no one to point fingers at whoever else may have been involved. It still doesn't make the agent less of an asshole.

Hooked up to monitors and an IV, my cut-up clothes somewhere in an ER trash bin, there's not a whole lot I can do but lie here—steaming. Which isn't doing the pounding in my head much good.

"Excuse me."

A nurse comes in, pushing past Fletch who was blocking the door. She comes straight to the bed and checks the IV.

"How are we doing? I noticed your heart rate go up quite a bit on the monitor at the nurses' station."

"I'm fine."

Far from.

Both my father and my right-hand man are in intensive care, James and Bo are forced to deal with the fallout of a shooting that saved my life, and the woman I love is sitting beside me instead of spending time with her son, who is already about halfway through his leave, and I'm powerless to do a damn thing about any of it.

"I'm sure you are, but maybe you should rest a little anyway."

Alex jumps to her feet right away, pulling her hand from mine.

"I should check in on your father anyway and probably give Jackson a call."

"Yeah. I'll see if I can get in to see Sully." Fletch is already on his way out the door.

I'm always on top of things—in control—but in the past week I've been blindsided one too many times. Had a few too many brushes with death. All it takes is the blink of an eye for fate to turn those cards on you.

"Alex, wait!" I call after her when she follows Fletch out.

"Are you okay for pain?" the nurse asks, blocking my view.

"I'm fine," I repeat sharply.

I'm sure she'll write something in my chart about being a difficult patient, but I frankly don't give a damn. I don't intend to stay here any longer than I absolutely have to.

I watch her march out of the room and figure I'm alone when Alex pokes her head around the door.

"Did you need anything?"

"Yes."

She approaches the bed. When I can reach her hand, I urge her down on the edge of the bed.

"What's wrong?"

Concern deepens the lines in her forehead.

"We were interrupted before."

It takes a second for understanding to put a flush on her face.

"Yes, we were."

Slipping a hand under her heavy hair, I curve my fingers around her neck and pull her closer.

"What you were saying before...about being afraid you'd never have the chance to use the words."

"I remember."

"I can't risk that either."

I cup her face in my hands and put my heart in the kiss I give her.

"Wasn't expecting you. Definitely wasn't expecting to fall for you. But I did and I did it hard."

I stare into those liquid brown eyes, which are able to see right through me, and I'm so fucking grateful to have this chance.

"Love you, Alexandra Hart."

Twenty-Seven

JONAS

I watch as the familiar vehicle rolls up my driveway.

I'm almost glad for the distraction.

Alex brought me home this morning after I was able to convince the doctor to discharge me. He initially wanted to keep an eye on me for another day, but I'd already alienated every nurse on the ward and I suspect they were glad to be rid of me. He did insist I take it easy for another couple of days which I brushed off, but Alex took as religion.

She took me to see Dad and Sully but forced me to sit in the wheelchair she'd rounded up for me. I conceded only because I was eager to see with my own eyes both of them were doing as well as reported.

I'm not sure which was harder, to see a strong man like Sully looking haggard and hooked up to monitors or my dad, who was always tough and larger than life, now a frail man barely taking up space in the hospital bed.

The good news was both are doing better. Sully should

be able to come home in a couple of days and Dad might already be released tomorrow. He and I still haven't had that talk but, according to what the cardiologist who was checking in on him said, it looks like we could still have plenty of time for that. As long as Dad sticks to his regime and takes his damn medication.

When we got home, Alex installed me on the front porch in a fucking rocking chair she hauled from the attic and ordered me to stay put. I guess I should be grateful she didn't cover my legs with a blanket, but she did leave a footstool so I could put my feet up.

I've been sitting here for five hours, watching everybody else work—even Alex's son Jackson is jumping in—and I'm getting damn tired of it. Every time I try to get up someone barks at me, and Ama pokes her head out of the house every so often, checking to see if I need anything.

So yeah, even though I easily recognize Wolff and Schroeder—who I haven't seen since Homeland Security took over—I welcome the distraction.

"Good afternoon, gentlemen."

"Not looking too bad for surviving a grenade blast," Wolff says dryly.

"Harvey."

The gruff greeting is from Schroeder, who looks a little ill at ease.

"Have a seat."

I wave at the wooden bench along the wall. Schroeder takes a seat but Wolff opts to lean against the bannister. Something has shifted in the power balance between these two.

It's confirmed when Wolff takes the lead.

"You'll be happy to know your man has been cleared. It's on the books as a justified shooting."

"About time," I grumble.

James and Bo had come by the hospital last night, but neither had brought up the shooting. James was even more quiet than usual and I hesitated to ask. It's never easy to take a life, no matter how justified it may have been. Being a pacifist at heart, I'm sure it's gonna leave a mark on him.

This morning I saw him briefly and took the opportunity to thank him, but all he did was nod and take off for the breeding barn.

"Agreed," the younger agent surprisingly concedes. "I'm afraid our colleague with DHS was a bit zealous."

"About Limpkin..." I glance around Wolff. "I would've figured he'd be with you?"

"As far as Homeland Security is concerned, the imminent threat has been neutralized so he's heading home."

"What about the third guy?" Wolff's eyes drop to the tips of his boots. "The general. He's gonna leave that hanging?"

"He may be satisfied to write this up as case closed, but we're not," he says decidedly, throwing a sharp glance at Schroeder, who seems less than happy with that prospect. "Thankfully the Deputy Assistant Director agrees with me."

So that's why Wolff is in charge and Schroeder has been relegated to second fiddle. *Good*. I put more faith in the young agent than his older colleague and Limpkin combined.

"We're you able to find anything in the shelter? Anything to give you an idea who you're looking for?"

"No convenient names or notes with plans, but we were able to recover a laptop our lab is looking at. We also found most of the stolen arms."

"Most?"

"Around eighty pounds of explosives have not been retrieved. Combination of TNT and C4."

Jesus. Properly placed, that's enough to take down a city block, maybe more.

"You're gonna want to find that," I point out the obvious. "Or find whoever the general is, I'm sure one will lead to the other."

"We're working on it."

Wolff pushes off the railing and holds out his hand.

"I hope you succeed," I tell him earnestly, giving him a firm shake.

I'm not enamored with the idea of some lunatic sitting on a pile of explosives in my proverbial backyard. The sooner they find him the better.

"So do I."

Schroeder nods before following the other agent down the porch steps.

"Oh shit, forgot to mention," Wolff remembers halfway to their vehicle. "Could you tell Ms. Hart we should be cleared off her property by later this afternoon?"

"Sure thing."

But when they drive off and I glance over at the corral, where Alex is working Phantom for me, I'm seriously considering not sharing that bit of information just yet.

I'd like to keep her around.

Unfortunately Ama, who just came back from a visit to the hospital, spoils it for me at dinner.

"Oh, Alex, by the way, I noticed on my way home it looks like they've cleared out at your place. Not a single vehicle in sight. Did you know?"

"Nope. Nobody told me."

Her eyes shoot straight to me.

She saw the FBI agents pay me a visit earlier and asked

me what they wanted. I may have left this bit of information from my response.

"You never mentioned that."

"Must've slipped my mind," I tell her.

Her eyes narrow on me. "That's a bit concerning, don't you think? Maybe we left the hospital too soon?"

I'm pretty sure I'm in the doghouse, and Lucy doesn't help when she says, "I'd kill to sleep in my own bed tonight." Then she darts a glance at me. "No offense, Jonas, but I swear the mattress in that cabin is still stuffed with horsehair."

"None taken."

In fact, she may well be right.

"You should've said something," Ama pipes up. "I would've got you a better one."

"Of course not," Lucy objects. "It was just for a few nights anyway. We've already overstayed our welcome."

Feeling my plan to keep Alex here a bit longer slip through my fingers, I throw out a last-ditch effort.

"It'll be dark soon after dinner. Too late to try and load up all the horses. Besides, you may want to make sure they didn't damage any of your fences first."

"So? We'll load up Ellie and Sarge, secure them in the barn and we can do a quick check of the fences tonight before we move the rest of them tomorrow morning."

Alex

Does he realize how transparent he is?

I have a hard time keeping the grin off my face as Lucy

tortures him. Serves him right, keeping that information from me.

I let him stew all through dinner and while we load up the horses in the double trailer we hooked onto the new truck.

"I won't be long," I tell Jackson. "If you want to take Sarge and help Lucy check the fence lines, I should be there by the time you get back."

As the truck pulls away, I turn to Jonas.

"I don't want you to go," he admits.

"I know. I don't particularly want to go either, but I don't have much time left to spend with Jackson before he's off. On top of that, I have a business to run, and so do you."

"Can't you do that from here?" he persists stubbornly.

"I don't know. I'm going to need some time to figure that out. Then there's Lucy to consider as well." I step up to him and slide my arms around his waist, lifting my eyes to his unhappy ones. "You may have noticed things have been a little hectic. Let's have them settle down a bit, give me a chance to spend time with my son and feel out Lucy, and then you and I can have a talk."

"You're making sense," he grumbles. "And I don't like it."

I make no attempts this time to hold back my amusement at his petulance. It's kind of cute this strong bear of a man can be reduced to childish pouting. Clearly, he's not used to not having things go his way, but he needs to know I'm no pushover either.

"And now she's laughing at me."

"Only because you're adorable."

His face scrunches in distaste.

"No grown man worth his mettle should be called adorable."

306

I press my body against his. "I just did, and as for your mettle..." I slip a hand between our bodies and cup his semi-erect cock, eliciting a hiss from his lips. "I can personally vouch for it's worth."

He growls from the back of his throat.

"Tease."

"Not a tease." I smile up at him. "A promise. We'll get it figured out, and in the meantime—once you've recovered enough—there's no rule against sleepovers."

He bends his head and takes my mouth. A hard, claiming kiss I welcome.

I've loved two men, lost one and almost lost the other. I feel incredibly blessed to be standing here, feeling his hard hands squeeze my flesh and his mouth bruise my lips.

"Man, you need to up your game. You've got a perfectly empty house and you're mauling her out here?"

I snicker as Bo lumbers by, shaking his head.

"I thought you went home," Jonas observes.

"Heading that way now. Have a good night."

I watch as Bo gets in his truck before I face Jonas.

"I should be going too. I'm just going to grab my bag upstairs."

It takes me two minutes to stuff my clothes spilling out back into the bag and sling it over my shoulder.

Shit, that's heavy.

That's right too, along with those blueprints I'd stuffed that lockbox in there. Never had a chance to check it—in fact, I all but forgot about it—but maybe I can have a look when I get home.

I find Jonas back on the porch.

"Do you need anything before I go?"

"I'm fine, Sweets. I'm a lot better, I can look after myself."

Maybe, but when I kiss him goodnight, promise to call him later, and leave him standing alone in front of that rambling house, I'm feeling a niggle of doubt. Not enough to stop me from heading home for some quality time with my kid.

I get in the truck, back out of my spot, and when I drive off, I check my rearview mirror to catch sight of Jonas tipping his hat.

Honestly, I wouldn't mind calling High Meadow my home. Don't get me wrong, I love the rescue, but I'm not particularly attached to the farmhouse. We haven't been here long enough for that. Besides, we still need to do a bunch of renovations to make it our own.

Or perhaps for Lucy to make it her own.

I feel responsible for her. She followed me here under the premise we would share the house and run the rescue together. If plans are to change, she would have to be the first person I talk to about that.

The work itself wouldn't really be a big issue, the drive from Jonas's to the rescue is not far. I just don't know how she feels about living in that old farmhouse by herself. What if she doesn't feel safe alone? Hell, after this past week or so maybe I should ask, what if she isn't safe alone?

Lots to consider.

I pull off the highway and in the waning daylight, the first thing I notice are the deep ruts plowed into what used to be the grass shoulder along our driveway. *Great.* Limpkin and his crew obviously don't give a shit about other people's property. Testament to that is the gate to the paddock, which is hanging half off its hinges.

As I pull up to the house, I do a mental tally of the lumber we have stacked behind the barn. I'm sure this won't be the only damage; I don't even want to think what they may have trashed in the back field.

The trailer is parked in its regular spot with the back gate open. I bet those two are already out there checking.

I grab my bag from the passenger seat and walk up the steps. The front door is still locked so they must've gone straight to the barn, hoping to get it done before dark.

Inside, I flick on the lights. I guess I should consider myself lucky Limpkin didn't demand access to the house as well. God knows what we could've come home to. Fortunately everything in here looks just as we left it. Kicking off my boots and tossing my jacket on a hook, I carry the bag with me into the kitchen, then I grab the kettle to make some tea.

With the water coming to a boil, I take my bag into the laundry room, pull out the rusty old box, and set it on the dryer. Then I grab the tool box and select a screwdriver and a hammer. I wedge the flat head of the screwdriver in the seam close to the lock and give it a few good whacks with the hammer, but nothing moves.

I hear the kettle whistle in the kitchen and slip out of the laundry room.

Only to stop dead in my tracks.

"Hey, what are you doing here?"

His smile is as friendly as it's always been, but I can't help feeling a little unsettled.

"Just dropping in to see how you were doing."

"Oh, we just got back, actually. How...uh...did you get in?"

He cocks a thumb over his shoulder.

"Front door was open."

Did I leave it open? I thought I'd kicked it shut. In fact, I'm sure. The hair stands up on my neck.

"I probably left it open so Jackson and Lucy could get in." I turn my back and go through the motions of pouring hot water in my teapot, but my hands are shaking so hard, half of it spills on the counter. "I don't think you've met Jackson? He's my son. He's in the military, just got back from Iraq. He's starting Special Ops training."

I'm rambling, hoping maybe mention of the military might scare him off.

"They should be back any moment now."

"No they won't. They just left on horseback before you got here."

A cold fist closes around my heart.

He was watching them.

"Turn around, Alex."

I swallow the dry lump in my throat and do as he asks. That jovial smile is still on his face, but now I notice his eyes are ice cold. As cold as the steel of the gun in his hand.

"Enough games. Where are they?"

Twenty-Eight

ALEX

"What are you talking about? Where are what?"

I left both my phone and my gun in my jacket in the front hall. Fat lot of good they do me there.

"The papers."

He takes a threatening step closer and I press my back against the counter.

The papers?

"The blueprints?" I'm guessing that's what he means. "The FBI has them. Or maybe Homeland Security does, I'm not sure. I don't have them here."

His hand is so fast, I don't have a chance to react to the sharp backhand to my face and it knocks me off balance. I twist away and manage to grab on to the counter, sucking in a breath.

Damn, that hurts.

"Stupid bitch. Of course I knew they had the plans, or they wouldn't have been all over this place. I knew it was

313

only a matter of time before those fucking pigs would find the compound. Left me no choice but to eliminate Pete and Terry—they could point the finger at me if the feds got hold of them—but Terry got away."

It takes me a second to clue in he's talking about the escaped prisoners and a chill runs down my spine when he starts to chuckle.

"Fate took care of him for me," he continues, apparently finding it all very amusing. "Dead weight anyway. Now the only thing left to incriminate me is in that box."

He jabs my back with the barrel of the gun.

The box. Is that why he was so eager to ingratiate himself to us? Help us with the cleanup?

"Where is it?"

If I tell him it's just a few feet away in the laundry room, I might as well be signing my own death certificate. He's not going to leave any witnesses behind.

My only chance is to stall him and hope that when Lucy and Jackson return with the dogs, Chief and Scout will alert them something is off.

"What box?" I play dumb.

"You wanna play that game? Fine. We can just wait until that blonde tease and your kid come back. We'll see how good your memory is when I put a gun to his head."

The image those words evoke have me bend over the counter with bile crawling up my throat.

Change of plans. I will do whatever it takes to keep that from happening.

Whatever it takes.

I notice my hand is inches from the half-full teapot on the counter and an idea forms in my head. Maybe there is something I can do to get away from him.

Suddenly I can hear a muffled ringing and recognize my

phone, which is still in my jacket pocket, along with the gun.

"Leave it," he orders.

"But what if—"

"I said fucking leave it," he snarls.

After a few rings it stops. Maybe that was Jonas making sure I got home? For a moment I wonder if he'd worry I didn't pick up, but I realize that's unlikely. He probably figures I'm busy.

I'm going to have to get myself out of this.

"What is so important in that box anyway?"

I shift my body slightly so it blocks his view as I inch my hand closer to the pot.

"Pictures, not that it's any of your business. Uncle Clive was a paranoid sonofabitch and wanted insurance that if he went down, we'd all go down.

Uncle Clive?

"Thought he kept that box in the shelter until I was finally able to get in there once the snow started melting. It wasn't there so I figured he'd left it in the house, but unfortunately you'd already moved in."

My fingers close around the handle of the teapot and I grab on tight.

"I...I left the box in the truck."

For a moment I wonder if I made a mistake and he'll shoot me right now, but it turns out Clive wasn't the only suspicious one in the family when I feel the pressure of the gun in my back relieve and sense him taking a step back. He doesn't trust me.

"Show me."

I do my best to shield the pot in my hand and take a few steps toward the front, passing the laundry room. I hesitate for a moment, wondering if I should grab the box first, but then think better of it. My best chance is my gun in the front hallway.

When I'm level with the hook I hung my coat on, I don't hesitate and swing around, flinging the hot water at him. Some of it hits him in the face.

"*You fucking bitch!*" he yells, his free hand reaching up as the other pulls the trigger.

The gunshot is loud as I'm knocked to the floor.

∼

Jonas

It's been about ten minutes of feeling sorry for myself after Alex drives off when I come to my senses.

So what if all she'll let me do is hold her all night? Beats sleeping alone in my bed, surrounded by her lingering scent, and being miserable.

I whistle for Max and let him inside, making sure he has food and water to last him 'til Ama shows up in the morning. Then I leave a quick note for her and grab the new phone she got me. Then I shoot Fletch a message to let him know the house will be empty.

After getting a change of clothes and a toothbrush from my room, I grab my truck keys off the hook by the door. I'm sure Alex will be pissed I got behind the wheel—which the doctor advised against for a few days—but I feel fine. Besides that, she's just a couple of minutes up the road.

It only takes me one of those minutes to realize the flaw in my reasoning.

Fuck, those headlights are bright.

The US-2 is not a particularly busy highway this time of

night but it's not empty. Each time I encounter oncoming traffic, the lights blind me. When I catch sight of a large eighteen-wheeler in the distance, just a few hundred yards from the driveway to the rescue, I figure better safe than sorry and pull onto the shoulder. I turn my head away from the approaching truck and notice I'm right by an over-grown path to an old collapsed barn half hidden by the trees.

Clearly visible in the light of the passing semi is the pickup parked beside it. The logo plain as day on the side door.

Standish Automotive.

Now what would Hugh Standish be doing here, this close to Alex's place, and at this time of night?

I try to visualize the man I've had some dealings with over the years. Decent enough, knows his business when it comes to vehicles, and I know he helped the women find a new truck. I figured he was interested in Lucy; I recall them going out on a date.

Maybe it wasn't Lucy he was interested in at all.

I never had any flags going up around the guy, but now my gut is burning.

Planting my foot on the gas, I tear onto the road but when I get to the gravel driveway, I slow down to a crawl and turn off my headlights.

I have no idea what is happening, but the last thing I want is to announce myself.

The new truck and the dual trailer are parked near the barn, but Alex's F-150 is parked in front of the farmhouse. I see lights on inside.

Instead of driving right up, I pull off to the side of the drive and pull out my phone. The first number I call is Alex. It rings a few times before bumping me to her mailbox. It may not mean anything, maybe she doesn't have it on her, or she has her hands full, but I don't like it.

I don't like it at all.

I immediately dial Fletch.

"Yeah," he answers.

"Something is going on at the rescue. I found Standish's truck parked in the trees a couple of hundred yards from Alex's place and she's not answering her phone."

"Standish, as in Hugh Standish?"

"Yup. I'm gonna check it out, it may be nothing, but I wouldn't mind some assistance, just in case."

"On my way."

I open the glove box and feel around for my backup weapon, my sidearm is probably somewhere at the house. They gave it to Fletch at the hospital.

Then I slide out of the truck, easing the door shut.

The porch light is on, but the side of the house facing me is relatively dark so I stick to the shadows on my approach. I press my back against the brick, straining to hear anything from inside, but other than the pounding in my head that started up again, it's quiet.

Too quiet.

I press my fingers in the corners of my eyes, trying to get rid of the blur forming. Damn headache. I need to focus and keep my wits about me.

When I scan the wall behind me, I catch sight of the small window toward the back of the house. If I recall correctly, that's the laundry room. At best I might get a glimpse of the kitchen if the door was left open. However, if I can get to the big front window next to the door, I should be able to see most of the main floor, including part of the kitchen.

Tucking the gun in my waistband, I use both hands to

hoist myself up on the porch, trying to make as little noise as possible. Not easy, since my body is still sore from the blast, but the smallest sound could ruin the one advantage I have —the element of surprise.

Crouching as low as I can I inch my way past the door, when I hear movement inside followed by a shout.

"You fucking bitch!"

Suddenly noise is the least of my concerns as I jump up, throw my shoulder into the front door and push inside.

Just as a shot sounds and a bullet comes whizzing by my ear.

The first thing I see is Hugh, bent over with a hand to his face, but a gun still clutched in the other. Without thinking I launch myself at him, taking him down to the floor and try to pin the hand holding the gun.

Younger than me by about a decade, in good shape, and fueled by anger, he puts up a fight while I feel mine already draining. He's trying to twist the gun in my direction and the only thing that keeps me holding on for dear life is adrenaline.

Then I hear Alex's voice above me.

"All I need is one reason."

I lift my head slightly and see the barrel of the little peashooter she carries pressed between Hugh's eyes.

"Like you would shoot," he hisses mockingly.

"Without even a second's hesitation," she returns with ice in her voice.

He holds her dare for a few seconds before I can feel the fight seep from him. I easily disarm him and get to my feet, swaying slightly as I train his own gun on him. I risk a glance at Alex, who looks as fierce as she sounds.

"You wouldn't happen to have any handcuffs laying about, would you?"

Her eyes, which had been intensely focused on the man on the floor, flit to mine.

"What?"

"Handcuffs. Got any?"

"No. Of course not."

I grin while keeping an eye on Standish.

"Pity. Never thought I'd say this, but I'd let you cuff me if you used that voice on me. I like you bossy."

Before she has a chance to react, I hear the clopping of horse hooves on the gravel and the sound of barking.

"I'll never get that image out of my head, Momma. Remind me never to piss you off."

"Maybe now you know what I'm capable of you won't need me to remind you," Alex fires back.

She still sounds fierce—definitely a turn-on—but I can also hear the fatigue in her voice. Not a surprise after the events of tonight.

Her son and Lucy had been out in the back field when they heard the gunshot.

Jackson was the first one through the door, with the dogs on his heels. While he was still frozen in the hallway, slack-jawed at finding his mom with a gun to someone's head, Lucy came in.

She didn't hesitate, took in the situation with one look, and started kicking the shit out of Hugh with her heavy-duty riding boots until Jackson hauled her back. Probably a good thing, she looked pissed enough to kill the man.

Fletch showed up seconds later and was quick to secure Hugh, who was screaming assault at Lucy by that time.

Sheriff Ewing was the first law enforcement officer to

arrive—Fletch had made a call on the way here—and took Standish into custody, placing him in the back seat of his cruiser. Then the feds got here and they took charge of the lockbox Hugh had been after.

Alex explained she'd found that along with the blueprints. She seemed disappointed when Wolff said they'd hand it to the forensics team to open, but he assured her he'd fill her in on what they found.

It's almost midnight by the time the last vehicle leaves.

Lucy already went upstairs, she seemed very quiet after her outburst, and Jackson, his mom, and I are sitting around the kitchen table.

"I'm suddenly exhausted," Alex says on a yawn.

"It's the adrenaline letdown," Jackson explains. "It's what keeps you alive, but when the threat is gone, it leaves you drained. You'll be fine tomorrow."

She turns bleary eyes on her son.

"I don't even want to know how you know that."

He grins at her. "Then I won't tell you."

"Come on." I get to my feet, which are thankfully steady again, and take her hand. "Let's get you up to bed."

I'm surprised she doesn't object as I walk her to the stairs.

"Jonas?" Jackson's voice sounds behind me.

"I'll be right up," I tell Alex, giving her a little nudge upstairs before I turn to her son.

"Thank you," he says, his voice cracking. "If I'd come back and something had happened to her while I was out there, I don't know—"

"But you didn't," I interrupt him, clapping a hand on his shoulder.

"Will you look after her? After I leave next week?"

"Of course I will. I love her. Although, in all fairness, it's

321

a toss-up who looked after who today. Turns out your mom can handle herself pretty well."

"Yeah, I guess she can." He grins at me. "Glad she found you."

"Not half as glad as I am."

I shoot him a wink and head up after her.

Halfway up the stairs I call over my shoulder, "Lock up before you hit the sack."

I grin when I hear his response.

"Yes, *Sir!*"

Twenty-Nine

ALEX

"This one's new."

I catch sight of my son leaning on the gate and smile at him before turning back to the horse on my lunge rope. He's a bit skittish with Jackson standing at the gate.

"His name's Buster. Belongs to a dude ranch just north of here. He was dropped off this morning."

Jackson had still been in bed when Lucy and I got busy this morning. He's been up every other morning with us, helping with the animals, mending the fences, and fixing odds and ends around the house. He deserved to sleep in, especially since he likely won't get that chance once he flies out the day after tomorrow.

A heavy feeling settles on my chest. I've tried to enjoy this time with him without focusing on the end date, but it creeps in anyway.

"What's wrong with him?"

"Encounter with a mountain lion," I explain. "He's a

trail horse and normally quite docile, but the attack left him jumping at everything."

"I can tell," Jackson observes. "Think you can settle him?"

"Yeah, I think so. It's just gonna take some time."

Time I'm about to have more than my share of with Jackson leaving, and I also haven't seen as much of Jonas as I'd like.

He was here a couple of nights, joined us for dinner, and spent some time with Jackson getting to know him. Yet another reason I love the man.

I was at the ranch the day before yesterday to welcome Thomas home. He's looking a lot better than last time I saw him and seemed committed to sticking around a little longer. The likelihood is his heart will give out at some point, the damage already done is significant, but at least he's not actively helping time along.

Jonas has stayed home—understandably—and today Sully is supposed to be released so I'm sure he won't be over either. It's surprising how much I miss him. We talk on the phone, but it's not the same, and with Dan taking over working Phantom and Blitz I haven't been at the ranch much.

I hear the crunch of tires on gravel and start turning to the driveway when Buster rears, almost pulling the lunge from my hand.

"Whoa, buddy. Easy."

A quick glance over my shoulder shows Jonas getting out of his truck and my heart does a little skip.

Buster unfortunately requires all my attention and it takes me a few minutes to settle him down enough so I can walk him to the barn. It would be quicker to let him out in the paddock, but I have a suspicion he won't let himself get caught too easily.

By the time I walk out of the barn, there's no sign of either Jonas or Jackson.

I find them in the kitchen having a coffee. The conversation stalls as soon as I walk in and I eye each of them suspiciously.

"Okay, what was that all about?"

"Hello to you too, Sweets," Jonas says with a grin, hooking me by the neck to plant a kiss on my lips.

"Hi," I respond. "But don't think that's going to get you off the hook. What are you two hiding from me?"

"Nothing, Mom. Jonas was just giving me the names of a few contacts at Fort Bragg."

"Ahhh."

I'm feeling a little silly and suddenly sad, which is probably why they stopped talking in the first place.

Jonas tucks me under his arm.

"I was just on my way home from the hospital. Sully is coming home this afternoon."

I turn to smile up at him.

"I heard. That's great news."

"Yeah. His sister is staying for a few more days to see him settled in, and he'll still need physical therapy to build up some of that muscle tissue he lost in his leg, but he should be making a full recovery."

"Happy to hear it."

I notice his eyes slide to Jackson.

"I'm sure you'd rather spend some quality time with Jackson, but Ama is dead set on doing a cookout tonight, celebrating everyone's healthy homecoming, and made me promise to invite you guys."

I open my mouth to decline the invitation when I catch

the excited expression on Jackson's face. Spending the night with his mother and glorified sister, or eating grilled meat and drinking beer with a bunch of ex-special forces guys. Doesn't take much to imagine which he'd prefer.

"Sure," I find myself saying. "Why not? Anything we should bring?"

"Yourselves." He drops another kiss on my lips before he turns to Jackson. "Thanks for the coffee."

"No problem. Thanks for the contacts."

"Good guys. I already let them know to expect a call from you. Don't hesitate, even if you just wanna talk to someone."

"Much appreciated."

My heart warms to know he's looking out for my kid. It relieves some of my worry for him.

Jonas nods at Jackson before glancing at me.

"I should get going. Walk me out?"

He leads me outside with a hand on the small of my back. When we get to his truck, he turns me around and presses my back to the driver's side door and leans in for a kiss. A deep, hungry one that has me grab on to his shirt.

"That's better," he mumbles as he pulls away. "I missed you."

I smile into his blue eyes. "Me too. How does that happen? Two months ago we didn't even know each other."

"One thing I've learned in my fifty years: Don't waste time questioning your good fortune when you should be enjoying it instead. That's what I intend to do, enjoy every minute I can."

I tighten my arms around him. "You're absolutely right."

"Talking about enjoyment, I saw my doctor today as well."

"You did? I didn't know that was today."

"It wasn't, but I bumped into him in the lobby. He happened to have some time."

I almost laugh, I'm sure Jonas twisted his arm.

"And?"

"I'm cleared. No restrictions. Can't wait to get back in the saddle."

I narrow my eyes at him, not quite buying into it.

"Really?"

The cheeky grin tells the truth.

"Well, he did mention something about a riding helmet, but he's probably from New York or something. Besides, it would look ridiculous in bed."

I'm still laughing when a dark SUV pulls up beside Jonas's truck.

"Good. I caught you both," Agent Wolff says, exiting the vehicle.

I recognize Schroeder in the passenger seat but he's not showing any signs of getting out.

"I wanted to stop by before we head back to Kalispell."

"You're done here?" Jonas asks.

"For now. Department of Homeland Security is back in the picture."

"Limpkin?"

Wolff grins at me. "No. I heard through the grapevine his superiors weren't impressed when it became obvious he'd missed a few things. He's been suspended pending an internal investigation."

"Good," Jonas comments. "Guys like that give the department a bad name."

He glances at the darkened passenger side window of the SUV, where Schroeder's profile is just visible. Wolff catches it too.

"He's not a bad agent," he says in a low voice. "Old school, a bit sour, and probably worn—he's got eight more months 'til retirement—but he was a great mentor. Anyway," he continues at regular volume. "DHS took custody of Standish and the stash of explosives we found in the loft at his shop."

"Did you have a chance to talk to him?" I want to know.

Wolff explains how they discovered from both Hugh and the contents of the lockbox that Clive Jenkins was his mother's brother. She died in 2005 and he spent a fair amount of time with his uncle, until they had a falling out some ten years ago. It turns out they shared a dislike of government institutions, but the uncle was all about maintaining peaceful autonomy while Hugh was looking to overthrow the establishment. When the old man died, Hugh thought he'd inherit the property, not realizing at the time the place had gone into foreclosure. He found out after his uncle died, and I'd snatched it up.

My head is still spinning when the dark SUV drives off a few minutes later.

"I should go too," Jonas announces. "You guys show up any time you're ready."

With a peck on my lips and a tip of his hat, Jonas is off too.

"You pouting again?"

I turn around to catch Lucy walking up from the barn.

"I'm not pouting."

"Like hell, you're not. Whenever Jonas is around you look nauseatingly happy, but as soon as he's gone you get this woeful look on your face. I don't even know which one is worse," she grumbles. "When are you moving in with him already?"

My mouth falls open as I turn to her. She looks dead serious.

"We haven't even talked about that."

"What's to talk about?"

"Well, for one thing, how is that going to work with the rescue?"

She snorts loudly. "No different from how it worked before, except you may need to get up ten minutes earlier or, even better, I get to sleep in ten minutes longer."

I scrutinize her face for anything to tell me she's putting on a brave front, but there's no indication.

"It would mean you living here alone," I point out.

"So?" She shrugs. "I've got Scout and Chief—neither of whom, by the way, you're taking—I've got my gun and if it makes you feel any better, I can put in a security system. Besides, I'm used to living on my own."

"I'll think about it."

Lucy throws up her arms.

"What's to think about? He's a good man. Heck, may well be the last decent man left, and for some godforsaken reason he looks at you like you're the last drop of water in the desert. You wanna pass up on that?"

With an annoyed grunt she stomps up the porch and disappears inside.

Well...if you put it that way.

Jonas

"You're a cruel sonofabitch," Sully mutters.

"Hey, you're the one who wanted to sit out here," I point out, checking the racks of ribs on the smoker.

"Maybe Ama can grind you up a steak?" Bo suggests helpfully.

Sully is going to be on a low-fiber, soft-food, and no-alcohol regime for the next six weeks, which he clearly is not thrilled about.

"Fuck off, Bo."

"Gladly, I was about to grab another beer anyway. Want one, Jonas?"

I try to hide my grin from Sully. Poor guy is going to be tortured relentlessly unless he starts pretending not to care. Bo might leave him alone then.

"Sure, I'll have another."

"Hey, big guy," Lucy calls out, waving her empty bottle at Bo. "I could do with a refill."

"Gotcha," he mumbles before heading inside.

Bo doesn't mumble, he booms, so his muted response is unexpected.

I glance around the back deck, looking for Alex. She was sitting with Dad and Lucy earlier. Then I hear her laugh and glance in the kitchen window. She's standing at the sink and her head is thrown back as she laughs at something Bo must've said.

I don't realize I'm staring until I hear my father behind me.

"I used to look at your mother like that. Like I didn't know how I'd ever managed without her in my life. I'm sorry."

"Dad..."

I turn to him, seeing the emotion sketched on his face.

"Long overdue, Son. She's quite something, your Alex.

Not afraid to speak her mind either. Gave me what for, she did."

He pauses for a moment and stares at the mountains. I take a sip of my beer and wait; I can tell he's not done.

"Miss her somethin' fierce, boy. Thought time might take the edge off, but it hasn't. Seems the more I can feel my own clock ticking, the more I miss 'er."

I drop a hand on his shoulder. "I get it, Dad."

He hums. "Wasn't sure you would, but then that filly came along. I can see now how you might. Damn girl makes me wanna stick around a little longer to see you finally settled down. Bet she'll give you a run for your money. I figure it'd please your mother I can share some of that with her when I get to join her."

Jesus, he's killing me.

I clear my throat before I trust myself to speak.

"I'm just glad you're here, Dad."

He grunts and without another word heads inside just as Alex comes walking out. She tilts her head slightly as she approaches and slips an arm around my waist.

"You okay?"

I bend my head to drop a kiss on her pretty lips.

"I'm good."

It's not until after dinner, when I'm walking Alex and her crew to the truck, I have a chance to pull her aside.

"I want you to think about moving in. Soon," I add. "Don't wanna waste time, Sweets. I know your head's somewhere else now, but when you have a chance, give it a thought."

She smiles up at me but I can see the strain in her face.

"Okay."

"And Alexandra? I'm not gonna bother you tomorrow

—that's your time with Jackson—but I'd like to drive you guys to the airport Monday morning."

If she says no, I've already decided I'll put my foot down. No way I'm going to let her drive back from Kalispell by herself. She'll be a mess. But I'd prefer not to have to browbeat her into it.

She presses her lips together when she gives me a little nod.

"We're leaving at five thirty in the morning. You may as well spend the night."

Even better.

Thirty

JONAS

I've never been this happy to see the house at the end of my driveway.

In previous years I enjoyed this trek to Spokane, Washington. A little break from the daily routine carting Phantom and two of the other studs around to a number of breeders. This year my heart wasn't in it, although Dan seemed to enjoy coming along for his first time.

He was hesitant at first, not wanting to leave his mother, but Gemma insisted, pointing out there were plenty of people to look after her if needed. So he came, and I have to admit he was damn handy to have around. The kid's getting better with the studs every day. If not for Alex, he would've been wasted on grunt work. I had no idea Dan had the kind of affinity with horses he's shown. Maybe I just wasn't looking.

I've always been a skeptic and need to see to believe.

Alex, on the other hand, is a believer who can spot potential in a man, or a horse, a mile away. The pragmatist and the visionary. Opposites attract, guess that's what makes us work well.

Of course we only had one week to test out that theory before I had to leave for Spokane.

It took Alex two weeks after Jackson left to make the move. She needed the time to sort out what she wanted Lucy to have and what things she wanted to keep. She also wasn't going to leave without having a good security system installed, with an alarm notification here in case of a breach. Alex pointed out we could get to the rescue faster from the ranch than law enforcement.

I suppose two weeks is not that long in the grand scope of things, but it was definitely fourteen days too long for me.

Before I left for Spokane, she asked whether I would mind if she put a few of her personal touches on the house while I was gone. I told her I didn't give a damn what she did to the place as long as she was there waiting for me when I got home.

Turns out I lied. All week I've been wondering and I can't wait to see what she's done to turn the house into a home.

Last night I couldn't get to sleep and made Dan get up at two so we could get home. It's barely five thirty in the morning when I pull the trailer in next to the barn, but the moment I get out of the truck I can hear Max barking and when I glance over, I see Alex hoofing it down the porch.

Fuck. Morning hair flying all over, my old bathrobe flapping around her legs, she's the most beautiful thing I've ever seen. I'm frozen on the spot, unable to do more than open my arms and brace.

"Oomph."

She knocks the air out of my lungs when she collides with me. Or maybe it's the feeling of her lithe body wrapping itself tightly around me.

"I missed you so much," she mutters as she peppers my face with kisses. "I didn't think you'd be back until later today."

"Couldn't wait," I confess, keeping her in place with an arm under her ass. Grabbing a fistful of her hair in my free hand, I pull her mouth down to mine.

Coffee, a hint of toothpaste, and a sweetness that is all Alex.

I get lost in her taste, her mouth, her heat, when I hear a throat clearing behind me.

"I'll...uhh...just get the horses."

I can feel the smile on Alex's mouth before she lifts her head and peeks over my shoulder.

"Morning, Dan."

"Hey, Alex."

"Good trip?" she asks, jumping down from my hold.

I already miss her body, but I grab on to her hand to keep her close because I intend to drag her up to the bedroom as soon as she's done saying hello.

"Great trip."

"Good. I'm glad. Your mom is fine by the way. I took her for her blood work yesterday and her counts are up."

"Really? That's great news. I'll go check on her as soon as I've got the horses taken care of."

"Why don't I give you a hand with that?"

The frustrated growl escapes me before I can check it and it earns me a sharp, pointy elbow in my ribs.

Dan snickers but has the good sense to quickly follow it up with, "No need. I've got it."

As soon as he turns his back, I'm dragging Alex toward the house.

"That was rude," she mutters behind me.

Unfortunately, Dan's not the only one standing in the way of my plans. My father is standing on the porch steps.

"Good trip, Son?"

"Yeah. I see you were able to keep down the fort?"

His narrow shoulders straighten as he pulls up an eyebrow.

"I may be old but I haven't forgotten how to run a ranch. Been doing it more years than you've been around."

I grin at his feisty comeback. Never thought I'd say this, but I'm glad to see the cantankerous old goat is back.

"Coffee's in the pot and I'm making pancakes," he says. "Breakfast in ten minutes." Then he turns his back and walks back in the house.

"Awesome, it'll just give me enough time to show you what I've done before I have to hustle out of here," Alex announces.

So much for my plans.

"I hope you don't mind, but I moved that wooden bench. It's inside the hallway so we can sit to put on our boots. That thing wasn't meant to sit on for long, but these are super comfy," she rattles as she drags me to a sitting area she made on the porch with two Adirondack chairs, throw pillows, and a small table.

"Nice," I grumble, annoyed with my foiled plans.

Alex doesn't seem to notice and drags me into the house where she shows me the reconfigured entryway, and a beautiful enlarged, black-and-white picture of her horse, Sarge, grazing dew-covered grass in the morning mist. As far as I can see nothing has changed in the kitchen or dining room, but the living room seems...warmer. Fat candles, that weren't there before, are randomly grouped on the ledge of the stone fireplace and on the coffee table. A threadbare quilt is draped over the back of my leather couch, and a few pillows tossed in the corners.

With every little detail she points out to me my sour mood lifts. With simple, little touches, she's put her print on the house and I like seeing it here.

"I can take this down if you don't like it," she says a little nervously when she points out a grouping of photo frames, in all different shapes and sizes, in the far corner of the room. They're almost hidden by a standing lamp.

Pictures of Jackson as a baby, alone, and one where he's sitting on his father's shoulders. A snapshot of the three of them. Jackson is maybe ten or eleven and her husband is wearing his uniform. In the background are other families and couples saying goodbye. There are other pictures, but that one holds my attention.

"That was his last deployment, wasn't it?"

She nods, a sad-sweet smile on her face.

"Jackson was devastated. Bruce promised to take him camping the next weekend when he got called up. It's the last time we saw him. Just three weeks later he was dead."

I glance over her shoulder and catch Dad watching from the kitchen.

"I do think you should take them down," I tell her. Then I lean over the couch and lift down the large landscape I had hanging there. "I think they should go here where everyone can see them."

"I've got a box of Jonas's pictures growing up," Dad calls from the kitchen, a barely-there smile on his face. "Maybe we could add some'a those. Make it a family wall."

Alex buries her face in my chest.

"I love you so much," she mumbles in my shirt.

Over her head, I lock eyes with my father. He nods once and turns back to the pancakes on the griddle.

"If you want your breakfast hot, you'd better get your ass dressed, Filly," he calls over his shoulder. "This ain't no damn restaurant."

~

Alex

I can't wait to get home.

Luckily, we had a busy day, with Sam and his daughter, Mickey, coming to pick up Buster. Mickey was so happy to see her old horse back. It had taken about a month, he was slow to respond—his anxiety persistent—but once we started making headway, he turned around beautifully. Yesterday as a final test, I took him for a long trail ride and he didn't even spook when a large crow suddenly flew up from the underbrush just a few feet away from us. He was ready to go home.

Then this afternoon, Doc Evans dropped by for a follow-up check on Hope and the dogs, and to our surprise suggested the mare might be pregnant. Normally we would've suspected much sooner from changes in demeanor to the size of her abdomen. But Hope's anxiety overshadowed any telltale behavior and she'd been so underfed when we got her, it was hard to tell the difference between pregnancy gain and regular meals. A blood test confirmed it, but it's a mystery how she would've gotten pregnant tied to a post.

A surprise foal certainly perked up my day and Lucy was downright elated at the prospect. I haven't seen her that excited in...well, ever. I drive home—my new home —smiling.

Jonas walks down from the house with a massive picnic basket before I am fully out of the truck.

"What's this?"

"You'll see," he says after kissing me hello. "Anything important you need to do inside? Anything that can't wait?"

"Not really."

He grins, grabs my hand, and starts leading me to the barn. There he urges me up the ladder to the hayloft.

The loft doors wide open, I can see the sun sliding down in the sky, casting a rich golden hue over the magnificent view from up here. The waning light spills inside, touching my quilt, which is spread on the rough, wooden floorboards.

I turn to Jonas with a smile.

"Hungry?" he wants to know.

"Starving," I admit, although I'm not sure for food or for him.

He plants the basket in the middle of the quilt and starts unloading it. Containers of cheeses, dried sausages, crackers, and sliced fruits appear, followed by a bottle of champagne and two glasses.

"This is amazing. You did this?"

His eyes flit my way. "The basket is Ama, but the idea was mine. We've been so busy, I never properly welcomed you home."

Even without the romantic setting, those words would've melted my heart.

"I love it," I tell him. "I love you."

He smiles and kicks off his boots before sitting down on

the blanket, spreading his legs and patting the space between them.

"Come sit with me."

Following his example, I toe off my boots and sink down in front of him. His arm immediately pulls me back so I'm resting against his chest.

"Salty or sweet?"

"Salty," I answer as he loads a cracker with cheese and feeds me.

I feel his lips brush the side of my head. "Now, tell me about your day."

I'm not sure how long we're sitting like that, staring out at what rightfully is called, *God's country*, eating and drinking, and talking in muted tones. His warmth blanketing my back and the deep vibrations of his voice awakening every fiber in my body.

"I have something for you." I feel his hand fumble in his pocket. "The wife of one of my customers in Washington was working on this. I had to have it."

His hand appears in front of me holding the most stunning ring I've ever seen. A raw, uncut aquamarine set in a simple gold ring with randomly placed, hammered metal claws holding the stone in place. He slips it on my finger for a perfect fit.

"Jonas..."

"Not asking the question now, because I'm not sure you're ready to say yes, but your son's already given me his blessing when I asked him, and I want you to wear it knowing that I intend to make you my wife."

I twist around so I'm kneeling in from of him.

"You talked to Jackson? When did you talk to him?"

He grins. "The day of the cookout, in your kitchen."

I slap his shoulder.

"I knew you were hiding something from me."

"Only because I thought you weren't ready to hear it and your boy was leaving."

I'm not usually one for impulse decisions, but I'm not holding this back.

"I'm ready to hear it."

He looks surprised.

"Are you sure?"

I nod and try to stay calm but a bunch of Clydesdales are doing a polka in my stomach. Jumping in the deep end is not my usual MO, but I'm ready to leap.

"Try me."

His hands cup my face and his eyes take me in, like he's mapping out every line and feature.

"Marry me, Alexandra. You already own me."

I grab on to his wrists and smile like a crazy woman.

"I'd be happy—"

His mouth drowns out the rest of what I intended to say, but I don't care.

In no time he is divesting me of my clothes, layer by layer, until I can feel the cool breeze brushing against my bare skin. The waning sunlight is barely enough to warm me, but Jonas's body radiates enough heat for both of us as he fucks me in the fresh mountain air.

It's perfect—romance Montana style—and I've lost my heart to this man and his mountains.

"He's beautiful," I mumble.

We're sitting on the paddock fence, a mug of coffee in

hand, and a quilt wrapped around our shoulders, watching Missy's handsome little boy nuzzle the mare for milk.

The little colt has gorgeous coloring like his mother, but the stronger rounded lines of a quarter horse, courtesy of Phantom.

"Have you decided on a name yet?"

It's not the first time I've asked Jonas this question, but he keeps saying he hasn't decided yet.

"You choose," he says, glancing at me with a small smile tugging at his lips.

"Me? He's not my horse, he's yours."

"Exactly, and I want you to name him," he persists.

I roll my eyes at him and take a sip of my coffee.

"Mmm, I'll have to think on that."

He throws an arm around my shoulders, kisses the side of my head, and I snuggle into him.

Last night was amazing, but the chill eventually chased us down the ladder and into the house. This morning I was woken up by Jonas showing his appreciation again, but a lot slower and more thorough.

We grabbed the quilt and came out here to watch the sun come up again.

I straighten up and turn to face him.

"Thank you for a beautiful night."

His eyes smile, the lines deepening on his face.

"It was my pleasure." He drops a brief kiss on my lips. "And something I hope to repeat time and time again."

Oh yeah, I was right to take the leap.

"High Meadow," I suddenly blurt out.

"Sorry?"

"Missy's colt, his name should be High Meadow."

He looks at the foal and then back at me with a warm smile. He reaches over and tucks my hair behind my ear.

"High Meadow, huh? I like it."

THE END

Keep reading for a sample of the next book in the series:

High Stakes

High Stakes

COMING APRIL 18, 2022

When her sister, Pippa, goes missing, Nella Freling tells her boss she's taking time off from her job as a research librarian, hops in her sensible van, and heads south of the border to Montana. However, local police don't seem too concerned about a missing woman living in her motorhome. So Nella will have to look for Pippa by herself, unless she can convince a highly recommended tracker to help her, but sadly the rude and angry cowboy won't even listen to her at first.
But Nella can be persuasive.

The first time High Mountain Tracker, Fletch Boone, laid eyes on Nella, her ass was stuck in his grocery cart. The next time was at the ranch; she was wearing mud, head to toe. But when he catches sight of her a third time, hanging off a cliff, he can't turn his back again. What Nella lacks in survival skills she makes up for in sheer determination. Unfortunately, neither of those is enough protection when bullets start flying.
Fletch has no choice but to jump in before the woman gets herself killed.
And that would be a damn shame.

~

NELLA

"How can I help you?"

The woman behind the desk has a friendly smile, but her eyes are cautious.

"I have a reservation. Antonella Freling."

I picked the Sandman Motel because I can park right in front of my unit, which I prefer.

"Ah, yes. I have you here. Four nights?"

"Yes."

"You requested the end unit with a kitchenette?"

"That's correct."

I'm not here to see the sights or waste money and time on eating out. Much cheaper and faster to pick up some groceries and fend for myself. I keep a small cooler in my van for drinks and something to eat in case I'm out all day.

She slides a form across the desk and I quickly fill it out before handing it back to her.

"I'll need a credit card, please."

I look around the small front office and shudder at the pictures of proud hunters with their prize kills. My dislike must've shown on my face.

"Not here for hunting I gather?" she inquires, a little smirk on her face.

"No. Not a fan," I admit.

I'm the biggest hypocrite on two legs because I won't say no to a good steak from a poor anonymous cow, who never had a chance to start with, but I can't bring myself to try game meat from an animal at least able to live its life free.

Somebody offers me venison and all I can envision is Bambi with those big brown eyes.

My meat comes shrink-wrapped in plastic so I can keep my emotional detachment. I tried a vegetarian lifestyle for a little over a year but found it a challenge living in a small mountain town in British Columbia, Canada. My first juicy burger after that episode was a purely orgasmic experience.

She smiles, a sparkle in her eyes. "We cater to a lot of hunters, but they won't be coming in until next week when the season opens. Until the fifteenth only bowhunting is allowed and there aren't that many of those. Mostly locals anyway."

I mock-wipe my brow and smile back as she hands me the key card.

"Unit twenty-three is yours."

"Thank you. Oh, where can I find the closest grocery store?"

"Just down the road. It'll be on your right-hand side as you get into town. Rosauers, you can't miss it. If you need anything else, my name is Martha."

"Thanks so much, Martha."

I'm almost out the door when I think of the more important question.

"The police station, is it easy to find?"

After shooting me a curious look, she gives me directions. The station is only a few minutes from the grocery store, so I'll head there first and pick up supplies after.

My unit is nothing special. A generic motel room with an art-by-numbers painting on the wall over two double beds, a dresser holding a TV, a functional—and thankfully clean—bathroom, and beside it a tiny kitchenette with microwave, hotplate, coffeemaker, and a bar-size fridge. It'll do.

I spend twenty minutes putting my stuff away, toiletries lined up on the small vanity in the bathroom, some things in the dresser and the rest of my clothes on hangers in the narrow closet. It does little to give the room more personality. I don't own much aside from work clothes and those are all rather drab in grays, blacks, and some muted tans. No color other than the single pair of jeans I own.

Hiding my light under a bushel, that's what Pippa always tells me. She's my opposite in every way: colorful, exuberant, and adventurous. I'm a strictly inside-the-lines person, while she breaks every conventional rule she can.

I went to the University of British Columbia studying library and information sciences, while she went to trade school to become a mechanic.

As different as we are—coming from the same nest— we've always been close. Especially after our parents died in a house fire eighteen years ago. We're all the other has, which is why I can't simply sit around and wait to hear something. I need to find her.

The Libby Police Station is a nondescript red brick building and I snag a parking spot when a vehicle backs out.

"Yes?" The not so friendly officer behind the desk looks at me like I'm here to confess a crime.

I automatically feel guilty, even though I'm pretty sure I haven't broken any rules in the past few decades.

"Is Officer Franklin available? I spoke with him on the phone the day before yesterday. My name is Antonella Freling."

"He's on patrol. What is it regarding?"

"I filed a missing person report on my sister Fillippa Freling with him."

He types the name into her computer.

"Right. I have it here. It says she drives a motor home?"

"Yes."

"And you haven't heard from her since August twenty-sixth."

"Correct. I was hoping perhaps you'd found out something more?"

"Doesn't look like it. We'll continue to keep an eye out for the vehicle."

His tone is dismissive, much like Officer Franklin had been when I filed the report. I don't know why I thought a visit here would have a different result. Maybe a bit more urgency, but it doesn't look like that'll be the case.

I get it, my sister is a bit of a nomad, roaming the country, often staying off the grid but she would always let me know where she'd be and for how long. Exactly what she did this time. Except she was coming home, she said she'd be there on Monday. Only two-and-a-half hours to get from Libby to Cranbrook, British Columbia, it's not like she had a long way to go.

I know my sister. If she had run into any trouble causing a delay, or even in the unlikely event something changed her mind about visiting, she would've let me know.

Unfortunately, my gut feeling Pippa is in trouble doesn't go very far with law enforcement. I can't really blame them, from what I understand quite a few people go missing in these mountains, exposed to the elements, so they're not going to waste resources on a woman who travels in her home. Not unless I have something more concrete to give them, which is why I'm here.

My boss wasn't happy with the short notice I'd be taking time off, but that can't be helped.

My bread and butter is research so I'm not entirely unprepared. I know what to look for, I have every camping app downloaded on my phone, and I have the name of someone who might be able to help me.

If only he'd call me back, I've already left a couple of messages. If I haven't heard anything by tomorrow, I'll chase him down.

I'll do what I have to find Pippa.

~

Fletch

"Who the fuck do you think you are?"

I don't bother answering.

The punk is squirming, but I have my knee in the middle of his back with my full weight on it. I pull a few zip ties from my pack and strap his wrists together.

Then I sit him up, right next to the young bear he shot with his goddamn hunting rifle. I prop the rifle up against the bear as well. Next, I pull out my phone and take a bunch of pictures while the kid is swearing at me. Every time he tries to get up, I kick his feet back out from under him.

It's easy for me to tune him out, I have lots of practice. My hearing has gotten very selective after years of living in virtual silence. The only thing that penetrated it was the rifle shot earlier. Startled me so bad I fucking dove right for the dirt. It took me a few seconds to register what I heard, then I was on my feet and aiming straight for the excited laughing I heard down the trail.

Fucking poachers. No more than kids. Unfortunately, the second guy took off running while I was taking this one to the ground.

It takes me half an hour to get the kid and the bear back

down to the trailhead where my truck is the only one parked now. Catching my breath, I take my phone out. Only one bar, but enough to dial out.

"Sheriff's Office."

"Ewing, Fletch Boone here. I'm up by the Granite Ridge Trailhead parking lot. Got a dead bear with a bullet hole, the rifle that shot it, and the punk who fired it. Second kid got away. You wanna come pick this one up?"

Guess it was a slow day because less than half an hour later his cruiser rolls onto the parking lot, followed by a pickup. The kid loudly complains about his rights as Ewing hoists him to his feet and tucks him in the back of his vehicle. The deputy stepping from the pickup is already poking at the bear.

"Trust me, he's dead," I tell him dryly.

"Want it?" Ewing asks as he walks up.

He peeks in the back of my truck where I left my bow and the rest of my gear.

"Me? No. Still have plenty of bear from last season. Got a tag for a bighorn this year."

"Bighorn? No shit? Those are hard to come by."

"Especially for bowhunting," I add. "Tried every year for the past six and this is the first tag I got my hands on."

I only hunt with a bow.

Don't like guns. I may wear one, but I don't like it. It would have to be an extreme circumstance before I pull my weapon, let alone fire it. Instantly my mind goes back to the spring, when my boss had the barrel of a gun pressed to the back of his head. That counted as an extreme circumstance, but even knowing it would've been Jonas's life otherwise doesn't stop the sour burn in my gut. It was James who pulled the trigger, but we all carried that kill.

"It's a fresh kill, shouldn't be wasted," the sheriff points out before asking me, "Mind if I drop it off at Pete's?"

Pete owns a butcher shop and processes game for folks who don't like doing that dirty job or don't have room for it. Most hunters I know clean their own like I do.

"Have at it. And by the way, the second kid that got away? He's driving a rusted, blue Chevy pickup, my guess would be 1985 or thereabouts. Rear bumper is tied down with wire. Shouldn't be hard to find."

"Sounds like Willy Stubblefeld," the deputy suggest.

"Yeah. We'll go have a chat with Willy after I drop this other punk off. Don't know him, do you?"

"Never seen him," I answer.

It takes all three of us to hoist the bear in the back of the deputy's pickup.

"If there were any bighorns around, they're probably gone by now," Ewing observes. "May wanna check south of Cedar Creek. Talked to a guy the other day who spotted a couple of sheep up there."

"Thanks."

I've got a few other spots I want to try first, but if I'm running out of time, I know a couple of logging roads that'll get me close to that creek.

"See ya later, Boone, 'preciate the assistance."

I wait until they're driving off before packing up my own gear, but the moment I get behind the wheel, my phone rings.

"Yup."

"Fletch, it's Ama. Are you anywhere near town?"

"I'll be driving through in about five minutes. Why?"

"Would you mind picking up some coffee? I would, but I'm in the middle of dinner prep and—"

"Sure," I cut her off.

I need to get some stuff myself anyway. I've been putting it off because I hate fucking grocery stores. Always too many people getting in my way. I like to go in, grab what I need, and get the hell out of there.

"Ah, you're a lifesaver. Thanks. No coffee in the morning would've made for a grumpy bunch tomorrow."

"True."

She's right about that. All of us count on that big pot she always has ready to get us going.

"You stopping by for lasagna?" she asks as I start the truck.

More often than not I eat at my own cabin, instead of at the house with the other guys. I don't mind my own company, I'm used to it, and I happen to enjoy cooking, which I know the others do not.

Having said that, Ama's lasagna is legendary and I have to drop off the coffee anyway. She usually has dinner ready at five, before she heads home, which means I'll still have the whole night to myself.

"You bet," I respond, knowing it'll please her. "See you soon."

Ama is not only the wife of my teammate, James, but the den mother, manager, and housekeeper, for the entire crew at High Meadow Ranch. Jonas Harvey—my boss— owns it, but Ama runs it. She even tackles the office work for High Mountain Trackers.

Jonas Harvey was the commander of our Special Ops combat tracker unit. He was the first to be aged out and bought High Meadow ranch, building its name as a respected horse breeding facility. Then, one by one, he brought our former unit together to form High Mountain Trackers.

I was the last to join, running my own small tracking

venture just outside of Fernie, British Columbia. I liked being on my own. My cabin in the mountains was secluded and I kept my interactions with other people to a minimum.

But Jonas had been relentless in his pursuit to find me and, finally, convince me. Not with promises of money—which wouldn't have meant much to me—but by offering me the only family I've ever known; my team.

A lot of our downtime is spent running the ranch but these days we're hired more frequently to track down and rescue missing individuals. Some of them go missing accidentally, but in a few cases their disappearance had been intentional. A few months ago, we assisted law enforcement in tracking down a couple of escaped domestic terrorists responsible for a pair of deadly bomb blasts outside state buildings.

Over the summer we've had our share of missing hikers, not just around Libby, but all over Montana's northwest. I like the work, it's unpredictable, can be challenging, is mostly gratifying, and definitely feeds my craving for adventure. In addition to that, I get to take a couple of days off every fall during bowhunting season.

I grunt when I see the busy parking lot at the grocery store full.

Great.

For a second I contemplate stopping at the smaller Libby Empire Foods, but Ama prefers the coffee at Rosauers. Besides, I'm pretty sure the parking lot at the other store won't be much better. It's Saturday afternoon, everybody is out and about.

I find a spot around the side of the building and manage to snag a cart on my way in the doors. Afraid I'm going to forget otherwise; I aim for the coffee first. The din inside the

358

store grates on my nerves so I tune out, keeping my eyes focused on the shelf halfway down the aisle.

I don't even notice the woman hanging onto the shelves at first. Not until I accidentally brush my cart against her legs and she startles, landing with her ass in my cart.

"What the fuck?" slips out before I can check it.

Staring up at me are big eyes, that weird color somewhere between brown and green.

"No need to swear," she says in a clipped tone as she struggles to get out of her precarious position. "Especially since it was you who knocked me off."

"I barely touched you and I wasn't the one climbing the damn shelves," I grumble.

This is why I avoid people.

The woman's lips press tightly together as I grab her under her arms in an attempt to dislodge her from my cart. There is some grunting involved before I can set her on her feet. Standing in front of me she barely makes it to my chin.

I size her up in two seconds flat. *Middle-aged spinster*. She has a few silver streaks in her hair, is wearing ill-fitting clothes and serviceable black shoes, and has a pair of glasses on a chain around her neck. In addition, the contents of the half-full basket on the floor are as drab as the woman in front of me.

"I had no choice, they're too high," she huffs, shaking her shoulder-length waves from her face. "And my brand is up there."

She points at a single, red can of coffee sitting well back from the edge of the top shelf before smoothing her hands down the front of her plain, white blouse.

I reach up, grab the can, and drop it in the basket by her feet.

Without another word I move past her, tossing Ama's coffee in my cart as I aim for the produce section.

Fifteen minutes later when I push my cart out the doors, I just catch a glimpse of her behind the wheel of an older Dodge Caravan.

She's so close to the steering wheel, her nose almost touches the damn windshield.

Also by Freya Barker

High Mountain Trackers:

HIGH MEADOW

HIGH STAKES (*Apr 2022*)

HIGH GROUND (*Aug 2022*)

HIGH IMPACT (*Dec 2022*)

Arrow's Edge MC Series:

EDGE OF REASON

EDGE OF DARKNESS

EDGE OF TOMORROW

EDGE OF FEAR

EDGE OF REALITY

PASS Series:

HIT & RUN

LIFE & LIMB

LOCK & LOAD

LOST & FOUND

On Call Series:

BURNING FOR AUTUMN

COVERING OLLIE

TRACKING TAHLULA

ABSOLVING BLUE

REVEALING ANNIE

DISSECTING MEREDITH

WATCHING TRIN

Rock Point Series:

KEEPING 6

CABIN 12

HWY 550

10-CODE

Northern Lights Collection:

A CHANGE OF TIDE

A CHANGE OF VIEW

A CHANGE OF PACE

SnapShot Series:

SHUTTER SPEED

FREEZE FRAME

IDEAL IMAGE

Portland, ME, Series:

FROM DUST

CRUEL WATER

THROUGH FIRE

STILL AIR

LuLLaY (a Christmas novella)

Cedar Tree Series:

SLIM TO NONE

HUNDRED TO ONE

AGAINST ME

CLEAN LINES

UPPER HAND

LIKE ARROWS

HEAD START

Standalones:

WHEN HOPE ENDS

VICTIM OF CIRCUMSTANCE

BONUS KISSES

SECONDS

About the Author

USA Today bestselling author Freya Barker loves writing about ordinary people with extraordinary stories.

Driven to make her books about 'real' people; she creates characters who are perhaps less than perfect, each struggling to find their own slice of happy, but just as deserving of romance, thrills and chills in their lives.

Recipient of the ReadFREE.ly 2019 Best Book We've Read All Year Award for "Covering Ollie, the 2015 RomCon "Reader's Choice" Award for Best First Book, "Slim To None", Finalist for the 2017 Kindle Book Award with "From Dust", and Finalist for the 2020 Kindle Book Award with "When Hope Ends", Freya spins story after story with an endless supply of bruised and dented characters, vying for attention!

www.freyabarker.com